T0367883

Applause

ELIZABETH CAIN

iUniverse LLC
Bloomington

APPLAUSE

iUniverse books may be ordered through booksellers or by contacting:

iUniverse LLC
1663 Liberty Drive
Bloomington, IN 47403
www.iuniverse.com
1-800-Authors (1-800-288-4677)

ISBN: 978-1-4917-2859-8 (sc)
ISBN: 978-1-4917-2861-1 (hc)
ISBN: 978-1-4917-2860-4 (e)

Library of Congress Control Number: 2014904972

Printed in the United States of America.

iUniverse rev. date: 04/14/2014

To Joan Raymund, poet, mentor, and beloved friend, who did not live to read this story and who might have said, as she did from time to time about my writing, “Too rich for my blood,” but who would have applauded my themes and the poetry herein, most of which she knew like her own heart.

And to Leon M. Worden, one of my first ninth-grade English students who also did not live to read these words but with whom I shared, for many years after those junior high days, adventures, secrets, dreams, and a loving friendship.

Acknowledgments

Many friends helped with the technical aspects of this novel, and I would like to thank them heartily. Dr. Cliff Roberson, neurosurgeon, provided invaluable information about medical symptoms and procedures. Richard Yates, co-owner, Carrie Prelas, manager, and Felipe Barajas, chef, of the Opal Restaurant and Bar in Santa Barbara, California, allowed me to include their real names and menu items (delicious, by the way!). Chris Dombrowski, incredible young Montana poet who can change one's life with his words, loved the scene in which his name is used. Darla Hoff first found the world's only blue rose on her smart phone! Joseph Makusaro John, my Tanzanian "son," did most of the translation where needed from English to Swahili. Dorothy Worden, ninety-seven-year-old mother of Leon M. Worden, to whom the book is dedicated in part, approved of the fictionalizing of her son as Lee Henderson in the story. And I appreciate Mark Nepo, whom I don't know but who graciously let me, through mutual friends Jena and Carole Starkes, quote from his poem "Today I Feel the Pain of the World," from his book *Surviving Has Made Me Crazy.*

1

On a brilliant fall day on the campus of UCLA, I stood in a long line. I had been standing in that line every September for eight years, three of those from a half a world away. I stood there as a freshman, so far back I could barely see the man's face or hear his questions. I stood there as a sophomore, ten pounds lighter with a braid swinging down my back and a raw and sentimental sonnet in my hand. I stood there again just before my junior year and then turned and ran away with only tears to show for myself. I ran away as far as Africa. I felt that line pressed around me every year in Africa for three years. I earned credits. I wrote. I had a poem published in a safari brochure. I had an African lover who didn't mind in the night when I called out another man's name. I came home and stood in that line as a junior and then as a senior. I graduated before the line ever went down to a place where I could look into the face of Dr. William Langley.

Finally, on a cold Sunday morning, the year I began my graduate program, I sat on the quad in my sleeping bag at two a.m. with a book of his poetry. I was tenth in the line and could not sleep. There were reasons that it was so difficult to get into Professor Langley's classes. One couldn't just enroll online as with most of UCLA's faculty. He had a long-standing tradition of choosing his students by asking a question of them in person. Nobody ever knew what he would ask or what answers deemed a person fit to spend a year or two under his tutelage. He wasn't arrogant about it at all. The university allowed him only forty students in each of his three most popular creative writing classes, and he told everyone how much he enjoyed deciding who those 120 kids would be. By the time I knew I was close enough to at least have his question given to me, I had published two novels and one book of short stories and been accepted in several poetry anthologies. I could probably teach the class.

But I wanted more than an A on a story or a chair in one of his coveted metaphor workshops, limited to fifteen. I wanted more than a graduate degree or even a "well done" from his lips or his pen. I wanted to be important to him, to have him look at me and see my soul, to want to be with me, to miss me if I wasn't there, to call me with ideas, with poems. The thing is I can't tell you why. I tried to get over him every year when the line dispersed and those of us who hadn't made it went on to other things.

I would stay and watch him gather up his papers and books, file his notes neatly in his briefcase, fold up his table and chair, hand them to a couple of boys still hanging around, and head back up to the lit building. My throat would tighten when he put his arm around one of them or smiled at a passing colleague who would tease him about his singular way of gleaning students. I couldn't say the words yet, what I had felt for him since I was a teenager. What did I know of love? I only knew that if I didn't stand in that line, a little piece of me was going to die.

By the time the sun rose, I was practically frozen in my place. Kids were passing out coffee and donuts, practicing answers to probable questions. Professor Langley rarely turned someone down outright. He'd say, "I'll put you on an alternate list" or something kind and encouraging. After all, how bad can an answer be when you've waited all night to approach that table and speak to the man who holds your life in his hands? I guessed I was going to find out.

It had not been a good summer for Mr. Langley. (His students from past years always said he asked to be addressed as *Mr.* Langley.) Apparently he'd been rushed to the ER three times for symptoms related to dehydration. There had been a fire in Malibu Canyon that had burned his barn to the ground. No animals had been hurt, thank God. At a back-to-school faculty party, he had become desperately ill after two glasses of wine.

And then, barely a month ago, his wife had been following him home from a writers' conference in Big Sur in their second car, a gold Mercedes, courtesy of a trust fund. When he reached their home in the canyon, she was not behind him. She had been driving the wrong way up Conejo Grade and had crashed head on into a semi. How she had gotten on that side of the highway, no one knew. The police report said alcohol was involved, but the truck driver was cleared and lived with only a limb badly scarred by a deep slash where his leg got caught between the demolished hood and the brake. Langley had to live without his wife of almost twenty years. At least there were no children to mourn the lovely Natasha with her silver-blond hair and gray-green eyes and a penchant for a good martini or two.

I, of course, had fanaticized about holding his hand through these traumatic events, but when I thought of the reality of it all, it scared me. I didn't really know this man. Was I just one of a number of starry-eyed college kids who were always crowding around the amiable and handsome professor with his direct gaze and crooked smile that seemed to me to be halfway between laughing and crying? For most of the time I had been aware of him, he had been unavoidably married. That had held me back as much as anything from making a complete fool of myself and perhaps hurting him somehow. But everything had changed.

Light began to fill the sky. He was coming down the steps toward us with some young man—Lee Henderson, I think—whom I'd known since grammar school and with whom I'd shared many teenage games and secrets, but never this one, that I was so crazy about William Langley. I dared to look at the professor now from the closest I'd been in years. He was thinner than I remembered, and his hair was tinged with gray. There were shadowy places under his eyes, and he seemed not to be standing as straight as usual. I had better give a damn brilliant answer.

He arranged his notebook and pens, gave Lee a pat on the back, and looked up at a line that stretched down the campus quad almost as far as one could see. He grinned and said in a hearty voice that rather belied his appearance, "You're all accepted!"

A cheer rose up for his good humor. This was a gracious man. I heard most of the first questions, things like, "What do you think I can teach you?" and "What did you discover about language in the last book or short story you read?" and "Can you define these words—*untenable, rhetoric, erudite*?" One girl said she couldn't remember the last book or story she'd read. Her name was not put on the golden list. And then, I was standing before him. I was shaking.

"My dear, how long have you been waiting?"

"Eight years, three days, six hours, and twenty minutes."

"Now, *there's* a story," he said.

"Yes, sir."

He smiled. "Okay, now seriously, give me a line or two of metaphoric prose or poetry—yours, something you've read, or something you can make up on the spot."

I suppose he thought some of us wouldn't know what a metaphor was. So I spoke out in a clear voice, looking right into his eyes.

listen
the horses are circling circling
hooves thrum on the blossoms
white blooms from the night sky

listen
grey geese cry overhead going home
the cougar pads his soft retreat
snow whispers to the blind ground.

He did not look away but said, after a quick intake of breath, "Those are *my* words."

"Yes, sir."

"What's your name?"

"Sela Hart."

"Ho, now there's a metaphor," he said. He wrote my name with a flourish on his approved list.

I wanted to cry. It had just been so damn long.

"Thank you, Mr. Langley. I won't disappoint you."

"Oh, I'm quite sure of that, young lady."

His eyes held me as if he didn't want me to go, as if there weren't two hundred kids in line by now wondering why I was still there, but finally he said, "I'll see you fifth period tomorrow, Miss Hart."

Lee was sitting on the edge of the fountain, and he called me over. "Did you get in fifth period?"

"Yeah."

"Me too."

Lee had worked a couple of years before coming to UCLA, so we were both in about the same place in our upper education. He was a senior and I a first-year graduate student seeking a master's degree. I only had a few other friends with the same interests—my housemates, Melissa Wells and Anne Damon, both of whom I'd met riding horses at Griffith Park and with whom I'd shared midnight popcorn and poetry. But only Melissa knew how I had adored Mr. Langley all these years.

I had told her after I came back from Africa and we met again in Miss La Monde's Chaucer class, which happened to be next to Langley's Room 33. She noticed how I hung out in the hall before and after class, how I put my hand over my heart if he passed us on campus, and how I tried to get in his metaphor workshop, even though I wasn't one of his students. Late one afternoon after a long Saturday trail ride, we were brushing the horses and I leaned my head against my pinto's neck.

"Sela, what on earth is wrong with you?"

"Oh, Melissa, I have to tell someone," I said. "I have been dreaming about William Langley since I was nineteen!"

She jumped on me, telling me I'd better get over it or I could be headed for a lot of trouble. When I asked what on earth she was talking about, she told me that her mother had defended a schizophrenic woman years ago who had escaped from a prison mental ward and had tracked down her ex-husband and his new wife with a gun. She said, "I remember how freaked my mother was about that case, how close that couple had come to being killed. So I worry about you, Sela. Who knows what Langley's wife might do if… hey, I hear she's kind of weird and has a drinking problem. Just forget any *dreams* about that man."

"Do you want me to forget sharing stuff with you?" I asked.

"Well… no. I think he's a doll too!"

Now, I couldn't wait to tell her I'd gotten into his class. She and Anne were farther back in the line, deep in some discussion, probably making up answers to possible questions. I'd see them later. Lee had been assigned to keep the professor supplied with fresh coffee and maybe a sandwich or chips as the morning dragged on.

"This must be hard for him so close to… losing his wife," I said to Lee.

"He said he was okay, that he really loved choosing his students, and this year he'd be wanting some pretty special answers—'answers that make life worth living' were his exact words. What did you say?"

"I quoted the last two stanzas of one of his poems."

"You answered his question with his own words?"

"I think he liked it. He liked my name anyway."

"I remember how you got teased in junior high about your name," Lee said as he put his arm around my shoulders. "I guess you're glad you have it now."

"He said it was a metaphor."

"Nice."

"I hope he doesn't forget it soon," I said. I glanced back over at Professor Langley. He was shaking the hand of a tall, black, young man who I'd heard had just transferred from a university in South Africa. He was Xhosa. I was sad that I couldn't speak his language. I was fairly competent in Swahili but couldn't imagine when I'd ever use that language again.

"Hey, you, I was *saying*, if Langley doesn't remember your name, he'll for sure remember your eyes," Lee went on.

"Oh, yeah?"

"Yeah… exactly the color of this autumn blue sky."

"I don't know. By the time I'm sitting in his class, they may be the shade of the faded, blue chalkboard."

"Your gold hair curling down practically to your thin waist and your long legs in those black tights won't have escaped his memory, I'm sure."

I knew he meant it as a compliment, but I said quickly, "Lee, it was my *answer* I wanted him to remember."

"I'm just saying…"

"Well, get back to work for the exquisitely observant Dr. Langley," I said. "I need some sleep. I'll talk to you later."

"Okay, my friend. Love you."

"Love you, too."

We parted. He went over to fill Mr. Langley's coffee cup, and I headed for the house that the three of us girls had rented, just off campus. Melissa and Anne wouldn't be back for a while, and I could rest. But by the time I had let myself in the door, there was already a poem in my head. It began:

If first words are a metaphor
then we already soar above the common
& untenable paths
where death and loneliness
can strip us bare
of poetry.

Then it stumbled on:

But you and I are meant for poetry
connected by some fleeting but
endearing language
no one else can hear.

When could I ever show him that, for heaven's sake? What if I was just too much for him, metaphoric name or not? I thought, *How can I be amazing, inspiring, comforting, every day from now on?* But I was pretty sure he didn't expect that. Realistically, as any respected professor would, he could expect me to listen to him in the classroom and to write my heart out but never, never, never… to fall in love with him.

2

It was only a short walk from my house on Bruin Drive to the campus. Most of my classes were in the lit building: first period, The Literary Novel; second period, Classics from Around the World; third period, Quantum Physics Demystified (a ten-minute walk to the math/science building); fourth period, The Romantic Movement in Literature; lunch; fifth period with Mr. Langley, MWF, Writing the Short Story (semester one), Writing the Modern Poem (semester two); and sixth period, graduate studies with a faculty advisor.

If an advisor was not available on a particular day, students could use that time as a study hall but had to check in and out with someone from the English department. My graduate studies room was right across the hall from Mr. Langley's, but my advisor was Lois La Monde. I didn't have any other classes with her that year, but I knew her from my junior Chaucer class, and she had a reputation for a no-nonsense attitude about everything, demanding perfection in speech and dress—which most students failed to live up to—and strict attention to university codes. I had been around UCLA off and on for eight years, and I still didn't know what those were. I guessed Miss La Monde would inform me soon enough. I was already pretty sure that throwing my arms around Professor Langley was on the prohibited list.

That first day, I took a few notes in my classes but mostly marked time until I could be in Room 33 with Mr. Langley. I ate with Melissa and Lee at an outdoor café on campus, barely tasting my food. When the bell rang for period 5, we walked together, three utterly joyful lambs going from the sheltered grounds of what felt safe into the woods, where the wolves of despair and bliss stalked the unwary. Nothing wrong with *my* metaphors.

Langley was writing some very beautiful and succinct quotes from authors we all knew—Ernest Hemingway, Joyce Carol Oates, Virginia Woolf, Oscar Wilde, Annie Dillard—under a large, almost calligraphic heading: "WRITERS TAKE NOTE." His back was to us, and his desk was piled with books and papers and, sadly, a photo of Natasha in a red-sequined dress at some faculty function. The frame cut off part of one hand that perhaps held an alcoholic beverage.

Then I was absorbed in the words that hit me so deeply I could hardly breathe when he turned around. And there was that just-as-beautiful face and heart-stopping eyes, and he said, "Who knows where you can find all this advice in one source?"

No one moved. I raised my hand. I would be the first in my class to address this much-honored and quite adorable man.

"Yes… Miss Hart?"

So he did remember my name.

"Those words can be found in Ms. Oates's book *The Faith of a Writer*," I answered.

"Absolutely. Thank you, Miss Hart. First assignment—buy that book. I've ordered quite a few copies for the Student Union, and they can be found at bookstores around town. You have two days to read it. By Wednesday, I want you to find a truth that resonates with your experience as a writer, something that shows me you are going to know how to live with those words for the rest of your life."

Any other professor would have said "until the end of the semester," but not Langley. These were words for one's life, and maybe he and I were the only ones who knew it. He went on to other things—class schedules, conference hours, his free periods, writing requirements, make-up work, and late assignments. I could not take my eyes off of his face. He didn't look his age. His eyes were shining, and this was just menial information. I wondered what his eyes would look like when he showed his heart. Then I listened in earnest as he opened up a little more.

He told us he was named after the nineteenth-century British painter William Langley, that in his mother's room in the Santa Barbara hospital maternity ward there had been a Langley painting expressing the artist's favorite themes—sand dunes, seascapes—that his father was big into symbolism, took one look at that painting and said his son had to have that artist's name. Then our professor admitted that Langley was really his middle name. "No one knows my last name, unless they know my folks, who are 90 percent of the time out of the country. I've almost forgotten it myself."

We all laughed. He confirmed the rumor that he never gave a grade lower than a B minus. "But don't think that floats you a get-out-of-jail-free card." He said he expected great things out of us because we had given the best answers to his questions that he had heard in a long time, and he was ready to give us his all. This in the last minutes of that first class, his wife barely in the grave, his sorrow and his joy in the hands of twenty-something college students bound to frustrate and annoy and even dig at the tenuous foundation he had built for his life without Natasha Skinner Langley.

I put my hand on the story I wanted him to have. I only hoped, that first time, and maybe every time after that, for my words to be a net into which he could fall—oh, not to catch him, but to embrace him. He was straightening his desk but looked up with a smile as I came closer.

"Miss Hart," he said pleasantly. "I guess you won't need to buy that book."

"No... but I'll do the assignment, of course." I hesitated.

"Yes?" His sixth-period students were coming in.

"Could I turn in a story now?" I handed him a few typed sheets.

"'The Range,'" he said, looking at the title page. "If there are horses in it, I'll love it."

"Oh, yeah," I said, thinking, *Now I know something else about him,* and smiling to myself, because what I had wanted most was for *him* to discover *me*.

When I got home that day, I thought I must have been dreaming, sitting in William Langley's classroom, answering another of his motivating questions, seeing his beautiful smile. Anne had the TV on. Dr. Phil was saying, "This will be a changing day in your life."

Oh, my...

I had to look far back to conjure up that day in high school when Mrs. Jalen told our English class that she had a special visitor for the hour, the newly conferred Doctorate of Literature at UCLA, William Langley, who was to come read to us. I had no idea who he was. Could the power of words be such that I began to love him then?

He came through the door a little shyly, books under his arms, some with sheets of paper between the pages, maybe unpublished poems. He was very handsome, I guessed not quite thirty years old, with a sweet smile and sparkling brown eyes, if brown can sparkle. His hair was short, and he was dressed informally in jeans; a blue, tan, and white striped shirt; and a tan sweater slung around his shoulders. He moved with confidence to the center of the room, shook Mrs. Jalen's hand, turned to us, and said, "I greet you from the pages of your own work, where you will write better than I, in time."

Mrs. Jalen said, "Dr. Langley, we would be pleased if you would read some of your earlier poems and then a few later, published ones. I would like my students to hear the *development* that comes with learning the craft."

"Craft? Yes, it is a craft," the professor said, "but the heart of it is language that wakes you up in the middle of the night and will not let you go until you write it down! See what you think of this." And he began to read in a deeper, more provoking voice.

Webs

stronger than steel that filament
the spider leaves behind,
his fragile being bent on some design,
movements honed by dance far older than the grass
which holds the finished piece
released in dew like shattered glass

or higher up enhanced with boxes, honeycombs,
& Ferris wheels.
metaphors all
swinging in woods from branch to branch
or gardens between rose and wall
where running once I fell among the sinews
making ragged tears and crying home to Mother's call
ashamed to tell.
and later in a feverish dream I thought
of prison cells composed of lace
& sweetness pouring down my face
& flying where the sky is taut with twilight.
beautiful and magical as wishing wells,
but—
they are traps.
don't touch, my lovelies.

Hands went up all over the room.

"But what does that mean?"

"Why does it have rhyme? Mrs. Jalen doesn't like us to use rhyme."

"There's tons of alliteration!"

"I can feel the webs all over me, uck."

He smiled. "What word in the poem stands out to you?"

Several kids said, wisely enough, "Metaphors!"

A few said, "Traps."

I said nothing, lost in the beautiful and magical *released in dew like shattered glass.*

The young professor said, "You've almost got it."

"Metaphors are traps!" an excited voice said.

"The webs are traps!" another cried out.

Langley said, "That's literally true, but how 'bout metaphorically?"

"Some shapes are boxes. Lots of things get trapped in boxes."

"Like what?" he asked.

"Old letters, secrets, keepsakes..."

"*Poems!*"

"And honeycombs?" he continued.

Everyone went crazy vying for his attention.

"The sweetest things in life..."

"Made by creatures that sting!"

"And Ferris wheels?" he asked.

"Freedom."

"Joy."

"Loss of inhibition!"

Then, a usually reclusive boy said quietly, "They could break. You could fall out. You could die."

There was sudden silence, but the professor bowed to us and said, "I dearly hope I have some of you in my classes at UCLA."

Mrs. Jalen held up her hand. "Do you see what's happening here, young people? You are discovering the power of language. You are talking about a poem as if it's life itself."

"It is *so* life," someone said. "What about the spider whose home is ruined?"

"What about the boy who made 'ragged tears' in the sinews of the web?"

"Or maybe it was a girl! We don't know. Was she trapped by her emotions? She ruined the web. She cried," one of my best friends said.

"Does the poem trap *us* in its emotion?"

"What about the line, *don't touch...*?" Mrs. Jalen asked.

"The poem is a warning that things can break."

"Strong-as-steel webs."

"Ferris wheels."

"Honeycombs."

"The little spider."

"The little boy!"

"The *poem* itself! We are breaking it. We shouldn't touch it!" someone said.

"I think the last line is an opening," I said at last. "For sure we are going to touch it. I think the author is daring us to touch it."

Dr. Langley looked at me for a long moment and said, "Touch it, indeed."

In the end, he admitted that it wasn't a great poem and had been rejected by several magazines, but he said that he personally liked it and delighted in the reactions he got from students. Then he read from his latest book with more up-to-date, award-winning poems and signed a copy for every one of us. It was the book I had quoted out of to get in his class these almost eleven years later.

On Wednesday, there was a note on my desk in Room 33. It read, "Bravo! May I read your story to the class?" I looked up at my professor and nodded. As soon as everyone settled down, Mr. Langley said, "I'd like to start today with something Miss Hart has already turned in. I believe it will get us to the heart of things." He began to read as though he were William Hathaway, the very broken hero of my stories entitled "William and Angela: A Quantum Crossing." I didn't mean there ever to be a person so true.

The Range

I like the title immediately when I'm handed the script. It implies a vastness upon which we actors will imprint our lines in as true a manner as possible. I am William Hathaway. I've been in this profession for quite some time and know a good story when I read one. This story is woven from the fabric of the early West, where boundaries are unclear. Mexicans don't know what territory is truly theirs; cattlemen from north of the border lay claim to the land; rustlers from as far away as California and Nevada want the horses; jobless men and gamblers desire the women. Single women have very few options.

Our lead character is one of those, played by a lovely half-Mexican actress named Elena Ruiz, in the script

called Rose. My part says I am a businessman who has made enough money in the East to buy land and cattle but who knows little of the country and the people of the Southwest. I will court the lovely Mexican girl. Rose comes to Borrego City with her sister from a broken family. They are basically orphans and as vulnerable as newborn calves. A gambler, played by Jonathan Hunt, seduces her, but he is rough and controlling and does not count on the wild, protective spirit of Rose's sister.

But the theme of the movie is not what I wish to tell you. There are things beyond our understanding that *The Range* is calling out of the small company camped in the Arizona desert. You do not need to know all that is passing through the lenses of the cameras to come away with a profound sense of the conflicts during that time in history or of the relationships that are not of the screenwriter's design. The script is only a frame for the truer story that occurs without warning among veritable strangers who know how to act, even when they do not know what is really happening.

Mr. Langley turned the first page over and looked up at us. "Anyone have a quick response to that last line?" he asked back in his own voice.

"I think it's a damn huge invitation to keep reading," Blake Adams said.

And so he continued reading, seemingly satisfied that a small lesson had been learned.

Day one. Hot. Monsoonal rains expected. The set is intimidating at first. I've been around horses and ridden all my life, but at 45, I'm not as agile in the saddle. The horses mill around impatiently, blacks, pintos, palominos, bays. They've done this before. A wrangler is rounding up the prettiest ones for the first day's shooting, which will have lots of close-ups. I am supposed to race with the young, supporting actress (can't think of her name), Rose's sister, down a canyon stream known for its quicksand. "Ride on the outside of turns," they tell us. I have a lump in my throat. Here we go.

The cameras whirr with importance. I step out of the postal station and start loading my saddlebags with packages and letters from friends who thought I was crazy to set foot in this country. I hear the frantic hoof beats before I see the young lady flying down the street on the only grey in the company stock. She glances at half-drunk cowboys and old men, and then she sees me.

"Mister!... Mister! Can you help me? One of my sister's horses has broken his leg. There are two pulling our wagon, and the good horse won't stop, dragging the lame one without pity. Please come help us," she cries.

So I'm off with this frightened kid (well, she seems like a kid to me), skinny, dressed like a boy, riding like a boy, but definitely not a boy. The camera trucks are rolling beside us, trying to keep pace with two very fresh horses. Thunder booms some distance away. In two miles we reach Rose struggling with a striking Paint mare to keep her from charging ahead with the injured bay barely able to move.

I dismount quickly, handing Rose's sister my reins, and pull my Winchester from its scabbard. I remove as much harness as I can before ending with one shot the poor animal's life. Rose falls forward with her hand to her heart, and I try to calm the Paint, who is freaking out at the gunshot. Rose looks over the back of the horse at me. She is certainly beautiful with her Mexican brown skin and dark eyes. I know Elena from a few encounters in the studio and see that this will be a good role for her. She exudes strength but can seem as fragile as a butterfly.

The cameras close in, just the two of us in the eye of the lens.

"Gracias," she says breathlessly.

"De nada," I respond and then tell her I don't speak much Spanish.

"Bueno. I speak English."

"What are you doing here?" I ask.

"Our mother and father have many problems, other children. We are a burden. So we have come from Mexico to make a new life."

"Brava, muchachas," I say and tip my hat.

The sister has hitched her grey in place of the dead horse and climbs up next to Rose.

"What about the horse?" Rose asks.

"I think you'll have to leave it for the wolves."

She looks about to faint. There are other men and wagons on the road now, so she urges the horses on. She stares at me and asks,

"Su nombre?"

"Ryder... just Ryder."

"Cut!," the director calls out.

We are all parched from the sun. The horses are pulled aside and watered. We are led to shade and cool drinks. I am feeling strangely tired and hope we don't have to reshoot any of the scenes. The director suggests that the sister stay more out of the camera view and reminds her that her character is not as vital as the character of Rose. But I am amazed at the eloquent presence of the sister with fewer lines and less contact in the scene with Rose and me. Her passion seems to come from another world, and the director doesn't want any part of it. Rain gives us an early break, and we are driven back to our trailers on the outskirts of Borrego.

In the script I am haunted by Rose, catch glimpses of her calico dress floating into the mercantile or a hand on the harness of the Paint, called Spooky, and the sister's grey. I haven't been in Borrego City long when trouble starts. I walk out my front door one morning to a gruesome sight. Cattle lie scattered, dead, around the water tank, which has been poisoned. I lean on the porch rail, devastated. The girl, Rose's sister, appears out of a thick stand of saguaro to the south with her arms around a golden heifer.

"I saved one for you, mister," she says.

"So you did."

She starts to hand me the lariat holding the animal steady.

"No," I say. "Take it to Rose."

"Gracias," says the girl, "mi amigo."

She and the yearling blend into the blinding desert light as they move off toward the slumbering hills and Rose's small piece of borrowed earth.

The cows wake up from their tranquilized state and are herded away by the wranglers. In the movie it doesn't show what Ryder does with the dead animals, but he wearies of the friendless life. There are scenes after that depicting the hardships faced by Ryder and by the women alone in a harsh landscape. When their paths cross, there is a silent bonding that hints at something more.

I act the outsider, disdained by locals, but I decide to play their game and sit down one day at the poker table. Rose is at the bar alone. Her sister lingers in the shadows. She is barely old enough to be in the bar, but she watches everything. It's smoky and hot from the lights. I look over at Rose with compassion and admiration. Her betrothed, Wyatt, spits his line.

"Git your eyes off her, man, if you want to keep 'em!"

I feel dizzy, literally, and should ask for a reprieve, but I'm sure my discomfort fleshes out the scene. Wyatt is shoving chips at me angrily. I see that I've won, but I only want to talk to Rose. My head is splitting. Suddenly Rose is gone. I want to go after her, comfort her. Something is wrong. I push the chips back to the center of the table, stand unsteadily.

"You can have the money," I say and make my way to the door.

Just outside, Rose's sister grabs my arm. "Don't follow her. Wyatt'll find her. I know where she goes. I'll take you later. Sit here a while."

There's an old couch on the rotting boards of the porch. I'm relieved to sit down. My head is killing me (not in the script). Tears fall out of my eyes. The girl reaches a hand out and wipes them away (not in the script, but it works, the director says later).

I say to Rose's sister, "Are you real?"

"Some people think that I am," she replies.

"Cut!," we hear, still looking at each other.

Later she comes to my trailer with ginger. "Eat a little of this," she says, "for the pain." And then she lays cool cloths on my forehead and massages my shoulders. She sings something about a river with a hint of desperation that springs from the rough waters. I hear the rhymes but don't really understand what she's saying, just feel healed. Without question I fall in love with her. Her name is Angela Star. She doesn't have a name in the movie. She's just the sister.

She calls me William. Nobody does that. We don't have a lot of scenes together, but they're powerful ones. I think the movie turns on them, surprises the viewer with their emotional impact. Angela always touches me, in the movie and on the sets after shooting. She does it in a casual way, but it sends chills through me.

One day we both are off the set. It's raining anyway and not much is getting done. The horses are huddled against each other, muddy and spent. We stay in my trailer. No one seems to notice. I grip her hand and we don't speak for a long time. Finally she says, "I've had a crush on you since I was ten years old." She stands up and leans over me, slowly bending down to put her mouth on mine. I kiss her back with everything in me, and I don't know where I am.

"I can't be here," she says quietly, and I am suddenly alone with my pounding heart.

There's a scene one day where Angela puts on one of Rose's dresses and lopes away on Rose's Paint. Wyatt gets confused and angry and searches the hills and farms for his woman, while Rose and I make love in the basement of my ranch house.

"Why does she put herself in such danger?" I ask Rose.

"She protects me. She always has," she answers. She pulls me closer to her, while I yearn for the body and breath of Angela Star riding somewhere out in the fields, the camera catching flashes of her among wildflowers and beneath blue skies.

The movie feels like my life, the aching for love, the bad guys knocking down my door, killing my dreams like the poor heifers, and the unreality of playing a part. Who am I? I'm sure I'm giving my best performance.

Everyone says so, but I am counting the hours until Angela comes to me, caresses me through my fatigue and misgiving. Then we'll go to my door and hold each other for a long time. We don't have sex. *The Range* consumes us. We seem to need only those sweet embraces, but when she leaves, I weep.

One day she's not on the set.

"Where's the sister?" I ask.

No one knows, but the day doesn't go well. The horses are jumpy. We have dozens of retakes, and actors stumble on their lines. There is no dialogue or action for Rose's sister to hide Rose or keep her secrets or lie to the abusive Wyatt, but the company is falling apart. Without Angela in the wings, the show does not seem to be able to go on.

I wonder at this, but later that night Angela steps through my door. She has been crying, but I don't question her. I take her in my arms and kiss her wet face and tell her I'll love her forever. That seems to calm her. We have a big scene tomorrow, the last scene. Neither of us feels up to it. We go over a few lines, but then she throws one in that is not on the page.

"I have loved you for so long in my mind, I had never imagined what the real love could be. Don't let go of me, William," she whispers. "Don't let go of me."

And so, we lie together all night curled up and hungry for the consummation. When *The Range* is finished, we will find the part that is meant for us. For now, some kind of fantasy is playing itself out.

The morning shoot brings us back to reality. Even the horses know it's a big day, strutting around tossing their heads and whinnying. We mount up. It takes a while to get it right. It's a difficult and exhausting task. By afternoon we are certain of our portrayal.

The sister is on Spooky and I on the big black gelding that has been mine throughout the story. The director has called several times for a stunt double for Angela, but she refuses, saying, "I have to do it."

Wyatt has found Rose's hiding place and is ahead of us on the road with his "boys." We are galloping now. The trail is twisted, and it's hard riding. Once, Angela pulls up beside me, reaches over, and puts one hand over my hand that is on the reins (not in the script, and if the camera catches it, it will be edited out).

Rose is waiting by a crystal pool in a black and burnt-orange rock canyon. Wyatt is screaming at her, "I'll kill you!" when Rose's sister leaps from Spooky and slams Wyatt's body from his horse to the ground, snatching his rifle from his hands. Angela fires at the men, just grazing them, until there are only a few bullets left in the rifle, and she is the only one standing on the red-stained desert floor.

I am calling to Rose who seems frozen to the spot. She moves dazedly toward me like a person already drowned, her hair and dress dripping water. I throw the reins to her, and she swings up on the mare, her long, black hair flying out with the movement. She hesitates again.

"We're going to Mexico!" I shout, kicking the gelding forward.

She says, "I'll be a gringa there… scorned."

I say, trying to get her to grab the reins, "Would you rather be a live gringa or a dead Mexican in a foreign land?"

Her sister is turning all Wyatt's horses loose and holding the gun over a man on whom she didn't inflict a serious enough wound. We look at each other. Her eyes say, *Good-bye, my love* (not in the script). I slap the Paint's rump, and soon Rose and I are racing south. It's fifteen miles to the border. Of course, they don't let us ride all the way. They trailer up the horses, and Elena and I ride in silence in the truck, thinking of our final lines, as the sun flames down the horizon corralled by the blackness of night.

On the desert set a few miles away, the crew is arranging special lights so that the black gelding won't fade into the background. I cannot get Angela out of my mind. Even though it's just a story, I can't help feeling she is in actual danger.

Final scene. We are far out in the Mexican flats, the horses heaving and a dark night closing around us. We're safe now, but the script calls for me to turn my horse back and tell Rose, "We can't leave your sister. I'll go for her."

"Ryder…" she pauses. "My sister has been dead for twenty years."

Of course I know how the movie ends, but hearing those words shakes me to the core (a look worthy of an Oscar nomination but hard on the heart).

"Cut! Wrap!" the director yells.

"Where's Angela?" I ask immediately.

"Who's Angela?" somebody says.

"Angela Star, Rose's sister, the actress?"

"There's no Angela Star. The sister is played by Katie Turin," someone else answers.

And a young woman whom I've never seen approaches us and speaks through the sage-scented air, "Nice working with you guys."

"Yeah, Katie, good job," Elena says.

I dismount and stand on solid ground. The horse rubs his sweaty head against my shoulder. Somewhere

a coyote yips. The wranglers are handling the animals, the set being broken down, people drifting off in small groups. Someone slaps me on the back.

"Great work, Bill... Are you okay? This last day was a tough one, huh?"

I mumble something, but I am not okay. I will never be okay.

Everyone gasped at the end, and students were waving their hands frantically.

"Mr. Langley!"

"Mr. Langley, isn't that science fiction? Are we allowed to write that? That's just make-believe."

"Is it now?" Langley shot back. "Does anybody else have a different idea?"

Words were tossed about: fantasy, dream-state, even stream-of-consciousness. And then William Langley shocked everyone, including me, when he said, "How 'bout quantum consciousness?"

"There's no such thing!" Riley Starkes announced.

"I think you're looking at it," Mr. Langley said, holding up my manuscript.

"There's nothing about quantum dimensions in *The Faith of a Writer*," Suzi Han noted.

"But there is something about revelation and surprise, if I'm not mistaken," Langley said. "But let's start someplace else for the moment. What's the first thing that involves you in this story?"

"The movie script," Blake said.

"The history part about women not being treated so well," Melissa suggested.

"The actor, William Hathaway," someone else said.

"I don't believe so," Mr. Langley said and waited.

"I'll bet Sela doesn't even know!" Calisha Sims teased.

"Oh, I think she does." Langley looked at me. "Shall we say it together, Miss Hart?"

And we both said at the same time, "The title."

Risa Hollingsworth practically leaped out of her seat. "A *range!* A whole range of things—an actor's life, a story, or two stories within a story! Love with sex, love without sex, mistaken identity, the very *land,* the role of the horses, the role of *reality* itself..."

Langley broke in, "You got it, Risa, and yes, yes, yes, all of those things. The title dares you to find all of these themes."

"Range of emotions!" Lee called out. "Range of the actor's ability."

"Or believability!" someone added.

"The range of possibilities at the ending," Suzi offered.

"But what about the ending? Did you know when you started how it was going to end?" Lee asked me.

"No," I answered truthfully.

"Isn't that one of the rules?" Blake asked.

"There aren't really any rules that you can't break," Langley tried to explain, "if you have a damn good reason. Miss Hart, would you like to enlighten us?"

"To be honest, all the way through the story, as I was writing, I thought Angela Star was the actress playing Rose's sister. The whole ending came to me when the script has Rose say, 'My sister has been dead for twenty years.' That just led me to the double meaning of that statement, that Angela may be a ghost too."

"But is Angela real or not?" someone asked.

"Why does Hathaway not see the actress Katie Turin during the actual shooting of the movie?" Suzi continued.

"How do we know what to believe? There are so many levels... oh, wow, *dimensions,* to this story!" Lee said. He turned to me again. "Sela, it's genius!"

"Look what we're doing here, folks," Langley interjected.

"We're talking about it! We're captured by the story!" Melissa called out.

"Exactly," Langley said.

More hands went up, but Professor Langley said he needed to spend some time hearing our quotes from *The Faith of a Writer* that were especially engrossing for us. Almost everyone had found something meaningful, and the class ended on an upbeat note. There was excitement about writing, about language, about revelations. Mr. Langley seemed very pleased. When I passed his desk, he said softly, "Sela, may I keep this?"

"Of course. I'd be honored."

Then, even more softly, he said, "Are you real?" with his hand on the top page of my story. It felt like a caress.

On Friday, he looked tired. This first week of school must have been hard on him, having to go home every night to an empty house, fix his own meals, grade papers in the darkening silence. My heart just ached for him. I couldn't help asking him if he was okay when I went by his desk. His eyes sprang to life for a moment. "Nothing another story of yours wouldn't fix," he said.

"The next story will not be easy for you to read. I'm sorry." I noticed that the photo of Natasha was missing.

"I think I'll take that chance, Miss Hart."

So I handed him "A Story in Two Hearts."

"Sentimental?"

"Not at all. Just very literal. You'll see." And I took my seat.

Langley began telling us his plans for the first semester. He said there would be no tests, a metaphor workshop closer to the beginning of next semester, and independent projects for extra credit. He added that if a particular assignment wasn't working for us, he'd accept a poem.

"I'm also not opposed to short stories having a connection or running theme. Sometimes there's a novella or a novel developing in the writer's head."

Blake raised his hand. "Mr. Langley, sometimes it takes me a while to get anywhere with a short story idea."

"You may turn in drafts, first pages, or outlines. I understand you can't force the process, but today I have some ideas to help you. Thinking back to our discussion of knowing the ending before you begin, I'd like to suggest a few lines that could be endings. Actually, if you feel drawn to use them as first lines, that's acceptable. The idea is just to get you writing."

He read some lines, and we copied down the ones that appealed to us.

"and wine from the wounded deer"

"He held the rock as long as he could."

"She looked back once."

"no limits"

"a place for me"

"with everything undone"

I especially liked the last one. It was so inviting, mysterious, ambiguous. I might try it. Mr. Langley was saying, "Let's take some time to write other possible endings. I'd like to hear them aloud in ten minutes or so."

We set to work inventing endings. I could only think of one thing: the white bed in the white room waited.

Langley grinned when I read that. "My, my, Miss Hart," he said.

The bell rang.

But I didn't write that story. I had homework in my other four classes and a graduate project that needed some research. I thought maybe I'd turn in a poem where I'd written the last line first. I had plenty of those. I looked through the ones I'd written in Africa and tried to stay away from anything with death in it. My heart shuddered worrying about the story I'd given Mr. Langley. It would be a double reminder of the reality of death, and I wished I hadn't let him have it.

I was alone at the house. Melissa and Anne had a drama club meeting and probably wouldn't be home for a couple of hours. The phone rang. I didn't rush to get it, wondering who would call on a Friday home game night.

"Hello?"

"Sela."

I almost dropped the phone.

"How did you...?"

"Melissa gave me your house number. I hope that wasn't inappropriate."

"No, of course not."

"Sela, I loved the stories. I just had to tell you. I knew you'd have second thoughts about letting me read them."

"I did, Mr. Langley."

"I'll admit I cried a little, but then, I think I needed to. I'm going to read them again right now. I would be pleased to know you were reading them along with me. I had an idea for class, but I'm not sure I can do it."

"What's that, Mr. Langley?"

"I would read the first part as though I were William Hathaway, and then you'd read the next as if you were Angela," he said.

"I'm not sure I could get through that either, sir."

"Why?"

"It's a little close to home—parts of it anyway."

"When did you write this?"

"Last year, standing in line for your class," I admitted.

There was a moment of silence.

"Did you know the last lines of these two stories?"

"I did."

"Wherever did they come from?"

"From the characters themselves," I said.

"Well, they're amazing. You can use them for your 'last line first' assignment."

"I appreciate it, but I'm trying to revise something I started in Africa where the last line followed me around for days looking for the rest of the words."

"A short story?"

"No. A poem."

"I'll be interested in seeing that, Miss Hart," he said quietly. "Now, pick up 'A Story in Two Hearts' and read with me."

"Okay, sir… Good night."

"Good night, Sela."

I reached in my fifth period folder and pulled out my copy. I felt Langley's vision streaming through my eyes as I read the words. I knew he wouldn't call again.

3

We settled into our roles as student and teacher, but the phone call had changed everything. It was so personal, so honest. Neither of us had put up any walls as we had to do on campus. It was comfortable knowing that we could talk on a level deeper than lectures and assignments. It was the beginning of friendship.

And then he surprised me again. He put a scrap of paper on my desk. It read, "Everyone has my home phone. This is my cell phone. Keep it to yourself. WL." I memorized it, and then I put my cell phone number on a note card and wrote, "SH's cell phone. Call any time for any reason." I had always thought such a move by a teacher would scare me, even by this man whom I had dreamed of for so long, but I felt myself growing up by the minute. If I couldn't be what he needed, I had no business writing those words *call any time for any reason*. This was not a short story that I could revise here and there or delete with a punch of a finger. I had to write on the pages of his life the truest person I was.

For a couple of weeks, kids read and reworked their "last line first" stories. Finally, Mr. Langley called on me. "I believe Sela has taken me up on my offer to write a poem for this assignment. I haven't seen it, but I'll ask her to read it now, if she's finished her revisions."

"Yes, sir, I can do that," I said. It was true I had needed some time, but I still hadn't solved a problem. I had used a phrase from another poem. I knew I'd have to rewrite one of the lines sooner or later, but I hadn't been able to choose between the two poems. The lines fit both realities, just like my life fit so solidly with my two Williams.

I stood up in front of my classmates, some of whom knew nothing about my years in Africa. I would have some explaining to do. Mr. Langley moved to the back of the room, but he didn't sit down. It was so respectful of him. I began to read with my heart in Tanzania.

Holy Water

The sea stretched away in turquoise splendor
darkening at the horizon
where ships and dhows and fishing boats
plowed the waters unceasingly.
A few clouds bunched up on the curve of the earth
and I sat on the sea wall,
the tide lapping at my feet.

I had come to see lions,
to peer over the side of the jeep
at those golden shapes resting in our shade,
to touch the cave walls where Maasai set their stories
in vegetable paint 300 years ago,
to photograph the silver shadows of rhinos
on the Ngorongoro Crater floor.

There had been no rain.

Giraffes loped with long oar strokes
across the dry plains.
Wildebeests and zebras panted past predators at meager ponds
for a chance to drink.
Women in swaths of purple and red walked mile after mile
with water vessels balanced on their heads
under the merciless sun.

All water is salvation.

I passed through burnt-out land,
water trucks speeding in their suffocating clouds of dust
to parched settlements.
I reached for the Indian Ocean,
too salty to save anything
except my desire to have it on my skin,
my nonblack skin,
to wash clean my conceit from a world
that calls this *world unenlightened,*
this world that speaks to every man as a brother,
that protects one from harm in the blink of an eye,
that spins wasted plastic and glass into unimpeachable art.

And I wandered in their ocean
to be one of them,
a Tanzanian,
an assuager of thirst.

Mr. Langley leaned against a desk in the back row when I read the last line. Then he said, "Miss Hart, would you read the last line again?"

When I finished, no one spoke. I could hear Mr. Langley's footsteps coming up an aisle. He stopped and took the poem from my hand.

"Are there more of these?" he asked.

"Oh, yes. I was saving them for next semester."

"I don't know if I can wait that long."

"Neither can I," Lee Henderson spoke up.

Then others were full of questions, and Mr. Langley noted the metaphoric language, imagery, symbolism, and political and social inferences, letting students point these things out too when they could.

"And then, of course, there's that magnificent title," he said. "When did you write that, Miss Hart?"

"After I had finished the poem. At the end, I guess you could say."

"Ah," he said, as if that were a whole sentence, and then, "I guess that's where you would find it."

He slipped it into his briefcase as the bell rang, and I left with conflicting feelings. Africa was another story, one I was perhaps not prepared to tell.

In sixth period that day, Miss La Monde checked over my graduate project outline and said she didn't like it.

"Why?" I wanted to know. It was an idea for a metaphor workshop, if I were teaching it instead of Mr. Langley.

"It's just preposterous," she exclaimed, "taking thirty kids to the beach because the *sea* might be used as a metaphor!"

"That's not exactly it, Miss La Monde. The sea *is* a metaphor whether we go there or not. But I have found that being in the environment of one's poem can have astounding results."

"Like what?"

"Like getting in Mr. Langley's actual metaphor workshop because of the title of one of those poems. Like finding a new *current,* excuse the metaphor, to explore with your writing while a freshwater stream pours into the ocean or a tidal bore threatens to wipe out… something dear to you and in the poem *is* that thing, like your memory, your prized possession, your love."

"Oh, what would you know about it!" she said.

"I can show you a poem I'd use to get the discussion going," I said, and I handed her one called "Resurgence." It was short, so it didn't take her long to criticize.

"This rhymes!"

"So? That's not the point. It's full of metaphors," I said.

"Well, I don't see any," she said.

"'Salt streams' equals 'saline fields,' 'resurgence' equals 'swam the surgeon's element,' or 'ocean in his eyes' equals 'churning dark.' The horse grazes in waves and carves furrows with his hooves."

"That's just imagery," she said.

"Well, it's close, but I think a case can be made for metaphor if you look at it deeply enough in the light of the whole poem."

"Is this the title that got you in Langley's workshop?"

"No."

"Well... what was it?"

I hesitated and then told her, "Holy Water."

"I'd say you have a passion for water, don't you?"

"You'd be surprised what I have a passion for," I mumbled.

"What did you say?"

I didn't answer.

"Well, carry on. I don't suppose that kind of workshop will ever happen. You'll be lucky to stay in Langley's workshop. He usually pares the group down closer to the session."

She walked out as the bell rang, and I went straight across the hall to Room 33. Mr. Langley was seeing his kids out and collecting assignments.

"Sela! What can I do for you?"

"I didn't have time for lunch. Can I buy you some coffee or something so you'll sit with me at the café?"

"Sure. I'd love to. Hang on a minute."

He closed his inner office, grabbed his briefcase, and locked his door. When we passed Miss La Monde's room, she came rushing out. "Where are you two going?"

"To have a *private* conference, Lois," he said, and he put his hand briefly on my back.

Oh, God in heaven, I will not be able to eat a bite.

When we got to the little café outside the Student Union, he said, "Is there something I should know, Sela?"

You mean besides the fact that I am absolutely crazy about you? I thought, but I said, "Oh, Miss La Monde's being a bit negative about my grad project. All I wanted to do was be with you for a while. I hope you don't mind."

"I'm flattered, Sela. You are my A number 1... everything," he said.

"Really?"

"Hmm. Would you like me to write you a poem?"

We both laughed, but I said, "How 'bout just a title."

He thought for a moment while we pulled up chairs to a small table in the courtyard. Then he said, "The True Key."

I couldn't believe it. "That's one of my Quantum Crossing stories!" I told him.

"Well, let me think of another while you get my coffee, as you promised," he prompted me good-naturedly.

I went to the snack bar and got coffee and a chicken sandwich. When I sat down, he was smiling and said immediately, "Anchor."

"Oh, wow, I hope I can live up to that."

"I'm sure you will," he said with a look on his face that I couldn't quite read.

He sipped his coffee while I devoured my sandwich. I was hungry, after all.

Then he said, more seriously, "Only a true anchor would write the words *Call me any time for any reason.* That's perhaps more generous than I deserve."

"Look at you, sitting here with a weepy grad student who can't get along with her faculty advisor. You deserve the world."

"And you," he said.

We sat there a little longer, and finally he said, "You okay now?"

"I'm very okay, Mr. Langley. See you Wednesday."

"See you Wednesday, my dear."

On Tuesday, I dove into my metaphor project, La Monde be damned. I hadn't told Mr. Langley all of what had occurred between my advisor and me because I didn't want to put teacher against teacher. That was just petty. I searched the Internet and the library for titles that led me to the sea. Oh, there were so many. Of course, the work couldn't be just *about* the sea; there had to be strong metaphoric content or I discarded it. I also decided to limit the literature to twentieth- or twenty-first-century authors. Then I had a startling idea. What if I found evidence in the latter part of those periods, poems that hinted at climate change in the oceans—a line about more deadly storms, an unusual fire season where tankers scooped up buckets of ocean water to douse the flames, or a hiker wondering why his feet were wet where the tide had never reached before?

As excited as I got about that idea, I stopped myself and remembered the feel of Langley's hand on my back and his calling me his anchor. An anchor goes in the sea. An anchor holds something steady that is searching for calm water. The metaphors were killing me because I couldn't know all the meanings they would have for my life. Oh, how worth it it was to have stood in his lines all these years.

The thing that I had never been sure of from the beginning was that there would be an easy way for Mr. Langley to get to know who I was. We were strangers. I was over ten years younger. He was my teacher, and he was known for treating all of his students equally. Calling me his "anchor" went way beyond everyone's rules, but there it was. I guessed I should be grateful that crushes abounded where William Langley was concerned. I didn't really stand out, except maybe to him. How did this happen? I believe it was through my words, through short stories and poems. If I had not had that talent, or at least a talent he recognized, I would still be standing in a line going on nine years long.

Melissa teased me quite a bit.

"How's your secret love today?"

"Not very secret if you keep asking me things like that!"

"But you can tell he really likes you. You must be stoked."

"We have an interesting relationship," I said.

"Interesting? Girl, you're missing the boat. Go for it!"

I wondered then what she'd think of the anchor metaphor!

We always had something to say to each other after Mr. Langley's class. We'd walk down the hall arm in arm talking about how great he looked in jeans, how intensely he reacted to a good story, how sad he seemed some days when students' themes touched on death. Mostly we sighed with infatuation.

One day in the middle of October, we saw Lois La Monde leaning precariously close to *our* Mr. Langley outside her classroom. Melissa grabbed my head and put hers close to mine. “What does she think she’s doing?” she whispered.

Miss La Monde put her arm on Mr. Langley’s and said as we sauntered by, “I just can’t get used to lesbians on campus!”

We were not so far past them that we didn’t hear Langley’s response. “Sela and Melissa? They are definitely not gay,” he said.

We got a lot of mileage out of that.

Near the end of that week, I crossed paths with Mr. Langley on the quad just before fourth period.

“Hey, Sela,” he said as he recognized me.

“Hi, Mr. Langley,” I said in my best I-am-not-out-of-my-mind-excited-to-see-you voice.

“Here,” he said, motioning toward a bench. “Sit here with me for a minute.”

Whatever I had been thinking flew completely away.

We sat fairly close. It was a balmy day for October, but I was shivering.

“Miss Hart, you’re shaking. Have my jacket.” He placed his tan leather coat over my shoulders and said, “Are you uncomfortable with me?”

I looked right in his beautiful eyes. “No, Mr. Langley. If I could freeze time right this minute, I would.”

“Unfortunately, we both have ‘promises to keep,’” he said.

“Yeah, I know.”

“I just wanted to ask you if you’d read ‘A Story in Two Hearts’ with me today, for periods five and six?”

“You’re all right with that?”

“I think so,” he said. “Can we go through it? Are you free?”

“I can skip physics today,” I said.

I reached in my backpack and handed him “Chosen One.” After just a brief pause, he began to read. He became William Hathaway. No one walked by. I was mesmerized (nothing new there). I waited just a breath when he finished. Then I said, "Angela's Lament" and read the first line, "I don't know why I was so crazy about William Hathaway."

He listened as if he were hearing me for the first time. When I came to his name in the story, I was afraid to say it. How could he not know I was speaking *his* name? At the last line, he leaned back against the bench and closed his eyes. "Read the last part again," he said.

I tried to make the darkness of the story close everything else out. He put his hand to his eyes, you know, like you do when you're staunching tears. But he recovered quickly and said, "I love the way you say Mr. Hathaway's name."

"Your name," I said.

"Yes." He got up. "Keep the coat until class, Sela… I don't want you to get cold."

"As from-the-river cold?" I asked in Angela's voice.

"Yes," he said. "I'm sorry I can't say more now or stay with you. I need some time."

"I know," I said.

He reached over and pulled his jacket closer around me and then walked off toward the lit building. I hugged myself inside his coat. It smelled of aftershave and chaparral and a distant sea and him. I thought I had gone too far, saying his name like that, showing my heart. I needed to slow down.

Then, there was my roommate Anne coming up to me. "Sela, why are you wearing that coat?"

"It's Professor Langley's."

"I know *that*. I've seen him in it a jillion times. But why do *you* have it?" she persisted.

"We were talking about his short story class that I'm in, and I started shaking," I answered.

"Oh, yeah? From the cold?"

"Not exactly," I admitted. "I adore him. I'm trying to be a normal student, but the thing is I'm not. I'm older than most of my classmates, I've lived in Africa, I've written so much more than anyone in my class, and I really care about him. Anne, please don't repeat any of this. I'm just having a hard time with my feelings."

"Does *he* know that?"

"I'm not sure. He likes my stories, my ideas, the way I say his name, for heaven's sake."

"You call him *Bill*?"

"No. My stories have a main character named William."

"Oh, yeah, *that's* a coincidence," she said.

"It is really. I wrote these stories a while ago."

"Do you think he believes that?" she asked.

"I don't know what he believes. I have to be so careful. He's been through a lot, his wife dying in that terrible accident last summer."

"I heard about that. She was drunk."

"That's what everyone says, but I haven't heard that from him."

"Why would he tell you?"

"I think he needs someone to talk to," I said.

"Well, he's got Lois La Monde," she said. "She's always telling us how he's her boyfriend."

"I don't think that's what he wants."

"How could you possibly know that?"

"She... hovers. She's judgmental and prudish. I don't think he appreciates that."

"So you are out to save him?"

"I don't think of it like that," I said.

"Well, how do you think of it?"

"I think of it as saving myself."

She had sat down about halfway through that conversation. Now she shook her head and stood up. "Sela, I think you're headed for a fall."

"Maybe," I said.

"Just don't take him with you," she said. She went off to lunch with my little drama behind her.

I couldn't move. I had hoped Anne would understand, but I was sorry I had told her so much. I walked over to the house and put some soup in the microwave. I ate it with Langley's jacket still around my shoulders.

An hour later, I opened the door to Professor Langley's room. I handed him his leather coat. "It saved me," I said.

"Well, we'll see," he said with a twinkle in his eyes.

He raised his hand after the bell to quiet the room. "Here's what you all have been waiting for—'A Story in Two Hearts' by Sela Hart." I went up to the front. We faced each other, and he began with William Hathaway's words in "Chosen One."

The screen went blank. Lights came on, and people hurried up the aisles in inaudible conversations. Finally, the lights were dimmed, and I was alone in the dark theater, where I had been seated third row center for the premiere of my latest film, *Chosen One.*

I was tired. An ache had started up behind my eyes, and I couldn't face the crowd of fans and reporters just yet. This job had been debilitating. I'd lost twenty pounds and felt disconnected from the real world. The movie world wasn't much better, but it had been somewhat of a relief to be someone other than myself. My wife and I didn't sleep in the same bed, and my daughters came and went through my actor's life with barely a hello. I didn't blame them. I was not easy to live with. They accused me of loving my acting parts more than I loved them, and maybe it was a little true.

I was thirty-six but felt fifty. There was so much noise in my life, phones, directors, casting agents, sets full of shouting and cursing. I longed for this quiet, dark space, but it scared me too. People had expectations, desires. The movie was good. Everyone wanted a piece of me, not knowing I had already given everything to

the script. I looked deep inside to see what I had left. There wasn't much there.

Outside, fans waited beneath my name in lights, beside the posters with my double-sized image, though I am duller and thinner than I have ever been.

"Bill... are you coming? There's a party at Carino's."

"I know," I said. "I just need a minute."

But I stood and walked slowly up the aisle. I could see the crowd moving, shimmering, but I couldn't hear the sounds. The fans watched for me like a surrealistic painting both comic and sad. What would they see if they looked in at me? A fatigued, aging actor dreading to have any contact with them or a vital, handsome man as gregarious and fit as the man in my role in *Chosen One*?

I opened the door and stepped out into their world. I was mobbed. Theater programs and scraps of paper were thrust under my hand for a scrawl of my name. Sometimes I signed my movie name, wondering if they would be disappointed later when they got home and noticed the signature. I don't like a lot of people close to me. I feel a small panic, a pressure in my chest that threatens to overwhelm me. But that night I fought it back and made my way towards the limo. I was feeling some distress then, fending off questions and compliments as though they would eat me alive.

Suddenly, a young lady moved out of the crowd. I thought she was about twenty, but she wasn't screaming like the other women. She was serious and intent and looked right into my eyes. She had nothing for me to sign, but she reached out one hand and placed it softly on my arm and said my name, "William."

I froze. My pain was shed from my body like water from a desert draw. For a moment, I felt that the earth had stopped spinning and she and I had been flung out into space. Then she was pushed away from me, and I lost sight of the slim, raven-haired angel of a girl who touched me in a way no one had for a long time.

When I closed my eyes in the car, I could see her approaching with her eyes locked on mine and her heart seeking mine, as if it had done so for years. I was afraid to open my eyes, afraid of losing that image, that startling spark that had come from her hand.

I was home now. Everyone had gone to bed, but there was no way I was going to sleep. Fans were all the same to me, nameless, voiceless film addicts with a stake on my life. I remembered very few faces, very few remarks about my roles. And then, this... one... girl opened me up to some kind of truth. That I had value beyond the screen, beyond the sad bickering in my marriage, beyond the weariness I succumbed to day after day. She saw the real man that played the parts. She saw the real pain and disappointment, swept it away with a breathless word, and then gave me back to myself.

But I heard in the next few moments, from somewhere in my musings, an anguished cry.

"William... William."

I glanced at the TV. There was a mangled car being hauled out of the Chalice River and a broken railing where it had crashed through and into the water. I turned up the volume.

"...family of five returning from the premiere of *Chosen One.* All were rescued, except one nineteen-year-old daughter, who was swept away by the strong current..."

Then, I held up the other story and began to read.

Angela's Lament

I don't know why I was so crazy about William Hathaway. Whenever his face came on the screen, I had to hold my heart to keep it from leaping out of my chest. I was drawn to a world that was not my own by a stranger who was my own, my inexplicable fantasy.

I guess it started when I was about ten. My mom had a recording of William (I always called him William, even from the beginning) reading poetry. The first time I heard it, I cried. His voice was magical, a hint of pain, a breath of joy, a wrenching sadness. He must have been in his late twenties then, not very well known, but it wasn't long before he had a TV series and then starred in a few movies. My parents had to drag me out of the theater to keep me from sitting through another showing.

When I turned fourteen and knew what my body would do at the sound of his name or the sight of his face, everyone thought I'd get over it. "It's just a phase." "Just a crush she'll outgrow." But I didn't. I ached to be in the presence of William Hathaway. I cut his picture out of every place I saw it, stealing whole articles from office magazines and pasting them on my walls. I was afraid if something happened to him, the police would see my room and accuse me of being a mad stalker.

I tried to keep it reasonable, to watch his movies only twice a month, to stop whispering his name, to stop writing his name on my notebooks at school. I wrote to him, of course, and mailed pages of love poems for his agent to give to him. The poems got A's in English class but not a word from William.

He became more famous and solicited by important people. Fans idolized him in the usual ways. I loved him. Of course, he was married, even acted in a movie once with his wife, and I liked her. But I put myself in his arms night after night. I imagined that someplace in his glittering, whirlwind world, he needed the serenity of me.

In one of his films I saw when I was about seventeen, he'd been in a fight and lay wounded on a flat, white table. His friend, Toller, came to him and grasped his hand, and they looked at each other for a long moment. There was no intimation of homosexuality, but something fused between them, some loyalty, some secret caring, good acting I supposed. But then Toller said something I'll never forget. "I can't go on without you." I gasped. That was my line! "I can't go on without you... I can't."

I never watched that movie again. The desire to be just an actor on the set with William drove all my dreams waking and sleeping. I believed that wherever he was, whoever he was with, the light of my love would burst into his consciousness like the rising sun on a cobalt sea.

A few months before I was twenty, William finished a long-anticipated movie called *Chosen One.* I don't know how my father got tickets to the premiere, but he did, and we all (my mother, brother, and sister included) drove with some excitement and a great amount of teasing of me to the theater, where I might at least have a glimpse of the man I adored. I could hardly speak by the time we arrived. There was a huge crowd and ropes holding back the fans until the stars could be seated. William had already gone in, a reporter told me.

The movie was fabulous. I felt as I had at ten, looking at his beautiful face and hearing that magnificent voice. That he was sitting right there in the room with me was beyond my wildest imaginings. It was almost torture to realize how close I was to him.

When it was over, the lights came on, and people hurried out to get the best spot to greet William. I didn't see him. My father got us moving toward the exit. "We have a ways to go," he said, "and I'm tired." I walked as slowly as possible. I was dying inside. Fans were pushing against the ropes and calling his name. William... my William. He didn't appear. Some people left. Others murmured anxiously, "Where is he? Where's William Hathaway?"

Then, a swell of sound from the crowd told me he was there. A limo pulled up a few feet from where I was standing with my family, a little distance from the main throng. William was bending and signing programs and trying to smile. He looked exhausted. I found a space for myself beside his silver car and watched him come. When he saw me, he didn't speak to anyone after that. He almost seemed to recognize me. I waited without breathing until he was close enough to look in my eyes. The only thing I could do was reach out my hand and touch his arm and say, "William." It was enough. Because he really looked at me, as if he would remember me for some reason even he couldn't fathom. Then, he was rushed from me into the limo, and I leaned against my father.

On the way home, I put my hand that had touched him against my heart. Everyone was jabbering about *Chosen One* and seeing William and all the actors in their finery and what a night it had been. And suddenly a powerful image came to me as I curled upon my dreams in the back seat of the dark car, and I almost said aloud, " I will see you again, William... I will see

you again" at the moment my dad turned onto the old bridge over the Chalice River...

No one said a word. I went back to my seat, and Professor Langley turned to the class. "Why does this story work so well?" he asked.

Lee chanced an answer. "William and Angela lead such different lives, but they get thrown together in a strange way, an unbelievable way. But you do believe it. Something happens that changes their lives forever. But they don't recognize it. They don't make the connection. Good Lord, one of them either dies or is lost, and the other one only reacts to some TV news, he's so involved with *himself*."

"Very good, Mr. Henderson. Anyone else?"

Melissa said, "I just loved it. You know they are going to meet again. You want to know how, why. The suspense kills you."

"Now think about this a minute." Mr. Langley had the beginning of a smile on his face. "How old is Mr. Hathaway in these stories?"

Kathryn Markham found it first. "He says he's thirty-six but feels like fifty."

"Right," Mr. Langley said. "Now who remembers how old he was in 'The Range'?"

Several hands went up, and several voices called out, "Forty-five! He was forty-five!"

"They've already met! Angela came to him in the movie!"

"He didn't know who she was then!"

"And he didn't remember he'd seen her before, at the movie premiere!"

"So who can answer my first question—why does it work?" Langley asked.

Calisha said, as if the power of words was dawning on her for the first time, "You want to stay in their world, believable or not. You are invested in their dreams, their drama. Sela, you have a fan for life, girl."

"So there must be more stories," Riley added.

"There are," I said, but I didn't tell him how many. I didn't want to give away my ultimate metaphor.

"I'll fit them in as the schedule allows," Mr. Langley promised. "And thank you, Miss Hart, for the reading with me."

"I thought it was Angela," a small voice said from the back of the room.

Mr. Langley said, "So did I, Leticia. So did I." He set the stories on his desk and drew us back to the real world. He talked about the coming November's unit on Short Shorts, how challenging it would be to get big ideas in a small space. He mentioned an English Department story contest, the December fifteenth deadline, and the times he would be able to help us. I thought of William Hathaway with all the demands on his time and his heart. I would be Langley's Angela, who took nothing and gave everything.

A girl who rarely spoke up in class raised her hand. "Mr. Langley, for the contest may we use an ending line you gave us?"

"Yes, Carly, I think that would be all right."

"None of them are like Sela's endings," Blake said.

I spoke up. "It depends on how Carly *begins* the story and follows through. I think she'll surprise us."

"Thank you, Sela," she said.

"Very thoughtful, Sela," Mr. Langley said. "You people should be encouraging each other. Writing is very personal. No one's heart should ever be stomped on."

"Just like in life," Riley said.

"Just so," Langley said.

There was the bell.

"No homework this weekend. Enjoy the nice weather. You might read some short shorts. I've put a list on the board."

Kids scribbled in their notebooks. I held my short story in my hand, wondering whether I should give it to him now. After our reading together today, I thought he could use it. I thought it was the best thing I had ever written, and personal—oh yes, that too. A short short for the soul.

As his sixth period students filled the room, I asked Mr. Langley if he wanted the next Quantum Crossing story.

"I want it, Sela, but I'm not only feeling the emotional impact of your stories, but the emotional impact of *you*."

"I will only ever give you my best self," I said.

"Somehow, I know that, Sela. Now here we go again as William and Angela."

We read with a lot of feeling. The drama club would have been impressed. There was a good discussion afterward about the actual and the quantum dimensions. Some didn't think it was a viable literary device. Others thought it took reality to a higher level.

"What do we really know?" my housemate Anne asked. "Aren't there at least two stories or parallel stories going on all around us? Why not write about it, fictionalize it?"

"But when do those stories come together? Are there resolutions?" someone asked.

Mr. Langley said, "I don't know. The crossovers and resolutions are in Miss Hart's head. I guess we'll have to wait for those. I *do* have regular assignments for *new* writing, as she, as well as you, knows."

There was a rumble of laughter. The bell would ring in a minute or two. Mr. Langley walked me to the door.

"Of course, *you* don't have to wait," I said, and I held out "Survivors."

He looked at the title. "I love it already," he said.

I hadn't gone but a few feet when Mr. Langley came out into the hallway. "Miss Hart," he called. He held out his jacket. "I want you to keep this over the weekend."

"Oh, I'd love to," I said.

"I'll like thinking of you wearing it as I read your story. Fair trade?" he asked.

"More than fair, Mr. Langley. Thanks."

"See you Monday then," he said.

"See you Monday."

I slipped into the soft leather, almost crying with the thought of having it for two days. He had already stepped back into his room. I was beginning to realize that the *real* man was so much dearer than the fantasy.

Melissa caught up with me going home that day. "You're still wearing that coat!" she exclaimed. "How cool is that!"

"He just gave it to me after class because I gave him my next story, as if he needed me to have something of his."

"Are you going to sleep in it?" she asked.

"Oh, no, I'm not that weird," I assured her.

"He is such a sweet guy. I can't believe there aren't a few gays with crushes on him."

"Oh, Melissa, that's stretching things a bit," I told her.

"No, really. You know Andy Sloan?"

"Yeah, kind of."

"He told me his deepest fantasy was to love a straight man."

"You're kidding."

"I couldn't believe it either," she said. "He said we'd talk about it later, but he's been out sick for a couple of weeks."

"Oh, no," I said.

"Yeah, I hope he's okay. Anyway, about Mr. Langley. What's going on with you two?"

"I think we're trying to be just teacher and student, but it's not working too well," I said.

"But isn't that what you want?"

"I don't want him to get hurt," I said.

"You're more likely to get hurt, Sela."

"It hurts not to be able to touch him. Nothing could hurt more than that," I said. I smoothed a little ripple in the worn leather. "This is not quite the same thing as having his arms around me."

"Well, I'm on your side, Sela, whatever happens."

"Thanks, my friend," I said, and we walked on in silence.

The weekend dragged. I wore the coat to dinner. I folded it carefully and put it beside my pillow that night in bed. When I breathed, his whole person bounded into my consciousness. I dreamed that he came to the door and asked for it back. When I woke up, it was still there. Morning light poured into the room. Was he reading my story now? Was he smiling at the line "Dad, we're not seven!"? Was he weeping with the man estranged from his children for most of his life?

Melissa and I took a walk Sunday afternoon to get out of the house. Of course, I wore the jacket. We ran into Riley Starkes jogging the other way. He stopped. "Hey," he said, "isn't that Mr. Langley's coat?"

"Yeah," I said with no further explanation.

"You girls are strange," he said. He trotted on, shaking his head.

I didn't wear it at school Monday but kept it in my locker until fifth period. When I got to Mr. Langley's room, he was talking to Lois La Monde—something about the contest and that he didn't want to be a judge. "But you won't see the names. The stories will be coded with numbers for each author on a separate list," La Monde was telling him.

"I'd know *this* writer in my sleep," he said showing her my two pages.

"Oh, that girl again," she said, mildly peeved.

I handed Professor Langley his leather coat. La Monde's mouth fell open. "And what is the meaning of this?" she asked.

"Nothing that concerns you, Lois," Mr. Langley said.

She strode away in a dismissive manner.

Professor Langley said, "I think this is your best story yet, Sela. I'm going to read it first thing, if you have no objections."

"Of course not," I said. I couldn't wait to hear his voice speaking the words.

"All right, class, listen. I have a treat for you. Miss Hart's next story, a short short, which you will all be attempting soon. It follows the ones Sela and I read aloud on Friday so closely that I wanted you to hear it now."

Everyone quieted down as he read the title, knowing the key was in that word.

Survivors

After the premiere of *Chosen One*, my father seemed to come out of his bitter shell. He was still sitting in the

chair downstairs where we had left him after we got home from the theater. My sister and I moved cautiously around fixing our breakfast so not to disturb him, but he looked up.

"My girls," he said.

"Dad? Were you here all night?" I asked.

"Yeah. I wasn't feeling well... you know how sometimes you're just afraid to move, that it just might push you over the edge?"

"Like the flu," I said.

"Something like that... but I'm fine now."

He stood up and took a cup of coffee from Sela.

"Did you see the news?" he asked softly.

"About the girl?" I said.

"What girl?" Sela stirred her coffee absentmindedly.

"Oh, you missed it," I told her. "Some girl was lost in the Chalice River after her family went off the bridge in their car last night."

"Oh, God," Sela said.

My father flinched. "They'll find her," he said.

"But probably not alive," I said.

There was a small silence before he asked, "Are you girls doing anything today?"

Sela and I glanced at each other. Who is this man?

"No," we said in unison.

"Do you want to do something with me? Maybe... go to the Santa Barbara Zoo? I heard they have some new animals from Africa."

"Dad! We're not seven!" I said.

"There's a white rhino," he went on, undeterred. "There aren't many left in the world. Let's get out of the house. The grounds are really beautiful there. I'll go ask your mom."

This was new. The only thing he ever got excited about was acting. He and mom even slept in separate rooms. They never did anything together.

"Is this because of that girl? That daughter who drowned?" Sela asked.

"Maybe... does it matter?" he said, and he disappeared into my mom's room.

We could hear them arguing. Some things never change. But when he came back, he was cheerful.

"She doesn't like zoos," he said simply. "I'll go change. The gates open at nine. You ready?"

We just nodded and sipped our coffee. He returned in jeans, a white shirt, sleeves rolled up, and a hat that half covered his face. Who would make a fuss over William Hathaway at the Santa Barbara Zoo? Most people were probably in church. Actually, it kind of felt like that's where we were headed.

In the car, he started in again about the Africa exhibit.

"Dad, why rhinos?" Sela said.

"They're endangered," he said.

"But they're ugly," I added.

"Not to other rhinos," he said and smiled.

"Are you making a movie in Africa or something?" I asked.

"No, Denise... but if I did, I'd take you guys with me."

Well, that shut us up. Yea, rhinos.

There weren't many people at the zoo. We watched a mother giraffe nursing her six-foot newborn. That was awesome. Then, for at least twenty minutes, we cracked up over the antics of some Peruvian mountain goats. The tigers and lions were napping, of course, but looking gorgeous in their freshly self-washed gold and black and palomino coats. And there were the zebras. My father loves horses, so we spent some time analyzing their movements, their soft nickers, their unique stripes. We bought hot dogs and sat on a bench by a pond full of flamingos.

"Thanks for coming with me, girls," my dad said.

We used the excuse of eating to not have to say anything back. But we felt the change in our father. He did sign a couple of autographs (the hat didn't work), but he seemed to be more with us that day than with his fans.

Then he said, "All those people who admire my work just want my autograph. What do you girls want?"

"Your heart," we both said at once.

"Then you shall have as much of my heart as I know how to give," he whispered.

But his heart was to become entangled in a relationship that flung him between sorrow and joy with only brief spaces for Sela and me, which he tried hard to fill with what we began to call "zoo time." But the day after the girl drowned in the Chalice River was the closest we ever got to his heart.

A park attendant walked by saying, "One hour 'til closing. Have you seen the rhinos?"

We hurried along the bark pathway to where a small crowd was gathering, and there they were, two white rhinos swaying their heads disdainfully at the humans who saved them, sauntering off into corners out of reach of camera lenses, being great African beasts under the Santa Barbara sun. Our father put his arms around us and pulled us close. I barely remembered his touch. It felt strange but oh so comforting.

Then he said, very quietly, "Things that are so rare... need to be protected."

When he finished, Mr. Langley waited a minute before he said, "Comments?"

"That's really good," someone at the back of the room said.

"It's very good," Langley agreed, "but why? What's the heart of its power?"

"I think it's the last line," Melissa offered. "It ties in all the stories so far."

"It might. But what if we just stick to this story for the moment. What does the last line say literally?" he asked.

"That rhinos need to be protected," Marcella said.

"Yes. But what else is endangered here?"

Kids called out answers randomly, discovering things to their own amazement, as they clamored for Langley's approval.

"His relationship with his children."

"Their connection with *him*!"

"His marriage!"

"His health?"

"Yes. I think his emotional and physical health," Langley agreed.

"Oh, his acting career!" Melissa suggested.

"Possibly," Langley said.

"His self-confidence?" Riley asked.

"In what way?" Langley questioned.

"Well, he's been popular, but he's aging. Maybe he won't get the best roles anymore."

"Good, Riley."

"Other animals at the zoo," Lee said.

"Maybe."

"The discovery of Angela, real or not!"

"Excellent, Melissa."

"Oh, I know Sela. That definitely would have been in her head," my roommate added.

"Sela?" Mr. Langley turned to me.

"They're all true," I said, "but I didn't think of those things until after I finished the story, and I didn't think of everything that was mentioned."

"There are almost endless possibilities. That's the beauty of that last line," Langley said. "That's the beauty of the story."

Lee spoke up again. "Since we don't know if Angela survived… oh, man, the *title!* Anyway, she's endangered for sure, even though Mr. Hathaway doesn't get it yet. The daughter who's telling this story implies there will be a relationship that comes between him and his girls, but we don't know it's Angela."

"But do we know?" Langley asked.

"Only if we've heard the first few stories. We don't know from just *this* story," Lee answered.

"Does it matter?" Langley asked.

"I don't think so," Risa said thoughtfully. "There's something sad and endearing and yet hopeful about the whole thing. I'll never forget the image of Mr. Hathaway with his arms around his daughters. I … don't speak to my father, so *I* am also endangered."

"Aren't we all," Mr. Langley said into the hushed room.

4

One day in the first part of November, Mr. Langley seemed depressed. Gone were his usual sparkle, his appreciative smile at the end of a well-written story, and his patience with disingenuous students.

"Why am I wasting my time!" he snapped once.

The exercise was about dialogue tags. Someone started making up silly ones, like, "She shouted right in his face, turning her back on him." And "'This is the best drink I've ever had,' she exclaimed guzzling the martini through a straw." That one seemed to especially grate on the professor's nerves.

Blake read, "'I can see forever in your eyes,' he said, looking in his cell phone for her roommate's number."

I stood up and said, "But that could be fixed and be an interesting line. What if it read, '"I can see forever in your eyes," he said. Later, he looked in his cell phone for her roommate's number?' Then, the story has a life, a protagonist who's a con artist, a character whose friend might betray her, any number of possibilities."

"Thank you, Miss Hart," Mr. Langley said. "Now here's a page of dialogue tags. See if you can fix them as Miss Hart has just done."

He handed Kathryn Markham the sheets to pass out and then put his head in his hands. I couldn't stand to see him in so much distress. I went up to his desk, keeping my back to the class and sheltering his face when he looked up. I said quietly, "Mr. Langley, I can finish this class and take sixth period for you. You should go home."

"That's very thoughtful, Sela, but probably not a good idea."

"Can you tell me what's wrong, sir?"

"Today would have been my twentieth wedding anniversary. I'm the only one who knows it or remembers it... and now you."

"Can you write about it?"

"No."

"Just one line? Try. Words can heal."

"I believe that so much, Miss Hart, but I can't do it. Not about this."

"May I try?"

"Okay, but you didn't know her."

"It doesn't matter. I know you."

He smiled briefly, and I returned to my desk. He knew I could fix dialogue tags. What he needed was for me to fix his pain. I wrote out a few lines, and then I got it. It wasn't mine but something I'd read of the poet Mark Nepo's that stayed with me. I jotted it down quickly and went back to Langley's desk. He took the paper, catching my hand. "Stay," he said.

He read the lines twice, and I could see his body and his heart understand it and accept it. It read,

I feel more today
than one being should
and can't tell
if I'm in trouble
or on holy ground.

"That says it all, doesn't it, Miss Hart," he said softly.

"I haven't been there yet, but I see that you have. Now go home, Mr. Langley. Go home and find which ground you're standing on. I can handle your classes."

He grabbed his leather jacket off the back of the chair, gathered a few books and papers and my note, and walked out the door.

"What's going on?" someone asked.

"Mr. Langley's twentieth anniversary with the dead Natasha is today," I told everyone.

There was a murmur of sympathy. Then Blake said, "I heard she drank like a fish and preferred women. What's he so broken up about?"

"Maybe he loved her. Maybe this was going to be some kind of special day. We don't know, but we owe him our respect."

"Why did he leave *you* in charge?"

"Because I offered."

"I guess we learned two lessons today," Lee said.

"Okay, let's hear some of those revisions," I said, fighting my own tears.

The next class was a bit more mature about the whole thing. But halfway through, Lois La Monde stormed in. "What do you think you're doing, young lady?"

"A favor for Mr. Langley," I answered.

"Where is he?"

"I believe he went home, Miss La Monde."

"Why?"

"I think you'll have to ask him," I said. "Okay, everyone. Look through your short story manuscripts to see if you can find some of these 'tags' and tell me how you'd fix them."

I turned back. "Is that all, Miss La Monde?"

"I'll speak to you later," she said.

On the way back to my apartment, my cell phone rang. I sat down on a bench on the quad and put the phone to my ear. Mr. Langley said, "Sela."

"Mr. Langley, hi. Are you feeling better?"

"I'm getting there," he said.

"Classes went well, sir. I enjoyed being given the responsibility. Thank you."

"Thank *you*, Miss Hart. I didn't mean to draw you into my … whatever it is."

"I know, Mr. Langley. But who else did you have at the moment?"

"No one. I don't talk about my personal problems … and never about my wife."

"I understand, sir. I hope I didn't cross the line. I did explain to my class why you left, —a little less to sixth period because Miss La

Monde barged in and demanded to know where you were. I tried to be as vague as possible."

"Thank you again. I'll see you Friday, my dear."

"See you Friday."

I stayed there on the bench, my hand clutching the phone where his voice had been. He could have waited to thank me on Friday. Was this his way of touching me as soon as he thought I was alone? Oh, heaven help me. There is only one way to go from here.

Melissa greeted me with enthusiasm when I finally got home. "Sela, you were great! I hope Professor Langley appreciates what you did."

I held up my cell phone.

She gasped. "He called you?"

"Yeah."

"Sela, are you just jazzed?"

"We've talked before. You gave him our house number, remember?"

"Oh, yeah, but I didn't give him your cell number!"

"I know… I did."

"Oh boy."

"Melissa, the closer I get to him the harder it is. It was so simple when he was just a great-looking professor whose class I couldn't get in. Now we have a *relationship*. That takes honesty and self-control."

"But that's who you are, Sela," she said.

"I don't think I've quite passed that test yet," I said. But such a test would come, sooner than I expected.

On Friday, Mr. Langley seemed more at ease and apologized to the class for leaving so abruptly on Wednesday.

"Professor, you're only human," Lee said.

"Do you feel better?" Melissa asked, knowing I would want to know that.

"Much better. A little rest can give one a new perspective. Now let's start on those short short stories. Let's hear some ideas."

Students offered first lines, last lines, characterizations, and plot potentials. Mr. Langley seemed pleased and made complimentary comments. I sketched out a few plot twists I'd had in my head a while, but my heart was not in it.

"Sela? You're too quiet. Come on, get us going here," Mr. Langley encouraged.

"When I was young, I had a favorite stable horse that some kid ran to death. There might be a story there." Then I realized I had used the *death* word. "Or maybe not," I finished.

Langley hesitated but reminded everyone that the stories were supposed to be fiction. "I'm not criticizing, Sela, but you're so good at fiction, I'm surprised you chose a real event in your life."

"Maybe my whole life is a fiction," I said to him as the bell rang. I didn't stop at his desk or look his way. I felt out of control. I skipped my graduate class and went home.

Early Saturday morning, my cell phone rang. I almost didn't answer it but picked it up on the sixth ring.

"Sela, did I wake you?"

"Mr. Langley, no… I just couldn't find the phone," I lied. The sound of his voice just hit me like the sweet embrace it was.

"Do you want to go for a drive?"

Oh, I was in so much trouble.

"Sure. Where to?" I asked.

"It's a surprise. Wear something comfortable."

I could hardly keep a hold of the phone, but he pulled me in with each word, his voice gentle, kind of the way I imagined William Hathaway speaking to his daughters but with a hint of something else I couldn't quite place.

I dressed in a daze, changing my mind several times about what to wear. I had a pair of jeans with a sparkly design on the back pockets and a black cap-sleeved tee with the shape of a running horse in the same sparkles on the front. Black mary janes or black high heels? I chose the flats. The heels were definitely not comfortable. I put on a bit more make-up than I usually did for school and headed out. I felt as if I were wandering into a story that William Langley was writing.

He picked me up on a corner out of sight of the campus, not that that would really keep anyone from seeing me get in Professor Langley's restored '78 Mustang that, thankfully, had not been in the wreck on the day of the last summer solstice. He just said, "Hello, Miss Hart," and turned north on Highway 101. I was afraid he would hear my heart pounding, but the traffic was noisy and the windows were half down. He explained that he hadn't installed the air conditioning yet. I only nodded as he glanced at me with his golden brown eyes, perhaps a shade or two darker than the newly painted Sicilian umber Mustang. I slid a little closer to him on the white leather seats so the wind wouldn't mess up my hair. I was definitely in a short story I could never write down and do justice to.

Soon we were past the tall buildings towering into the LA smog, past the tree-lined avenues of Thousand Oaks, past the very place of his wife's demise a little more than halfway down the Conejo Grade. He pointed it out, swallowing hard. *Does he think I know the whole story?* I wanted to ask him about this adversity in his life, but no appropriate words came to me as we left the small, white roadside cross behind and veered north. Then, we sailed by a military base with its ominous drones, vast fields of strawberries tended by Mexicans—probably undocumented but working their hearts out to put that sweet fruit on our tables—and finally could see the ocean west of Ventura, waves lapping the shore for the hundred billionth time, and I began to guess the surprise. But when we actually turned through the gate at the Santa Barbara Zoo, I let out a cry.

"Steady, Sela," he said. He must have known what it meant to me. Well, maybe not entirely.

"I've never been here," I told him with my hand on my heart.

"You've been here," he said matter-of-factly, "in that complicated mind of yours. Just never with me."

We parked and got out, and Mr. Langley waved off the tour guide. "We'll find what we want," he said.

We followed the signs, passing the colorful displays of flowers and screeching primates, the sad-eyed antelopes, and a lonely black bear, until we came to a huge, double-fenced enclosure behind which stood a veritable tank of a mammal—an African white rhino. We leaned on the outer rail, our shoulders touching, and watched the endangered animal root around in a muddy pond, ignoring us and the whole world. I didn't know if Mr. Langley wanted me to be in the real world with him or in my story.

There was a bench a few feet back, so we finally sat down, still not speaking. The seaside hot noontime bore down on us; the tour group wandered by. We heard the guide tell everyone that the square-jawed rhinos were called white and the pointed-nosed rhinos black, that both were endangered and poached profusely throughout Africa, just their horns being sold to Asian countries for medicinal properties touted since the Middle Ages. It always devastated me, hearing that, and everyone heard the one sob I couldn't contain. Mr. Langley put his arm around me, pulled me against him, and said, "Things that are so rare need to be protected." He paused and then added softly, "You know what I mean, Sela." It was not a question. He squeezed my shoulder and then took his arm away, but the message was quite clear.

Then, he said, "You used your own name in that story, one of the actor's daughters."

"Yes... and later too, in one you haven't read."

"Kind of fitting, I guess," he said.

"I wanted to be in that story," I said, "and now I really am."

"With a lot more at stake in your personal life, huh?"

"You got it," I answered.

"Sela, I want you to enter that story in the English Department contest."

"But does it make the best sense without the stories that precede it?" I asked, now that we were back on safer literary ground.

But he caught me off guard. "Do *we* make sense?"

"At this moment... yes," I said with as much strength as I had. I felt very faint from the sun and his oh-so-life-changing words.

"Sela, let's get you in some shade," he said and started to help me up, but we were shocked back into the precarious nature of our story when a large, red-faced man approached, seemingly rushing someplace but halting breathlessly in front of us, shouting, "Langley, you old codger! You didn't waste much time!"

"Hello, Randall. What are you talking about?" Langley said, rising suddenly.

"Here with that darling girl, so far from home, so soon after..."

"Randall, this is Sela Hart, one of my lit students. We came to follow the sequence of one of her short stories."

"Un-huh," he said, not convinced.

"Sela, this is Professor Hall, head of the Math Department across campus," he said, as if that separated the underlying reasons we were all here in the same place.

I just stared at him.

"Well, whatever," Hall said. "It's a nice day for an affair, anyway. Mine's a bit younger... but you'll never see *her* in broad daylight, if you get my gist. Just meeting here and then off to... well, never mind. We didn't see each other, right?"

Mr. Langley nodded in assent and then sat back down next to me.

"What a crude man," I said.

"Married too," he said.

"I'm sorry, Mr. Langley. Do you want to go back to LA?"

"No," he said quickly. "I won't let that man ruin our day. Let's go see the 'little horses.'"

Of course, he meant the zebras so enjoyed by the William in my story because Mr. Hathaway loved horses. We gave a last look at the giant rhino rummaging in a pile of grass hay. I thought of the few white rhinos I had seen in Africa hiding in the tall bush grass, rubbing their tough hides against thorn trees, and eyeing us warily. If, to save them, we had to imprison them and make them bear the pointing fingers of humans, who were all poachers to them, then shame on us.

"Look, Sela," Mr. Langley was saying with renewed excitement.

In a grassy enclosure with some semblance of a running creek and acacia trees were several zebras frolicking about. But what amazed us was a smaller pen where two zebra mares stood, each with a tiny foal. Inside the pen, a black man shoveled manure and spoke to the foursome in a language I knew so well. We grew nearer, and I greeted the keeper, asked how he was doing today, in Swahili. "*Habari ya mchana, baba?*"

"Mama, you know my language," he replied. "You are African?"

The color of my skin meant nothing to most East Africans. I was simply of a different tribe. "No," I answered in English. "I lived in Tanzania for three years. I wanted to talk to your people, so I learned as much of the language as I could."

"Oh! My country, Tanzania! And these *pundamilia*," he said pointing at the zebras, "also from Tanzania!"

"*Baba, unaitwa nani?*"

"I am Daudi."

"I am Sela, and this is… William."

"Oh, *Karibu! Karibu!*" he said with his welcome in Kiswahili.

"Tell us about the zebras, baba," Langley said, politely calling the caretaker *father* in the man's African tongue.

"They were captured on Serengeti, already carrying little ones, six months ago. I was chosen to sail with them, to protect them. They accepted me but not tame. Their babies two days old, that one." He indicated the smaller mare. "And three days old, the other mama's." Then, the African held out his hand and said, "*Nifuate!* Come with me! I am giving grain now to mothers so earn babies' trust."

We looked at each other, and William reached for my hand as we entered a dark hallway behind the exhibit. Daudi led us into a small stall where the four zebras crowded around us, the foals not as sure of us as the dams. The African brought out pans of oats mixed with molasses.

"The little horses need more energy here in strange place, to endure watchers and construction," he explained. "Hold very still. If they touch you first, that is best. Don't startle them."

"Of course," we whispered together, holding our pans of sweet feed.

One foal turned his back on us and began to nurse. He was so new to the world, his black and white stripes sharply defined in the dim light. The other foal, a filly, stretched out her limber neck and touched William's hand where the mother was cautiously nibbling out of the pan.

"Oh, look," he said.

The foal pricked her ears, stepped back, and then came forward again.

"Is okay. You can talk," Daudi said.

"Sela, run your hand down my arm, and put it on top of my hand where the baby touched me," Langley said.

It felt like making love. The filly licked my hand but kept her eyes on us. No one breathed. Then Daudi said, "Is enough."

When we went back out into the sunlight, William didn't let go of my hand. It was symbolic of so much, but I said, "Mr. Langley, don't take a chance with your career. I'll feel your hand long after you let go."

So he did, and we walked slowly, with the African close behind, back into reality.

"Do you want something to eat?" Mr. Langley asked, and then he said to Daudi, "Come with us. For lunch."

"Not allowed, sir," he said.

"Well, it seems to be a day of 'not allowed.' Why stop now?"

The African laughed. "I have better idea," he said. "I have small cabin on beach. Zoo pays. I cook dinner for 'not allowed' sir and mama. I go at four. You find blue house, end of Oceanside."

"That would be wonderful, Daudi," William said.

We went back to the bench by the white rhino and shared a bag of trail mix. That time, we noticed another, smaller white rhino hiding behind a stand of eucalyptus. *Did we slip for a moment into the roles of William Hathaway and his daughters?*

"You're going to win the contest, you know," William said.

"You're just saying that because there's more to the story now."

"Maybe. Joyce Carol Oates would be proud anyway."

"Except we have no ending," I reminded him.

"Not yet, my dear Sela… not yet."

Then we drove to the end of Oceanside and sat in the car. The sun was slipping down through the haze and low clouds into the Pacific.

There was a moment of orange and gold and pink that spread across the horizon, centered by the image of our lovely star magnified by the atmosphere.

"Our little flash of joy," William said.

"Something rare," I said.

Daudi beckoned us into his sparsely furnished, three-room beach house whose board porch reached right out onto the sand. He had only three chairs to his name, all different shapes and colors, but he had brought in fresh flowers, courtesy of the Santa Barbara Zoo, to put on the small round table, and he began to cook some savory-smelling African dish. He apologized. "Can't find right things here."

"I know," I said, remembering the incomparable taste of African mangoes, sweet onions, potatoes, and chicken.

Soon we were eating, silently at first, and then Daudi and I were chatting away in Swahili, stopping to translate now and then for Mr. Langley.

The African described his Bantu village in Manyara, how he went to university in Moshi and became a park ranger in the Serengeti, far from his wife and five children. After years of providing for his family in this way, he was asked to make the ultimate sacrifice by helping with the transport of the zebras to the United States, where he would stay with them through their adjustment and foaling. Now, he felt obligated to be with them until the babies were weaned and healthy.

Daudi asked William about his family. Mr. Langley hesitated and then said simply, "My wife and I were never lucky enough to have children... and then she died a few months ago." He didn't detail the crash, and I was grateful for that. Daudi said, "*Niwieradhi.*" And no one had to translate.

It was warm in the little kitchen, so Daudi invited us to sit outside while he cleaned up. Mr. Langley seemed suddenly tired, getting up unsteadily from his chair and wiping what may have been tears from his eyes. We sat down on a dilapidated couch and listened to the restless waves rolling in toward our feet. I thought of the times I had walked in the Indian Ocean at Dar es Salaam, picking up shells and pieces of sea glass as if my life depended on them, the warm water rising with the tide swiftly to my knees, my African driver out there with me with his pants rolled up, protecting me from harm. Now here I was beside the cold Pacific with a man I surely loved and a Tanzanian protecting us from the judgmental eyes of the world.

"Mr. Langley, are you okay?" I asked.

"I am, Sela," he said. "Just trying to figure out the end of today's story." He pressed his hand to his stomach. "Maybe a few butterflies in here."

"Maybe we should go back," I offered.

"Maybe," he said.

He pulled me to my feet, and we stood in the dark night facing each other. I could barely see him, but I could feel the heat from his body, the ocean breeze making us shiver a little. And then—oh dear God—he kissed me. All my words, all my poetry, vanished from my head, and I took the feel of his mouth somewhere deep inside me and sealed it before he could stop.

Later, in the car going home, we spoke of other things.

"Sela, how did you learn so much Swahili?"

"Well, I cheated a bit. I bought a *Rosetta Stone* program before I went to Africa, so I had a head start."

"Do you still have it?"

"I do."

"Can I borrow it?"

"Really? With all the English you have to read, how can you have time for Swahili?" I asked.

"I don't know. I just feel excited about speaking to Daudi in his own language whenever we see him again." He paused. We were past the crash site now and headed into the crowded lanes still an hour from LA. "Here's something else I've been thinking about. He's probably the only black man on that street. What will the racism he could encounter in Santa Barbara do to him?"

"Oh, you're right. He'll feel any racism because in his country, there is no racism. Seriously, there's no color bar. He'll never understand why people might cross the street when they meet him or why a policeman might question him for the slightest 'out of place' behavior, like bringing flowers home from the zoo or some other innocent thing. How can we help him?"

"I think I should tell my classes about our trip… well, not *all* of it, but enough to make it about short story writing, our experience in *your* story, the potentials in Daudi's story. We'll bring him to school, introduce him to some diversity that works, ask him to talk about his life, his animals on the Serengeti, and how he got here. He could stay at my place. Not a lot of diversity out *there*, I'm sorry to say, but at school he'll be respected."

"I think it's a great idea," I said as we passed what I thought was the exit to his canyon home in Malibu.

"Don't think I didn't think about turning off back there," he said softly.

"So much for your butterflies," I teased.

"To be honest… I don't think those will be going away any time soon," he said.

I didn't know what to say, so I put my hand on his back as he had once done on mine.

"My anchor," he said. Then he asked when he could see my next quantum story, and I told him I'd bring it Monday but that he'd better have something else planned because it was really short.

"You sure? Discussing your stories seems to fill up the time quite nicely."

"I don't know why," I said. "They're so personal."

"But that's why, Sela. Yes, it's fiction, but there's some kind of *soul* in them."

We were still a ways from UCLA. "Do you want to stop for some ice cream or something?" Mr. Langley asked.

"I'll take a rain check on the 'or something,'" I said.

"Sela, Sela, you are a delight."

"Just a poem in search of a page," I said.

He reached up and took my hand from his back and didn't let go, even after we pulled up to the curb in front of my house near the campus. There were no lights in my roommates' windows. He stopped the car and turned the engine off.

I said, "I guess I can't ask you to come in for a while."

"We're in a tough spot, Sela."

"You could lose your job."

"Yeah... and I've got about twenty years to go," he said.

"Guess what, Mr. Langley," I said. "I'll still be here." Then I went on before he could say anything. "Thank you for today... for everything."

"*Karibu*," he said. He'd been listening to Daudi's and my Swahili and figuring out words.

I hated releasing his hand, but I did and slid out across the perfect, white leather seat and opened the door. "See you Monday, Mr. Langley."

He said, "Hey... Miss Hart."

So I stuck my head back in the window and said, "William."

I went into my empty apartment and sat down on the couch in the darkness. I loved him so damn much and didn't know how I would ever tell him. Twenty years from now seemed impossibly far away.

5

On Monday, Mr. Langley told his short story classes about our trip, so by the time my class started practically all my friends had heard about it and were pressing me for details. The professor held up his hand, "Okay, okay, young people. I'll tell you about our adventure. Settle down."

In William's voice I lived it again. When he got to the part about the zebras, he told a version of the truth, that it had been Daudi's idea for me to put my hand on his and let the filly explore our united arm, not scare it with two arms reaching out. A couple of the girls glanced at me meaningfully. I didn't give them the satisfaction of a meaningful smile back. He explained that we had gone back to the white rhino exhibit and tried to imagine William Hathaway and his daughters watching the endangered beasts lumbering around the pen and how he had put his arms around his girls and told them how rare things needed to be protected.

Then Mr. Langley said I had promised him the next story about William and Angela and that we had just enough time to hear it. It was only two pages long but unlocked part of the mystery, if one could believe it. I thought, just before I began reading it, *If William Langley can kiss me on a beach in Santa Barbara at the cabin of a Tanzanian, anything is possible.*

I began in a shaky voice and then said to the class, "Wait. This is a strong voice. This is the gatekeeper." And I continued with the purposefulness and clarity of William Hathaway's wife.

The True Key

I should never have married an actor. Half of his heart was always someplace else. I tried to understand it, to forgive his absences, his lack of focus on our relationship. I knew from the beginning, I was not enough for him. Or maybe he was not enough for me. I thought when the children came, things would be different. But he withdrew even more, or perhaps his career was blossoming and his heart was needed elsewhere.

He was a good actor, I will admit that. He made people cry. His intensity could be exhausting for me. I can't imagine what it was doing to him. When the girls fussed, he would leave the room. I know he suffered during that time from severe headaches, but he refused medication. He said he needed something, and when he found it, he'd let me know.

But he never did. He never told me about Angela. Oh yes, I knew. Surprised? It was a slow process, figuring out why Bill was so unhappy. Even when he came home from Arizona after finishing *The Range* a distraught man and I asked what was wrong, he just said, "I lost something very precious to me." He never said her name. He dreaded confrontations with fans. He learned his lines on his own, no reading partner. He went on long rides on his lovely mare alone. He was offered role after role. Everyone adored him.

As the years passed, I couldn't seem to forget about the girl that was lost in the Chalice River. She had been a fan. The newspapers said the walls of her room were covered with Bill's pictures, that she had seen all his movies twice or more, that she spoke no other name but William. My God, no one called him William!

For a while after she drowned, Bill really seemed different. He did more things with the girls, he tried to engage me in conversation, but I kept thinking all the time of those walls full of his pictures and that girl who told everyone how she loved him. I could never be that girl. I did not have that passion in me. It just wasn't my nature. Of course, Bill and I were attracted to each other at first, and we had some good times. But I didn't know how to heal him when he would plunge into despair or pain.

Now I know you won't believe this, but I am the one who asked Angela to come back. It's the one great thing I did for Bill. I went to the Chalice River, and I found that girl. She was quite a ways from the bridge, sitting in a field of lupine and paintbrush, soaking wet and dazed. I put my sweater around her and started talking to her as if it were perfectly normal.

"You're Angela Star, aren't you?" I said.

"Yes." She was shivering.

"Do you know who I am?" I asked.

She looked at me with such gentle eyes.

"You're William's wife," she said.

"I am... and I will tell you truthfully that he does not remember you. I am the one who kept you alive. I saved all the news articles, I taped all the TV shows with psychics and state troopers trying to find you, I kept the shirt Bill wore to the premiere."

"But why?" she asked, incredulous.

"Because I knew some day he would need you. You must go to him. You must find a way. You have my blessing."

"I... don't want to come between you," she said.

"You are already between us. He just doesn't know it yet. He has struggled so to find his place in the world,

with me, with his daughters, with his acting, as fine as it is. He's still haunted. I believe he is haunted by you. You just have to finish the job."

Her eyes were so real in the fading light.

"Perhaps… you love him more than I do," she said softly.

"Perhaps I do… but that is something he'll never know."

The bell rang. I gathered up my books. Mr. Langley said, "Good job, Sela. A powerful key, for sure."

"I have something for you," I said. "It's a gift… for Saturday." And I handed him a poem I had written in Africa. I thought he would appreciate the imagery and that I could later show him that the metaphor of the sea could occur hundreds of miles from any ocean. I planned to use it in my grad study project, but I also planned, from now on, to show him everything in my graduate work. Miss La Monde could just wonder why.

"Just you being in my life is gift enough for me," he said, and that carried me through the next two days.

On Wednesday, the poem was printed on the blackboard. Professor Langley had the eraser in his hand when I came in. "Just say if you don't want me to use it."

"No, please use it." No one else was in the room yet. But that wasn't the biggest surprise. After we students were seated, he opened the door to his inner office and out stepped Daudi! He had on traditional clothing and looked like a king. I was so proud of him. And then, while everyone looked at the English version on the board, Daudi read the poem in Swahili.

Serengeti

We sail the short grass seas
with kopjes set like ships
against the sky,

gazelle-waves leaping from our prow
with dust and wind-drifts.
Cheetah waits on islands
chirping to cubs hide hide.
Tawny eagles swoop like albatross
upon the tiny creatures in our wake.
Zebra swims for safety,
drowning in the jaws of lions,
hyenas treading water for the chum.
On our stern are lilac rollers,
grey crowned-cranes and ostriches.
And then the long grass rocks us
with the jackals and the elephants,
a tide of wildebeest still paddling paddling,
harriers hovering in the salty air,
topis rising here and there
on copper legs.
Warthogs chop the pool with quick strides.
Giraffes are the tsunamis
of acacia troughs,
turning their soft eyes
toward our passage
or loping away
with long oar strokes
back to the fount of creation
where all the others, named
and unnamed,
gather in the arks
of our imagination.

When he finished, we all stood and clapped and cheered. Daudi bowed and then sat down in a chair Mr. Langley had rolled up beside his desk. Blake's hand was in the air.

"Yes, Mr. Adams?"

"That's very nice, but what does it have to do with writing short stories?"

"Who'd like to answer that?" Langley asked.

Melissa said without hesitation, "The imagery! Even short stories should be *seen* when you read them, maybe with less poetic language depending on the style of your particular story, but still with mental pictures, something to give the story life."

"Good, Miss Wells. Anyone else?"

Riley Starkes spoke up. "That poem *is* a short story! Think about it. It's the story of those animals, the lions eating the zebras, the eagles swooping down on prey. It's the story of *survival*!" He seemed quite pleased with himself, and Mr. Langley complimented his insight.

"Now, here's a challenging assignment," Langley continued. "I want you to choose a poem, any poem, and write it as a short story. I believe you'll find the poems with the most imagery will be the easiest to do. All right, folks, this lovely gentleman is Daudi from the Santa Barbara Zoo, a character from Sela's and my story."

Everyone clapped again, and questions soared. William looked at me once, and I knew then I wouldn't have to wait twenty years to be in his arms.

The stories that week were just wild. Leticia and Blake created two completely different tales from Longfellow's "The Tide Rises, the Tide Falls." Marcella Ruiz turned Frost's "Mending Wall" into an immigration drama. There were several taken from Edna St. Vincent Millay and Chris Dombrowski. I tried "The Panther" by Rainer Maria Rilke. In my story, a schizophrenic turns on all fours from corner to corner in a padded room with one small window for years. When she is released, she continues pacing, now upright, along walls of buildings and hedges in parks facing said barriers. She boards up all the windows of her house and repeats her journey hour after hour, first inside and then outside the perimeters of the structure, until one day a board is loosened and torn away by a recent storm, and she looks in and sees herself wandering on all fours and is suddenly healed.

The first thing Mr. Langley asked after hearing these read aloud was, "Why do you think these stories are so good?"

Riley, who was really becoming quite intuitive, said right away, "Because those poems are good."

"That is the heart of it," Mr. Langley said. "And why did you choose those poems?"

"Because of the imagery," Alice Barnes piped up.

"If you can *see* the poem, you can feel it. It's the same with the short story. I realize you are working on short shorts and your contest entries, but I'd like you to develop some imagery in your work."

I handed the professor one of my quantum stories—a little out of order, but it fit the assignment the best. I said to him, "Will this work for you? I'm swamped with my graduate project."

"Of course, Sela. Just how many of these are there?" he asked.

"Eleven."

"The known dimensions of the quantum theory!"

"Yeah. I didn't plan it that way, but when I finished the last story, the characters went back into whatever dimension they came from, and I happened to have eleven stories."

"You are a surprise a minute, my girl."

"Surprise and revelation. That's me."

Before Mr. Langley shared my story with the class on Friday, he asked everyone to make a mark on a piece of notepaper every time he or she heard the use of imagery. And then he read.

The Beginning

In the summer of 1862, a soldier's wife was carrying her first child. When they learned the news, she and her husband, a captain in the Union Army, were pleased, and for almost two months talked of nothing else—names and cradles and christening clothes and room colors. It was a blessed time, but it was not to last. The captain

was called to duty and died in September at Antietam on a bloody field with his wife's name on his lips. The child had not been named.

Now the mother dreaded raising a child in those uncertain days, so she sought remedies to release her of it. Nothing worked. A midwife told her to swim every day in the river, that sometimes the swirling water would pull a child out before its time. So afternoons, even in the coming winter, the wife slipped away to the beckoning water, undressed, and thrashed about where she could still touch the ground. She couldn't swim, but she wasn't afraid of the water. She prayed to the water to take her child.

Without her husband she became crazed with longing for him and loathing for the baby that continued to grow unperturbed by her schemes. She closed up the house that had been the married couple's dwelling and moved in with her parents and two siblings even closer to the river. Her family had money and they indulged her, ignored the baby and all its signs of life, the kicks, the swelling of the mother's girth. The river was the only solace for the child's mother. She spent hours in the cold water, studied the shoreline maples and crows on the leafless branches, so she wouldn't have to look at herself.

The months passed. No one spoke of the baby, although everyone secretly wondered about it and what would happen if it were born alive.

"Darling," the mother's mother said one day, when the fetus was about six months old, "shouldn't you be seeing a doctor?"

"Why?"

"For the baby."

"There is no baby."

And so it went, until a glorious spring day in the ninth month, the baby's mother plunged into the rising river and twisted breathlessly among the clogging plant debris and parts of carriages that had washed down from counties far away. There was so much turbulent water around her that she didn't feel her own water rush from her or the pain of labor, only a sudden weariness that made her reach for the shore, grabbing at bushes and weeds hanging upon the edge, inching her way up the muddy bank, crying out to her manservant, who always waited a discreet distance away. He came running and pulled her out, exclaiming, "Ma'am, look!"

Between her legs hung an infant female. The servant cut the cord with his kitchen knife and tried to place the child in its mother's arms. It did not cry but seemed healthy and most certainly alive.

"Maybe we should draw the water out of its tiny lungs," the servant suggested.

"No! Let it be!" the mother cried, unwilling to touch this foreign river baby that she and her husband had conceived.

"Captain, what should I do?" she begged the now silent woods and suddenly calm river, but no answer came, so she and the manservant struggled toward the main house with the child barely supported between them.

Everything was in chaos at first, the mother weeping, the grandparents soothing her, the servants left to maintain the child in some sort of comfort. Nursing, for the mother, was out of the question, so a black neighbor mammy was fetched to feed the child. The woman cuddled her and sang to her and could be heard cooing, "You po' lil' river-baby, still wet and slashed by those ole cut-weeds. What'll we do now?" The baby drank and thrived.

She really never knew her mother. No one named her. She was called Riverbaby and passed from hand to hand for feeding and diapering and bathing and clothing. But the child didn't seem to care. She seemed to have other things on her mind. People noticed when her dark curls began to lengthen and her gray eyes looked out of her pretty face, but all sympathy went toward her clearly unstable mother, who still called out for the captain in the middle of the night and never acknowledged their child.

When Riverbaby was three, she toddled off down to the river and slid in. Some thick branches saved her from drowning, while she laughed and slapped the water like an old friend. When she was in the river, she began to speak. They were the first words she had uttered. She said, "I'm coming, William."

The family was shocked. Her grandparents had a greyhound named William, so they tied him by the bank to watch over her, day after day. Sometimes when they went to retrieve her, she'd say, "Where's William?"

And they'd say, "He's right here, baby. He'll never leave you." But she looked right through the dog and shook her head.

Another year passed. The four-year-old began to swim. No one had taught her. She used an odd stroke, like someone battling a strong current, even when the river seemed as sluggish as a snail. She would come back to shore when someone called her but emerged from the river with a secretive smile.

"Someone so young," they said, "knows who she is!"

At five, they sent her to school. The teachers praised her for her manners, her fine speech, her gentleness, her capacity to love because of her generosity toward the other children, but the only thing she ever put on her paper were scenes from the river, more detailed and vivid as the years went by.

She could do math in her head and had memorized all the states, their capitals, and their *rivers* by the time she was seven. One day that year she turned in a drawing of a river that no one had ever seen. It had a hard-railed, flat stone stamped bridge that no one had built yet. It had trees on its banks that did not grow in that county. But most surprising, it had no name. Her rivers always had names. When the teachers asked her, "What do you call that one?" she said, "I don't know yet."

"Where is that river, child?"

"Not here," she would say, caressing the paper.

When she was eight, the other children avoided her. She had no name, and she spoke in a language they could not comprehend. It was English, of course, but too advanced for most third graders. She mostly drew the unnamed river, and once she sketched in a metal carriage with small wheels at the entrance of the bridge that looked like no horse carriage anyone had seen.

"What is that?" they asked her.

"I don't know," she said, "but I am in it."

"You are in it?"

"Yes... see, there."

And she pointed to the figure of a girl faintly outlined in the back seat.

"Boy, that Riverbaby, she do have an imagination," her mammy said.

"She's smart as a whip," her grandparents said.

"We need her to have a name," her teachers pleaded.

But her ninth year came and went and no one named her.

"The captain would have named her," everyone said.

So they read through all of his letters and his charred diaries from the battlefield. There were no suitable child's names there. But the mammy said, "Let me see 'em. I'll find somethin'."

The child was ten. She stopped going to school and spent her time at the river. There was no dog William to protect her anymore, but she was overheard saying those first words she'd ever spoken, "I'm coming, William." They left her to her imaginings.

One day her own mother asked her, "What is your name?"

"I know it, but I am saving it for someone who will love me."

"Oh, child, do you know what love is?"

"I do," she said and turned away, running for the river.

The mammy came into the room just then. "I foun' a word that maybe make a name. Looka here, somethin' the captain call you in his last days. The page is burnt, but you can see fo' letters. It only be one thin'."

But it was too late. Riverbaby had leaped into the murky water and struck out toward the bridge. She had a name on her lips, but no one heard it. They heard nothing, not a cry or a whisper. Under the bridge the child was swimming through the maze of a carriage that had long ago crashed into the water. Splinters licked her face and spokes entangled her arms. She surged fiercely, as was her nature, finally floating free, her clothes impaled on the wreckage, her body not given up by the relentless water, the swift spring current taking her out of their lives forever.

They searched for ten days, one for each year of her life and at last named the dead child and put a marker on the rough bank under the bridge:

Here lies our only child, born in the river April 6, 1863
Lost in the river May 11, 1873

ANGELA

Mr. Langley set the pages gently on his desk and asked, "Does anyone have fewer than ten marks?" No hands went up. "I rest my case," he said.

That night was the homecoming game. Big deal. I was really over football, but my roommates and some other friends, mostly lit majors, were going and dragged me along. It was bitterly cold for LA, below 40 degrees everyone said, so we carted blankets and thermoses of coffee and hot chocolate. The players would probably love the cold, but sitting on a metal bench in the grandstand for three hours was not appealing to me. We girls huddled together and avoided the boys who wanted to huddle. They were too young for me anyway. As the band marched onto the damp grass with the teams ready to burst in behind them, Melissa nudged me and whispered in my ear, "Look! Look who's here!"

Mr. Langley climbed the first few rows, scanning the crowd. Melissa, bless her, waved and called out, "Professor Langley! Mr. Langley! Here! Come sit with us!"

One of the faculty women had invited him to the game to help her hand out the king and queen trophies, he told us after he sat down next to me, but he had lost her in the crowd and didn't want to miss the kickoff.

"You *like* this?" I asked.

"Not especially," he answered, "but I like *this*." And as we spread the blankets out to include him, he grasped my hand underneath the mass of down and plaid wool coverings. He must be so lonely, cut off from his wife almost six months now. I didn't hesitate for a minute. I pulled his hand over into my lap and put my other hand over both.

"I could never write a story like this one," he said. No one else heard amid the cheers for both teams warming up on the field.

The game was close, teams trading touchdowns until halftime. I got to dreading touchdowns because I'd have to let go of Mr. Langley's hand to stand up and yell. Then, during the band drill, Lois La Monde noticed William and beckoned him down. He was too much of a gentleman not to oblige.

"Thanks for the hot chocolate, my favorite writers," he said to us gallantly and went down the bleacher steps.

Melissa swooned teasingly and turned to me. "So?" she said.

"So, damn those touchdowns anyway," I said.

"Sela! You're crazy!"

"Crazy about that man," I said, but she didn't hear me.

After the game, there was a party at one of the frat houses. UCLA had won the game, so everybody was going. I told myself I'd only stay thirty minutes, but the first thing I saw was Mr. Langley dancing with Miss La Monde. They were laughing. Oddly, I thought she looked older than William and out of place, but I was a writer, after all. I would just write myself into the scene.

I moved closer to them and then stopped. *I could put his career in jeopardy,* I thought. I turned to leave, but I was too late.

"Sela!" I heard his lovely voice call out.

"I didn't think I'd see you again tonight," I said when he reached me.

"My special girl," he said softly in my ear, and we began to dance. He didn't hold me tight but looked into my eyes and moved his hand ever so slightly on my back. The band was playing a slow number, but the noise was deafening, and people kept bumping into us.

"Just think of the beach and that night at Daudi's," he said. "We'll be all right."

Even before the music ended, Lois was clutching his arm and shouting at me over the din, "He's my date tonight, young lady! Why don't you mingle among the *boys*!"

Mr. Langley replied, as nicely as he could, “I think our date is over, Lois. I’d like to walk Miss Hart home.”

“Is that such a good idea, Bill?” she asked, lowering her voice somewhat.

“I believe it’s the best idea I’ve had all night,” he said easily.

We headed for the door and the brisk winter night, which revived us after the stuffy frat house.

“Do you know what I’d like right now?” Mr. Langley said, avoiding touching me in front of all the party-goers stumbling in and out, smoking on the patchy lawn and being generally obnoxious and drunk.

“I’m afraid to ask,” I said.

He laughed generously. “There’s always *that*,” he said. “No, seriously, I’d like to go someplace, preferably quiet and warm, and hear those two stories you turned in today. They’re in my car, just up the hill a ways.”

“We could go to your office,” I offered. “It would seem... like schoolwork.”

“I think the building’s locked by now, but the Student Union is always open during homecoming. There probably won’t be too many people there—unless you’re too tired,” he added.

“I’m never too tired to be with you, Mr. Langley.”

“Hey, I meant to tell you, back in the frat house, your eyes looked kind of aquamarine in that awful light. It was the most beautiful thing in the room. Out here they look... cobalt.”

“Well, I like your imagery, professor, but people have told me that all my life, that my eyes change color, with the tides, one might say.”

“Another mysterious detail about Sela Hart.”

There were only two couples at the juice bar when we walked into the Student Union. In the back by the book section were a well-worn couch and some reading lamps.

“This is perfect,” Langley said. He reached into his briefcase for my stories, the ones titled “Beyond the Range (Part One)” and “Beyond the Range (Part Two),” and we sat down, probably too close for student and teacher, but I knew we were well beyond that. Every story I gave him was a turning point in the lives of William and Angela, a revelation and a surprise. I looked at the first line, and then I handed the stories back to *my* William, realizing that the words needed to come from his voice. He began to read.

Beyond the Range (Part One)

About six months after I finished shooting *The Range*, I went to a psychiatrist for the first time in my life. I didn't really think he could help me, but I needed to tell someone what had happened, to try to make sense of it all. I couldn't sleep, and I felt so disoriented and lost. Then, the director called with an idea for a sequel—the story of Ryder and Rose in Mexico running from the law and their own failed dreams.

I felt a pain surge through me when he said the name Rose, because, of course, I thought of Rose's sister, my love, Angela Star. I had to sit down in his plush office with the pain coursing through me like rogue lightning.

"Are you all right, Bill?" he asked.

"I don't know," I answered. "Do you know a good psychiatrist?"

So that's how I ended up in Dr. Sheldon's office a few days later. He introduced himself with a welcoming handshake and a complimentary reference to my latest movie. He seemed serious but open, so I jumped right in.

"I believe I am being haunted," I said, shaking even to say those words.

"By what?" he asked.

"By a young woman."

"Do you know who she is?" he asked as if this were a reasonable topic of discussion.

"I made a film last year... *The Range*."

"I remember it. Quite a powerful performance," he said.

"If you only knew," I began.

"Tell me."

"Do you remember the supporting actress, Katie Turin?"

"I believe so. She played Rose's sister, correct?"

"Yes, but not to me. I mean, I never saw her. I saw a girl with dark hair and gray eyes galloping toward me, stepping out of the shadows of the movie saloon, coming to my trailer at night, calling me William, which no one does, soothing me with soft words when my head ached from the difficult scenes and the erratic weather. She said her name was Angela Star and that she had loved me since she was 10 years old! When I embraced her, I felt whole. I felt that lifetime of love she had for me. I held her all night. We didn't have sex. Our relationship seemed too... sacred. What we had were fleeting moments alone and hours of action and dialogue, if you count all the retakes, as Ryder and Rose's sister."

"I do remember how intense I thought your performance was," Dr. Sheldon broke in.

"But, of course, there was no Angela Star," I said, almost choking on the words. I told him that last week, when I was riding my horse in the San Gabriel Mountains, I came to a creek crossing, fairly wide and turbulent. Some riders were crossing a rough bridge, but I froze. And I remembered. I remembered the night years ago at my premiere of *Chosen One* and the girl who was swept away in the Chalice River. I never knew her name. "Dr. Sheldon, this is what I need from you, perhaps the only thing. I need you to find out about that family, that girl who disappeared in the water."

"Do you think this is the woman who is haunting you?"

"Yes… but there's more. When I came through the crowd after the showing of *Chosen One*, there was a young woman a little apart from everyone. When I saw her waiting, I couldn't look at anyone else."

"Can you describe her?"

"Not very well. It was dark. She was away from the theater lights, but she held my eyes. I went straight to her. The noise of the crowd disappeared. I thought she wanted my autograph, but no—she just reached out and put her hand on my arm and said my name. She just said, '*William*,' and I was pulled toward the limo. What made me remember this was that I suddenly recalled hearing my name cried out, a desperate cry, just before I saw the news and heard that a nineteen-year-old girl had been the only one not rescued in a family of five who had plunged into the Chalice River that night."

Dr. Sheldon nodded, interested but skeptical.

"This was ten years ago! I'm so confused about it. I must know that girl's name."

"What do you think it has to do with your current… young lady?"

"If her name was Angela Star…"

"You could find that information yourself," he suggested.

"But I need someone to believe me. If *you* find that old story about the girl in the Chalice River… and if her name is… well, then you wouldn't think I was crazy."

"I don't think you're crazy," he said matter-of-factly.

"What do you think?"

"I'm intrigued, frankly. I've never had such a bizarre request. I'll do it. Give me about a week, Mr. Hathaway. I hope there is an explanation that will comfort you."

"And then I'll know what to do."

"About what?"

"About making a sequel to *The Range*," I said. I stood and moved to leave.

"Wait a minute," he said, reaching for a notebook. "Write the young woman's name and the date you told me about her."

My hand shook as I wrote *Angela Star* on the blank white page. It would be a long week.

I took the time to read the script. It was titled *Beyond the Range*. *Fitting,* I thought. Ryder and Rose are on a vineyard in Mexico, cut off from family and friends. One of the men Rose's sister had shot in Arizona has died, and we are both wanted for accessory to manslaughter. We are bone weary from running and hiding. No one likes that Rose has married a white man. She is called a *gringa* after all for being with me. Rose talks to her sister who is, of course, not there—no actress playing the part anyway. Ryder feels trapped. I put the script down. It is too close to the truth. Can I play this part without going mad myself?

I returned to Dr. Sheldon's office with great anxiety. I sat in front of him with my head in my hands.

He said, "Her name was Angela Star."

"Oh, God."

"Mr. Hathaway, there is a long article about her family here. Would you like to read it?"

"No. Let me tell you what else I know, and you see if it's there."

"All right."

"Angela told me she'd had a crush on me since she was ten years old."

"Yes… I remember you saying that. And it's here."

He quoted a line from the news clipping. "'Angela's parents showed reporters their daughter's room. The walls were covered with photos of William Hathaway. They said she began collecting them when she was about ten, and they didn't understand why she never outgrew her childhood crush.'"

"Dr. Sheldon, do you know what this means?"

"I don't. What else do you remember?"

"That night, at the premiere, was she the one who touched me?"

"It says, 'The Stars were trying to get Angela to leave the theater, but she was determined to see Mr. Hathaway. 'Finally, he did approach us,' they said, 'and we think she took his arm and said his name. It was the last word we heard from our daughter, the name *William*.'"

Dr. Sheldon put the clipping on his desk and looked at me. I could barely breathe.

"Bill," he continued, "it's only a black and white photo, but would you like to see it?"

I took the paper from his hand and stared into the face of my love. It was not a ghost. She had touched me, and I had embraced her ten years later not knowing who she was. I wouldn't make that mistake again. I went home and called the director of *Beyond the Range*.

"When do we start?" I said.

Beyond the Range (Part Two)

My first day on the set, my heart was in my throat.

"Bill, speak up. You're whispering," came the director's voice.

"It's just the dry air," I said.

We were on location in Mexico, the green vineyards an oasis, those scenes a relief. The rest of the time would be spent in barren canyons and wasted fields. Elena, the actress again playing Rose, brought me a glass of water and said with sympathy, "Bill, I think I know what's happening here, but it's okay. Just focus on me. Forget everything else. I'm supposed to go crazy in this story. That should be easy to react to."

"What if I'm the one who's crazy?" I said, taking the glass from her hand.

"You're not crazy," she said. "You had a dream, and it touched your heart. Leave it there."

"I'll try."

But it wasn't as easy as Elena had proposed. The pain in my head exploded, even more fiercely than it had in the Borrego City bar when Angela had first hidden herself in the dark corners of the room. We only had six hours in before I had to quit.

"Get some sleep, Bill," the assistant director called out. "We have a long way to go."

The trailers were parked in a circle out of sight of the vineyard in a depressing hollow with barely a saguaro or a manzanita to its ten acres. If those hardy plants couldn't survive here, how could I? It was dusk, still hot and hazy. I sat on the edge of the bed as still as I could to keep the pain at bay.

There was a light knock at my door. I was afraid to open it. Then I heard her voice.

"William..."

God in heaven... I reached the door in an instant and opened it to the flesh-and-blood Angela Star. She rushed into my arms without another word. I clutched her to me and buried my face in her hair. She smelled like fresh rain, although the desert stretched around us like a dusty cloak.

Then I looked at her. "I knew you'd come... but how?"

"Your pain brought me in… just as it did in Borrego City. I am sensitive to your pain. It frees me from my own. It draws me to a place where I can touch you."

"The pain is gone."

"I know."

"Angela… I know who you are," I said.

"Do you?"

I told her that I knew she had disappeared in the Chalice River ten years ago, that she had called my name just before the car went off the bridge but that I hadn't known then that she was the girl in the crowd outside the theater. "I didn't know last summer that you came to me as Rose's sister. Because I didn't know your name, and I didn't recognize you!"

"William… I called your name *after* I fell into the river too. I've been calling it ever since. I broke to the surface to be with you when you made *The Range*, and now you're here, in Mexico, with Elena, a new script, and a heartache. What can I do?"

"Stay… stay with me."

"I want nothing more."

She had reeds in her hair, and her clothes were torn. We undressed and got into the shower. We made love in the element she knew best. Then we slept in each other's arms, and time stopped.

In the morning, there was only a pillow pressed against me.

"No… no!" I cried, but there was a note on the table: *I'll be back, A.*

I got ready for the day's shooting and wandered onto the set. Angela appeared as a worker in the vineyard, as a servant in the vine master's house, as a soldier on a bay horse in the shimmering sun. At night, she caressed me and whispered my name. Her secrets remained unspoken.

One day, when we passed in the courtyard while the cameras were rolling, I said, "Are you real?" And she answered, "Some people think that I am," with a secret smile.

"Cut!" The director walked over. "Bill, what are you doing? Talking to that maid is not in the script!"

"Sorry," I said, but I was full of joy.

I had a few days off, and I told Angela there was someone I wanted her to meet.

"I can't. You know I can't."

"He's my psychiatrist. He knows about you. He's the only one. I want him to see you."

She agreed. We drove up to LA to Dr. Sheldon's office. I hadn't told him we were coming, so we waited in the outer room holding hands as if that were the only thing keeping us together. When Dr. Sheldon said good-bye to his last patient, we stood in his doorway. He gasped and reached out to Angela.

"Your hand is wet, my dear," he said.

"Yes, it would be to you," she said softly.

"Are you all right?" he asked.

"Only when I'm with William," she answered.

"May I… hug you?" the doctor stammered.

"Of course," Angela said and stepped into his arms.

"This is beyond anything I know," he said, "but it is a healing for me—I who try to heal others. I am now healed by Angela Star, the girl from the Chalice River. Thank you, Bill, for trusting me… and for giving me this gift."

We sat down and talked for a while. Dr. Sheldon did not take his eyes off of Angela. It got dark, but we didn't turn on any lights. There was a light in the room.

"I will never forget this," he said as we rose to leave, and he put his arms around Angela once again.

In the car later, I could not hold back my emotions.

"I know what I have to do," I said.

"William?"

"I have to go into the Chalice River."

"No!" she cried. "No… I can only come to you if you are alive! You would never find me in the river. No one ever found me in the river. It's not possible!"

"How possible is this? A girl who loved me most of her life and died before she was twenty and now is sitting here wiping away my tears?"

"You're right. We don't know what's possible. Just love me, William. It's what I live for, when I live."

"I will become an old man…"

"And I will still come to you until you take your last breath. It's the only thing I know how to do."

"Are you an angel?"

"No, I am the real love of William Hathaway."

We headed back to Mexico. She rested her head on my shoulder. Just before dawn I put my hand over to touch her. I felt only a leather seat drenched in river water and tears.

When he finished, William took my face in his hands and said, "Are you Angela?"

"No, Mr. Langley."

"You're not going to disappear on me?"

"Never."

I hated that he had to drive all the way to Malibu, but he assured me he didn't mind, that he'd sleep in on Saturday.

"It's already Saturday," I reminded him. The clock on the wall read 12:37.

He walked me the rest of the way to my apartment. There was no one home yet. When I opened the front door, I took him with me into the dark entry hall. We stood there for a minute without saying anything, all the possibilities hanging in the shadows. I kept thinking that whatever we did, someone was going to get hurt.

Then he said, "May I have this dance?"

He held me as close as he had wanted to at the frat party. I could feel his heart beating against mine. We danced to the music of all the poetry we knew. Finally he stopped and put both arms around me. I knew that when he left, I wouldn't believe it.

"Sela, can I stay for a while?" he asked. "I don't seem… quite ready for the drive. I think someone might have spiked my punch at the frat house."

"Oh, no. Of course—here, sit on the sofa. I'll bring you some ginger ale. I have Vernor's. It's great stuff."

"Yeah, sweetheart, I think that might make my stomach feel better."

I went toward the kitchen but glanced back and saw him pick up my old, self-published book of poetry and flip through the pages. When I came back, he took a long swallow of the soothing liquid and turned to page twelve.

"Sela, will you read this one to me?" he asked and leaned back, still in some discomfort.

"Okay." I sat on the coffee table just opposite him. Our knees touched.

To W. L. 2006

There is the man, just vanishing in the crowd,
whose eyes have sparked a fire in my bones,
who may know love, but mine is not allowed,
and if I speak, my words are dead as stones.
His hands have never brushed my tears away

or touched me passing in the halls or opened doors
where I could thank him, whisper stay
and let me hold you. *Only silence roars.*
His lips I kiss in dreams and never tell
a living soul how dear he is to me
or how I've followed from a distance, dwelt
on every step he takes by brook or tree.
If he is real, then I am nothing, ghost
of what my real heart wants the most.

He reached out and took one of my hands in both of his.

"It's not a very good sonnet, I know. But I was only twenty," I said.

"Twenty?" He seemed surprised.

"It was the second year I tried to get in your class. I guess I wouldn't have gotten an A back then… for that kind of work anyway."

"I think it's lovely, really. The emotion is… staggering." He looked away from me, seemingly choked up, but spoke clearly. "I remember a day years ago. I stopped along Ransom Creek. It was windy, and there were huge red and gold leaves landing in the water. And then I saw a face… your face, Sela?"

"No… I was too far away."

"I wish I had seen you. I wish I had known someone felt this way about me. It had been a terrible day."

"No, Mr. Langley. I was afraid of hurting you or scaring you. You were happily married."

He shook his head. "It was the day Natasha told me she was gay… that she loved someone else. I felt… well, as if I'd been hit by a truck. Oh, God, bad choice of words. But then, I saw that face in the water. It was blurred by ripples and leaves, but it gave me courage. I remember thinking, *If I can see a face in the brook, I can get through anything.* And here you are, Sela Hart, as real as can be, all these years later."

"There's a time to mourn and a time to dance," I said.

He leaned over and kissed me, as if really letting himself kiss me for the first time. Then he smiled. "You're missing an iamb in the last line."

"Yeah, I know. I figured if Shakespeare could have irregular lines, so could I."

"Good reasoning, but you really can't, you know."

"I'll fix it for you. Just give me a few years."

"That I can surely do," he said, and then he almost whispered, "Sela, I want you to know that no matter what happens, I do love you, you with the quantum blue eyes, burnished hair, and the loveliest lips I have ever kissed, the most memorable words on the printed page, and a touch that heals."

"Mr. Langley, stop, I'm not a saint."

"You wanted to be in my life for a long time, but you didn't interfere. You didn't seduce me with your poems, which you might easily have done. You were honorable. It's why I have to be honorable now and go home alone."

"But do you feel okay?"

"Not too well, but that kiss will take me right to my door... to my bed... to my dreams."

"I love you." Somehow I was unable to say his name.

"I know you do, sweet girl."

He wrapped his arms around me again as we stood up, and I felt the sobs before he even knew they were in his throat. "Thanks for the dance," he was able to say.

"Thanks for the kiss," I whispered.

He left quickly and did not look back. Oh, God in heaven, how could I not go with him? I put my hand on the door, and Melissa and Anne bounded in from the other side.

"We saw Langley leaving. What's going on?" Anne asked.

"He walked me home from the party, mostly to get away from Lois La Monde."

"But, I mean, what happened?"

"He kissed me. He said he loved me. What are we going to do?"

"Goodness, girl, what do you think comes next?"

"I don't know," I answered truthfully.

"You sleep with the guy, silly," Anne said.

"It's so much more complicated than that," I said.

"Don't you want to have sex with him?" Melissa asked.

"My body says one thing, and my mind says another. I'm sure this is a university rule that can't be broken."

"Don't tell me you don't know students are sleeping with their professors."

"Their *married* professors," Anne added.

"Well, I just hope he really cares about you and isn't just looking for a replacement for Natasha," Melissa said.

"Goodness," Anne responded. "I know he doesn't want a lesbian... not that there's anything wrong with lesbians, but... you know what I mean."

"Oh, Lord, let's sleep on all this," Melissa said wearily. "Is Mr. Langley all right?"

"I think he's a little sick from something he drank at the party. I wanted to go home with him so badly," I said.

"Maybe he'll call you tomorrow. Don't worry too much. Guys can take care of themselves."

"Oh, I know that. Love clouds all reasoning," I said.

The phone was ringing, ringing. I was dead to the world but suddenly thought of Mr. Langley. I grabbed the receiver.

"Sela, I'm okay. I just needed to hear your voice."

"Oh, William, what a great way to wake up!"

"You called me William... without thinking about it."

"Oh, Mr. Langley, I didn't mean..."

"I like it. Everybody calls me Bill. But *you* are not everybody."

"It has nothing to do with the stories, you know," I told him.

"I know, honey, but I'm glad to be a William for you, and I don't mind if there is a certain quantum crossover between William Hathaway and me. That's life, isn't it? Speaking of which, I have to come back into school to do some planning for the metaphor workshop. Do you want to have lunch and read me another story?"

"I'd like that. I'll fix lunch here. We won't be alone. Anne has to study for a couple of big tests, and Melissa will be in and out with her younger sister who's applying to UCLA next year."

"That'll be fine. I think I can take a break about one. I'm not quite recovered from last night, so I don't know how much work I'll get done."

"Why don't you stay here tonight? You must be exhausted driving to and from the canyon so much," I said, thinking of the pleasure of having him in the guest room, stealing a kiss in the hallway, and going over to the lit building together every morning.

"Thanks," he said. "I might take you up on that. The traffic is so bad this time of year, and the weather slows everyone down. Sometimes I feel as if I just get home and it's time to come back. How much trouble do you think I'd be in staying with *three* of my students?"

"Not any more than you are already in kissing *one* of them."

"You're probably right about that," he said. "I'll see you later. What's the name of your story?"

"Elena's Role."

"Who is *she*?"

"The first person, besides the psychiatrist, who believes William about Angela."

"Does that make Angela more real?"

"You decide."

"Okay, see you in a while, sweetheart."

"Bye, William," I whispered.

How had we slipped so naturally into this relationship? Was it always there, just waiting for our paths to cross? I would never have wished Natasha harm. Maybe I am what Natasha wished for her husband. *This is not a story,* I reminded myself, and I started making plans for lunch.

William, whom I must remember to call Mr. Langley at school, arrived a little after one, and we all sat around the kitchen table eating grilled cheese sandwiches, fresh tomatoes from our windowsill garden, homemade ginger cookies, and lemon tea. I'd invited Lee Henderson, because I knew he cared a lot about Mr. Langley, and Marcella Ruiz, thinking she would like the compassionate and strong Elena with the same last name in my story. Our professor took a place by Lee saying, "Hey, there're a lot of females here."

"And who's bringing you sustenance, mister?" Melissa asked with good humor.

"For which I am very grateful, believe me, and I really enjoy doing things with my students outside of the classroom. Miss La Monde was telling me one of her grad students had this ridiculous idea, her words, about taking a group of kids to the beach for a metaphor, a *sea*-metaphor, mind you, workshop, and I said, 'What a fantastic and clever idea. Whose was it?' And she zipped her lips so fast. Maybe she'll never speak again! But that doesn't solve my problem of finding out who wants to do such a wonderful thing."

"Would anyone here like to venture a guess?" I said. "Extra cookie if you get it right."

"Sela!" Lee cried.

"Sela?" Mr. Langley looked at me with his eyes widening. "I should have known. I guess you'll be helping me on Saturdays now. Because that's the workshop I want to do!"

"Why don't I just change my faculty advisor to you. Wouldn't that simplify things?"

"Somehow I don't think so, but it's worth a try," he said. "Now how 'bout that story, Sela."

"Let's go in the living room," Melissa suggested. "It's more comfortable."

I sat with my back against a big pillow and my friends around me on the sofa, chairs, and other pillows. This did not feel like a story that should be read standing up or looking down at people.

Elena's Role

> **When Bill comes back from LA, he is a mess. I mean, the guy is beyond talking to. He goes straight to his trailer without saying a word to anyone, and I feel so bad for**

him. He's a really great person and has been a good friend to me. Once, my ex kept my children two extra days, and I didn't know where they were. Bill took me to lunch and let me cry on his shoulder.

I know he had a kind of breakdown on the set of *The Range* last year. He tried to tell me about a girl named Angela Star, but I convinced him it was a dream because, after all, the girl *wasn't there.* His marriage is shaky, but he has two daughters he speaks fondly of, though they are somewhat estranged from him.

I love working with Bill. He becomes the part so effortlessly, saying his lines and ad-libbing like he is in another body. He's not too hard on the eyes either. He smiles at you as if he really means it. It's very endearing. And in a scene, he pauses and gives you a chance to get into your own character, doesn't hog the limelight, you know.

I wait a couple of hours and then walk across the dry compound to his trailer. I knock softly. Maybe he's sleeping.

"Angela?" he cries hoarsely.

"No, Bill. It's Elena."

"Oh, Elena. I'm not very good company right now."

"I don't care. I think you need a friend."

He opens the door. He definitely does not look any better.

"Bill, what happened in LA?"

He doesn't answer right away. We sit down in a couple of oversized chairs, and I wait for him to break the silence.

"Elena," he says slowly. "It's not a dream. She's real."

"Who?" I ask, though I know deep down.

"Angela," he answers in such a way that I want to believe him.

"She had an accident years ago," he continues, "but no one ever found her. She loves me... and so she stays on this side of... oh, God, I don't know. It sounds delusional. Haven't you seen her? She's been here for two weeks."

"No. What does she look like?" Going along with him seems to calm him.

"She has long, dark hair and gray eyes. She's slender, maybe twenty. My psychiatrist saw her yesterday. He hugged her."

"Then she must be real," I say.

"When we were driving back, suddenly she wasn't there. It's like my soul drains out of my body when that happens."

"Bill, I believe you. Does it help if someone believes you?"

"Yes. It's why I took her to see Dr. Sheldon. But if you believe me too, Elena, it would mean the world to me."

"This has happened before?" I ask, trying to keep drawing him out of his dark place.

"Yes... remember last year? I thought she was Rose's sister during the whole shoot."

"I told you it was a dream."

"You didn't know. You didn't know she was as real as you."

"Where does she come from?"

"The Chalice River."

I gasp. "The girl who went off the bridge with her family and was never found?"

"You remember that?"

"I do. I always thought they'd find her. Oh, Bill, just hold onto her when you can. Be grateful someone loves you like that. I've never had one hour with someone that I would cry to lose."

And I mean it. I want so badly to put my arms around Bill, but I know it's not what he needs. We sit there for a while. Tears still fall from his eyes, and I have a lump in my throat. This sweet man has told me the greatest secret of his life. And I will guard it. And he will know when he looks at me, wherever we are, that I believe him.

When I finished, everyone spoke at once.

"She loves him, no doubt."

"I think she's just a loyal friend."

"She's just acting. She doesn't believe that stuff about Angela."

"She says she'll believe him wherever they are."

"She's a great Mexican character for the movie."

"That girl has a good head on her shoulders."

"How can she not believe him? You always believe your friends."

Mr. Langley, as usual, came to their rescue. He said. "What do you think is the most significant line in the whole story?"

I had given everyone copies, so each person poured over the paragraphs searching for the answer.

"I think I found it," Lee said, and he read, "'Be grateful someone loves you like that. I've never had one hour with someone that I would cry to lose.'"

"Doesn't that just grab you?" Langley said. "How true that line must be, smack in the middle of the story of a ghost. It's brilliant."

Marcella asked, "Mr. Langley, may I read it in class Monday?"

"I think that would be fine," he said.

"I really like this girl… character," she continued.

I said, "Marcella, why don't you write a short story about her?"

"I think I could do that. I'd like to try. Will you help me, Sela?"

"Sure, but I want you to feel free to take Elena's story in any direction you wish. I don't want you to hold back because I'm in your head."

"I'll do it too," Anne said suddenly. "I'm in a different class. I haven't even heard all of Sela's stories. I think I could be objective."

"You girls can do this as an independent project. It can take the place of any other assignment."

"Oh, thank you, Mr. Langley," Marcella said. "I'm very excited to try this."

Then I said, "I'd like someone to tell me what Elena's role is?"

"To listen."

"To be a friend."

"To do her acting job. That's a *role,* isn't it?"

"To cry on Mr. Hathaway's shoulder, so he feels needed?"

"To help him with *his* acting role?"

Finally, Mr. Langley gave them the deepest understanding of the story and answered the question himself. "To give William hope," he said.

Melissa turned to her favorite professor and said, "Mr. Langley, I want to tell you something, and I think I speak for all of us. Of course, Sela's stories are great and some of the other kids' are too, but it's what you do with them, the things you make us see and feel, the way you find the ultimate meanings, the powerful truths in *fiction*—well, it's just life-changing."

"That's why I'm here," he said.

He hugged everyone as the group broke up. Melissa had to pick up her sister; Anne retreated to her room to study; Marcella went with her as she had one of the same classes; Lee said he had planned to go running with Riley, so at last, William and I were left alone cleaning up the dishes side by side in the small kitchen. His cell phone rang. He dried his hands and opened it.

"Yes, Lois... no, I'm not sorry I left the party early. I was, uh... getting sick. No, I was glad I was with Miss Hart. She's a good friend. She lets me be who I am. Can we talk about this later, Lois? I'm busy right now. Okay ... okay, good-bye."

"I'm sorry, Sela. She can be a problem. I don't know why she thinks we're an item. I only ever walked her to her car after an evening lecture, sat next to her at a faculty dinner once, things like that. She's been a little paranoid and possessive lately. It's something I don't need right now… or ever, for that matter. I don't seem to understand women very well," he said. "Except for you. What did I do to deserve you?"

"You let me in your class," I said.

"I should have done that years ago."

"Maybe… I had no idea what I wanted. And you were married."

"I was married and sleeping alone for most of twenty years."

"I'm so sorry, William. You are such a wonderful and desirable man. You must have had lots of women with their eyes on you over the years."

"I was waiting for the girl in the brook," he said and embraced me.

He left for Malibu, and for hours afterward there was the scent of a river throughout the house.

6

After Marcella read "Elena's Role" and we had a lively discussion in period 5, Professor Langley didn't read any of my stories that week, although a lot of students asked him to. He used Melissa's and Riley's work, which fit his lessons better than mine, and I was glad. I wasn't comfortable with all the attention. I didn't even want to enter my story in the department contest.

Lois La Monde started some talk about me, to which the math teacher, Mr. Hall, seemed eager to add. Mr. Langley got himself assigned as my graduate faculty advisor. La Monde seemed determined to denigrate us and gossiped about us being seen together in Santa Barbara sitting as *close* as two people could be on a bench at the zoo and raising her eyebrows to suggest what that might have led to. Of course, telling that tale backfired on her since everyone on campus had heard the story of the rhinos, the zebras, the Tanzanian, and the actor William Hathaway and his daughters. There was even an "in joke" going around among the friendlier of his colleagues about Bill's "zoo time." That kind of talk was no threat.

Christmas break was beginning the next week, and we wrote like mad to finish Langley's "theme" and "character" exercises. Sometimes he and I would be together during sixth period for my graduate study program when his class was doing a reading assignment, and we planned and replanned for some kind of sea-metaphor workshop. He was careful not to touch me as other students and advisors were in and out of the room, and I missed his touch. I hungered for it as for nothing else and was anxious about not seeing him over the holidays.

The day before vacation, I found a box on my desk in plain wrapping. “Open it later, Sela,” he said as he passed by me handing out story projects and book lists. Then he sat on the edge of his desk, his shoulders rounded slightly, his face pale. I wondered why I hadn’t noticed the change. Maybe it was the gossip, the jealousy of some in the department of his genuine rapport with his students, and the fact that three from his writing classes had made the finals of the short story contest (my story, “Survivors,” was one of them), or maybe a deeper pain was surfacing at this coming season without Natasha at his side. Maybe he was just surviving in ways I could not know.

“On one of your handouts,” he began, “is some information about ‘voice.’” He wanted us to give him a voice he could care about that was *not our own voice*, to develop a character so different that he wouldn’t be able to figure out who wrote the stories. His examples sent a buzz through the classroom : “If you are female, write a male voice; if you are straight, a gay point of view; if you are a white atheist, a black Christian. You get the idea. I’ve put my home phone number on the page if you need some help. I’m not guaranteeing I’ll answer it!”

“You got big plans, Mr. L?” Sam Chu asked.

“Big enough,” Langley said and gave him an unreadable smile.

I was already writing my story. It was easy for me after living in Africa, but William would know it was mine. I scribbled down the line that crashed into my head: “For as long as I can remember, my father has been wanted for murder.” And I knew the ending. The boy would come face to face with the father he had never known. I wrote a few more lines. Then the bell rang, and Langley’s next class started to come through the door. I pressed the package to my heart.

William said to me as I went out, “Merry Christmas, Sela.”

I tried to smile. I wanted to take that haunted look from his eyes. There was no time. I was out in the hall with his gift, alone. I sat down on the cold floor and tore off the brown paper. Underneath was another wrapping, blue paper the color of the sky on that September day four months ago when I quoted the lines of his own poem in answer to his question. He had remembered my eyes. I was having a difficult time breathing.

I removed the paper slowly and couldn't believe my eyes. It was a highly polished mahogany box with a white rhino carved on the lid. That would have been enough. But inside was a key and a note.

> My dear Sela,
>
> This may be another "true key." I won't keep you in suspense. It is a key to Daudi's house, his gift to us. He said to me when he stayed with me in Malibu Canyon, "That lady love you very much. Something between you rare and divine." He made me cry, and then I promised him I'd give you this key. You can choose when to use it. Please don't wait twenty years.
>
> Because I have to tell you, I have to show you, my precious girl, how much I love you.
>
> William

I hesitated only a moment to gather my courage, and then I texted him right there outside his room: "Can we go before Christmas?" I didn't know what he was in the middle of, and we all had to turn our cell phones off in class, but almost immediately came the reply: "How 'bout tomorrow?" I could hardly think straight and only had the strength in my fingers to press "OK."

I waited in my darkening apartment with my phone in my hand. I knew William had a faculty meeting after sixth period and a conference with another faculty advisor about the metaphor workshop. I held the mahogany box in my other hand, the box with the white rhino and the enigmatic key. Of course, I knew what the key meant. It meant that I would soon be in a place with William Langley from which there was no turning back. Wanting to make love to him, dreaming about it for years, and actually doing it were entirely different things.

The phone rang. *Oh, please be him,* I said to the god of such connections.

"How long can you stay with me?" William asked as if that question had been in his mind all day.

"Forever," I said without a second thought.

"Sela, my girl who doesn't know the ending of her stories at the beginning."

"I'm getting better at that," I said.

"Don't you have plans for Christmas?"

"Yes. My mom's mom lives in La Puente. My folks are coming in from New York for a few days. I'm supposed to spend Christmas Day with them at my grandmother's and then fly back to New York to see some good friends that I haven't seen since I was in Africa. And sometime next week I have to do *homework*," I reminded him, "and pack and wrap presents... and oh, William, the box! I love it. And the key... so special, just as you are, my dear Mr. Langley. Just say you'll have Christmas dinner with my family."

"What would your folks think of that?" he asked.

"Oh, they're used to me living life on the edge. It would just be par for the course."

"I haven't lived on the edge for quite some time. I may not be what you really need," he said.

"Are you kidding? Remind me to tell you about the first time I stood in line to get in one of your classes!" I teased.

"Hmm, I can't wait to hear *that* story. But do you have time to go to Santa Barbara with me?"

"It's the only thing keeping me sane right now."

"We could go tonight," he said.

"Oh, William, I promised Melissa I'd go riding with her in the morning. Could we meet there? Do you know where she lives?"

"Somewhere in Moorpark."

"Yeah, just off the freeway. I'll text you the address. And don't worry. She won't ask why I'm meeting you and leaving my car there for a few days. She knows how I feel about you. I had to tell *someone*," I said.

"I know. You girls can always share these things. Who could I tell? You saw how Randall Hall acted, and I hadn't even kissed you yet!"

"I trust Melissa. She's as loyal as they come."

"Okay, then. What time should I be in Moorpark?"

"I think we have to be through with the horses by noon. How 'bout twelve thirty?"

"I'll be there."

"Until tomorrow," I whispered, still in some kind of shock.

"Until tomorrow," he said.

Melissa and I rode out into the green hills behind the stables on rented horses. At first we walked along in silence, my Half-Arab, Chisholm, waiting with great sensitivity for a rent horse for the cue to stride out. Melissa's Paint mare tossed her pretty head. They were both frisky in the early morning winter air. To lease those particular horses, you had to be a rider. We had both had lessons growing up, and Melissa had owned a horse for many years that had died on her first day of college. We had met at Griffith Park, both trying to keep horses in our lives. It kept us together as friends, even though she was a few years younger and just now a junior at UCLA. Horses can do that.

After a couple of miles, we started loping down a winding dirt road. Some recent storms had made huge puddles in our path. I felt reckless and brave. I let my gelding leap the smaller ones and plunge right through the bigger ones. The chaparral glistened in the morning light. The trail was lined with blue junipers and endangered California oaks. Raptors glided on unseen currents overhead. I let Chisholm gallop on toward a tall stand of birches, his exuberance giving me heart for what was to unfold in my life. Melissa had to urge her Paint to catch up. The sun began to warm the air, so we pulled up under a sprawling oak to rest the horses.

"What is with you today?" Melissa asked as soon as we had dismounted and led the horses to a seasonal creek nearby.

"I need to tell you something—ask you, really."

"What?"

"I need to leave my car at your house for a few days."

"And why is that?" she asked.

"Melissa, Mr. Langley's meeting me here... and we'll be gone until maybe Wednesday."

"Sela! Where are you going? And why, for heaven's sake? Did you hit on him?"

"No! It's nothing like that," I told her. "We're just friends—well, maybe a little more than friends. But honestly, we like to spend time together. We like the same things."

"Yeah, short stories and poetry, oh, and... metaphors!" she joked.

"Slow dancing, the beach, rhinos, zebras, speaking Swahili... and..."

"Never mind, I get it, but there must be something more, Sela. I *know* you, remember?"

"We have a connection. It's kind of mixed up with my short stories, being older than his other students, having lived in Africa, him losing his wife like he did, and lots of things."

"Yeah, like sexual desire," Melissa added.

"He kissed me that day at the zoo, and you know I've always wanted to know *what comes next*."

"He kissed you that far back? Boy, you know how to keep a secret. But Sela, you know what comes next. You told me you had a lover in Africa!"

"I want to know what comes next with William," I tried to explain.

"But don't you think it's risky for him to spend a week with you?"

"Probably. But what if this week is all we ever have? Don't I have to leap into this story like it's my last?" I asked.

"But it's not a story, Sela. This is his *life* you're messing with."

"It's just a few days on a deserted beach," I told her.

"Oh, yeah, right." She paused to let that sink in. "Of course, you can leave your car at my place. Far be it from me to deny young love. What time's he coming?"

"Twelve thirty."

"We'd better get back. You might want to fix your hair a bit for the gorgeous Professor Langley!" she teased.

"I knew you'd understand," I said.

"Oh, I get it," she said dramatically. "But I know you won't tell me the details."

"Probably not," I said.

When I got into Mr. Langley's car, I felt suddenly really aware of what I was doing. Just looking at him made my whole body ache. He smiled his half-humorous, half-serious smile and said, "Today your eyes are ocean blue."

"We're not even close to the ocean yet!"

"And your hair, I just noticed, is kind of the color of my car."

"I promise you my hair doesn't change with the tides."

He laughed. "How was your ride?"

"Incredible, although I was a little distracted. William, please tell me you're all right."

"I'm finally *all right*, my dear Sela. Why?"

"Just this last week, I got the idea you were upset by something or maybe not well."

"Boy, I can't hide a thing from you, can I?"

"I hope not."

"I was a little under the weather, probably from that damn frat party. Please don't worry about me."

"It's kind of hard to stop now, after eight years," I said.

He put one hand on my knee. A fire hit me where it had not been in a long time. I wondered if one could have an orgasm without being naked with someone in a bed. Santa Barbara seemed a lifetime away, but William drove slowly, especially down the Conejo Grade.

"She was a good and gracious person," he said as we passed the place where Natasha had died. There was that white cross on the turnout and what looked like fresh flowers. He glanced at them. "Her family keeps something there," he explained. "I can't stop. Never have been able to. I suppose they blame me somehow, but she was troubled. Alcohol put her in the grave, not me."

"That stuff has not been kind to either of you," I said.

"Man, isn't that the truth. It's just poison for me."

He had to take his hand away to shift gears at the bottom of the grade, but then he put his arm around my shoulders and pulled me closer to him. "But you… are an antidote for so many things, even things you don't know yet."

Camarillo, Ventura, Montecito—all went by in a blur. William asked if I had an idea yet for my "story in another voice."

"I had the first line in class and the ending before class was over."

"Will I know it's yours?" he asked.

"Probably. I'm working on another one that I don't believe you'll ever guess."

"Enjoy a challenge, do you?"

"I guess you know *that*," I said. "But I can read you something you'll know is me."

"Can I hear it and drive?"

"I hope so."

I reached in my purse and got out the folded piece of notepaper I had written the poem on last night. He squeezed my shoulder. I took a deep breath and then read.

Eyes, yes,
& lips & hands
& voice that haunts me
Voice, yes, that I do love
& kiss that is a blessing
god or no

Words are never enough
but if they are
I love you William—
my fiction my poetry
my dream of you
my real William
my beginning
my ending
my endangered heart

Eyes, yes,
but more—
ideas and spirit
& pain
& everything you are
I love

He tried to wipe away the tears, but I saw them. Then he said, "Read it again, slowly."

Soon we were parking on Oceanside Lane and walking up to Daudi's door.

"Your key or mine?" William asked.

"I'm shaking too much," I answered.

"I'm not much steadier," he said.

He opened the door. The rooms were full of flowers. There was a note on the table.

dear ones karibu
i stay at zoo tonight
please be your home here
tomorrow 5 i fix dinner
upendo
Daudi

"Upendo?"

"It means 'love.' The whole thing is like a poem," I said.

"Upendo," William repeated as if fixing it in his heart.

In the bedroom, all the flowers were white, the white bed linens freshly pressed and the white curtains billowing in the afternoon breeze.

"It seems to me you made up a line like this once," William said. "Something about a white room and a white bed."

"But I didn't know we were going to be in it," I whispered.

I could hear the high tide rolling in and then my own blood rushing in my ears as William put his lips on mine and then on every part of me as he undressed me, still standing in the mimosa-scented room.

I know you want to know what happened next. Just think of the words I read to William—eyes and lips and hands and voice and kiss, beginnings and endings. And even though at the end of that first afternoon, he cried and cried, and I felt like Angela Star knowing that when it was over, she'd have to go back into the cold, dark Chalice River, a piece of our story fell into place, a piece we had wanted but not expected, a piece we had feared but could not resist, our endangered hearts coming home.

The room got dark, the sea air cold and damp, but still we lay tangled in the white sheets, finding the places on each other we had imagined we wanted to touch, maybe even from the first day. William held my face and tried to name a color for my eyes. I put my fingers on the mouth that had said, "How long have you been waiting?" last September. And how might I have truly answered that question? Had I been waiting to be in William's class or waiting for this, this utterly incandescent union?

"Ultramarine," William said at last. "Your eyes tonight in this light. Do you know the definition of that color?"

"No."

"Beyond the sea," he said. "I just remembered that I found that once when Natasha was in her painting phase. I wanted to know how marine blue could be 'ultra,' so I looked it up. The number one meaning in Webster's is 'beyond the sea.' I wondered then if the painter William Langley knew that. But oh, how it fits your eyes here in this place."

"And it fits us. We are 'beyond the sea' for sure. We are beyond everything."

A sudden gust of sea wind blew out a candle we had lit earlier. William got up and closed the window. I fell asleep for a few minutes. When I opened my eyes, he'd put on his jeans and was sitting on the edge of the bed.

"Are you hungry?" he asked.

"For you," I said, running one hand over his smooth chest. He closed his eyes and leaned into my hand as if he needed more pressure to ease some kind of pain.

"I just keep thinking of William Hathaway with his Angela, making love to a ghost," he said.

"And I am thinking of Angela pulled away from her beautiful William by that icy river… I have a story where they meet on this very beach," I told him.

"Oh, I've got to hear that one!"

"I'm waiting for the right assignment," I said. "Tell me some of your lesson plans."

"Somehow it doesn't seem right to discuss my lesson plans with a naked wo… excuse me, student!"

"Does this mean you are looking for humor, Mr. Langley?"

"Well, that's not a bad idea. But I don't want stand-up comedian routines or ha-ha anecdotes. I want humor that is so deep it hurts."

"Stop right there," I said. "Go get my manuscript. It's at the bottom of my duffel bag. Try not to look at my night things."

"You brought things to wear in bed?" he asked.

"I didn't suppose we'd be naked *all* the time. Besides, I thought men liked to remove frilly outfits from their women," I teased.

"I guess I wouldn't have any experience with that," he said.

"Oh, William, I'm sorry. I just always imagined your wife being thrilled with you in bed."

"She liked sex all right… but with women."

I started to speak, but he broke in. "Don't get me wrong, Sela. She loved me, and she tried really hard to... please me, as I tried to please her. Then she met Mikeala. I think they were tennis partners or something. After games, they'd go out for drinks. She'd be gone for hours. One night, she didn't come home. I was really worried because she was drinking pretty heavily by then."

He looked away from me when he told me how Natasha had admitted having sex with Mikeala, how it had been the best thing ever, and how she wanted to stay married but be free to have a relationship with that woman. "I was just bowled over. I mean, I don't have a problem with gays, but my wife? It just didn't make any sense. We'd been married almost fifteen years by then."

William lay back down next to me. He said he just wanted her to be happy. Maybe she'd stop drinking. But the two women loved drinking together, loved the alcohol. They were both a mess, but he was trying to get tenure at the university, had a huge load of students, and had no idea how to help her. He added that several of their gay, and some straight, friends had watched over them and counseled them. He wanted me to know he wasn't blaming "gayness" for Natasha's downward spiral.

"I was so overwhelmed in those days, I think I just accepted the first hundred and thirty kids that showed up in September, no matter how they answered my questions."

"No wonder I couldn't get in one of your classes," I said.

"I wish you had," he said with some emotion. "When Natasha wasn't behind me coming home that night, I thought she'd turned off in Thousand Oaks to see Mikeala. I found out later, at the funeral, they'd broken up. If I had known that, I would never have let her get in her car."

"I'm so sorry, William. There was so much I didn't know standing in those lines."

I put my hand on his forehead. It was warm, the fever of remembered pain.

"Hey, sweetie, we forgot about your story," he said.

"It's okay. It'll keep. It wouldn't be so good right now."

"I don't mean to spoil things by talking about Natasha," he said.

"She was a part of my life too, in a way."

"You probably could have saved her... and then where would we be?"

"Well, she might be alive, but she'd still be gay," I reminded him.

He pulled me over on top of him, and the feel of his hard belly, even through the sheets and his jeans, was so sexy. He wound his hand through the twisted linens until he found the small of my back and laid his palm against my flesh. He hooked his other arm across my shoulders and moaned. I was aroused again with the pleasure of that move, his holding onto me through all the doubts and missteps and undeniable expectations that had led us to the white bed in the white room.

In a little while, William threw on a sweatshirt and some warm socks. I got up and looked for my black fleece tights and a yellow winter tunic that I had tossed in with a nice black dress, spiky heels, some lived-in jeans, and on-the-edge-of-revealing tops. At the bottom of the duffel was my manuscript, *William and Angela: A Quantum Crossing.* There were only two left that William hadn't heard.

"Sela! Bring your story!" he called to me from the kitchen.

I went in to the little table in the center of the room. William had made a tray of cheese and crackers, strawberries and kiwis, and a couple of Vernor's ginger ales.

"Good job," I said.

"We'll go out to dinner later, someplace special," he said.

"This is special, William. My favorite cheese and fruit, and you."

"Eat, girl. Your compliments will get you nowhere," he said as he handed me a cracked plate.

We ate a bit in silence, listening to the tide retreating in its endless journey. William had pulled the old porch couch inside out of the bitter weather. We moved over there and tried to get comfortable. William leaned back in one corner and put my yellow-stockinged feet in his lap, caressing them as if he'd been doing it for years.

"If you put those hands anyplace but on my feet, I won't be able to read," I told him, settling back in my corner. I opened the manuscript to the tenth story and tried to conjure up Sylvie's tone.

Sylvie

When Angela drowned in the Chalice River, I was fifteen. I adored my older sister, but I did not cry. I saved my emotions for revenge. William Hathaway murdered Angela as sure as I'm writing these words. She had lived for him, dreamed of his voice, his smile, his touch. And she got all those things in one moment, and then she died.

My whole life became about making William Hathaway pay. I had no plan in the beginning, just anger. I imagined the way I would do it—make him pay. The only way, finally, that appealed to me was to kill him.

A year went by, then two. I drew pictures of William with a dagger in his heart. Too messy, and I could get caught. I thought of poisoning him, but just my luck, he'd make it to the hospital. I didn't know anything about guns, but I figured I had time to learn. I had all the time in the world. He didn't.

And then, when I was eighteen, I got a break. I was in university (I decided to major in drama), and a classmate and pretty good friend of mine got a job in a TV studio where William Hathaway was working on a movie. Oh, boy. The young man, I'll call him Joe, was sure he could get me on the set. They always needed extra hands, and I was attractive and efficient.

While I waited for the chance to be in the same room with William Hathaway, I spent some time at the shooting range. I almost scratched my plan at first, because handling guns was really difficult for me. I'm small and not physically strong. I didn't want to ask too many questions, like, "To kill someone, do you need a heavy gun?" Finally, I found that a .375 Magnum would do the job. And then I would throw it in the Chalice River. Ha!

One day, Joe said some stagehands had been called to a different set for the day, and they were short on Mr. Hathaway's set. Could I come? I almost dropped the phone, and I got really scared. I was almost nineteen and looked a lot like my sister. Would William remember seeing her in the poor light outside the theater the night of his premiere of *Chosen One*?

I noticed him immediately when I made it through security with Joe and walked onto the set. He was starring in some murder mystery (appropriate) and was very visible. I did a few errands, brought people lunch, put away props. During a short break, William Hathaway asked for a glass of water. Of course, I volunteered to get it.

When I held out my hand with the full glass, his head was down in the script. I cleared my throat. He looked up and jumped like he'd seen a ghost. A little of the water spilled.

I said, "Sorry."

He said, "Who are you?"

"I came with Joe. We're in the drama department together at school. Thought I might learn something."

"What's your name?" he asked.

"Sylvie."

"Thank you for the water, Sylvie. My throat was getting dry."

"Glad to help."

"You remind me of someone," he said.

"I get that all the time," I replied and turned away.

I had forgotten what a charismatic man he was, handsome and sincere. What Angela would have given for that brief exchange! Her life, I guess. I remembered the place on his chest where the bullet would go, into the heart of a dream, into the heart of a killer.

Shooting practice went great after that. I honed my skills. I slept like a baby. Another year went by. After all, I couldn't buy a gun until I was twenty-one. Mr. Hathaway got used to me being around. He relaxed his guard and was quite friendly. I hated him. I hated that beautiful face that Angela only had a glimpse of before being carried away by the Chalice River. I would have my revenge.

I bought the gun. I won't tell you where or how, but I kept it close to me. William Hathaway was in the middle of some difficult scenes on a new movie. He had to ride a lot of different horses and spend hours in the sun. He seemed depressed or exhausted or something. My graduate drama class was involved in the project, but he scarcely noticed me.

One morning, I heard him say, "I'll be back in a couple of days. I'll be out of phone contact."

So I got in my car and followed him. The gun was hidden, but luckily he didn't break any speed limits on his way out of town. He drove up the coast to Santa Barbara, stopped in an isolated spot, and walked down to the beach.

He took his shoes off and sat down in the sand. The gun and I slipped behind some rocks that had tumbled from nearby cliffs. Shielding his eyes from the sun, William Hathaway stared at the waves and the coastline curving away in the afternoon mist. A figure approached from the north. He turned slightly, so now

my target was his back. Might still work. I held the gun steady and balanced it in the cleft of two boulders.

The man in my sights stood up suddenly and held out his arms. A young woman about my age approached and then quickly hugged him to her like it was the end of the world, little did she know. My finger was on the trigger. The girl lifted her face from where it had been buried in his shoulder. She was dripping wet, as though she had just emerged from the sea.

A scream rose in my throat. The girl continued caressing William's back and kissing him, her love for him radiating out into the bright beach air, and the gun fell to the ground.

It was Angela.

I closed the manuscript and looked at my teacher.

"That's exactly what I'm looking for! Assignment completed, A+!"

"You are biased, Mr. Langley," I said, poking him with my toes.

"Sela, can I ask you something really personal?"

"Sure."

"Where did William and Angela come from, in your head? What got you into the story?"

"Why do you want to know that? Won't it spoil the writing for you?"

"I don't know. I just know they are so real to you. They must connect to some true experience."

"There's one line that's true, and I guess that was my entry point. In the first story, 'The Range,' Angela tells William Hathaway in his trailer, 'I've had a crush on you since I was ten years old.'"

"I didn't remember that, but I do remember the girl Angela Star having the photos on her bedroom wall of William Hathaway. And her parents said that her interest in the actor had started when she was ten. But what does it have to do with *you?*"

"Why does it have to have something to do with me?"

"Because I *know* you. This is not a made-up line."

"Well, William Langley, you always find me out," I said. "But this is kind of weird."

"Okay."

I don't know if he wondered at my reluctance, but I told him that when I was ten, I had collected photos of a famous actor and that when I was about fifteen, I had actually met him, but he'd seemed… distant. He hadn't said one word to me, even after I'd told him I'd been a fan of his for almost half my life. I didn't know what I'd expected. His wife had told me he didn't like signing autographs at horse events. It had been right here in Santa Barbara, at Earl Warren Showgrounds. I had been so hurt that I tried to forget about him. Later, I got to thinking that I wasn't being fair. Maybe he'd been tired. Maybe he'd looked at me so strangely because he was surprised or curious. Maybe I'd misjudged him.

"So I wrote a story about William Hathaway, an actor who meets a fan like that, where they don't speak but have some kind of connection. The fiction just grew. I couldn't stop it."

"What was his name, your actor?"

"Boy, you don't let a girl off easy. It's William."

"Tell me more, Sela," my true love said.

"It pleased me to reinvent that actor, to put him on a horse, to give him a ghost to love, a place to hold onto his children. It may not please him if he ever reads my words, but I don't know, maybe he'll be honored."

"So who *was* he?"

"I don't think you'd know him. Can I just keep that in the past?"

"Do you still have his pictures?"

"Probably, someplace. I haven't looked at them since I went to one of your poetry readings in high school. I'm afraid this is already ruining the stories for you."

"The stories are magical, Sela. What matters are the stories, not how you got there. They have a legitimate life of their own. I shouldn't have questioned you."

"If you had been cool to me that first day in class, I would have been devastated. I had already waited longer for you than for that other William."

"But you and I had something in common—ideas and spirit," he reminded me.

"And language and loneliness and white rhinos and zebras and a perfect kiss," I said.

"Well, I can't argue with that," he said.

I moved over to where I could tuck myself under his arm. "We have so little time here. I'm going to stay as close to you as I can."

"Fine by me," he said, and he hugged me even closer.

The tide was farther away now, curling itself into the larger ocean as I had done with the dreams of my childhood William. I didn't want to say more about that fantasy William, because the truth was that from the age of nineteen, all I had thought of was William Langley. Some people would think that was just as inappropriate "fan" behavior as my crush on the actor. The thing about fanaticizing is that you are in control. You can make things happen and then go back and make them happen a different way. You can kill someone off or have him marry you. You can adjust the ages and sizes of people in the conscious dream. You can put a whole scene on pause and go back later to the exact place. I was tired of it.

I craved something real, and so a terrifying thought began to enter my mind. If I had William Langley in my life, I wouldn't need the fantasy of him or any other William. Where would I get the power to write? What kind of stories could I devise when I had the living, breathing, loving William Langley in my arms?

It came down to what gave the most pleasure—writing stories or being *in* a story that challenged and delighted me and gave me the best reason for getting up in the morning. But so many things had gone wrong in Natasha's story with her William. Could I have William and my stories too? Was that possible?

William kissed my forehead and said, "I know it's late, but let's go get some real food."

"Just a jeans place, okay?"

"Whatever you want, Sela. I'm just the chauffeur."

"That's what you think!" I turned my head up so he'd have to kiss my mouth and just melted. I didn't know how I could go back to the classroom and sit demurely, knowing where William's hands and lips had been.

We parted reluctantly, had to shower separately (Daudi's shower was barely big enough for one), and changed. It was dark out when we climbed into the Mustang and headed into town. We found a restaurant on the pier that was full of college kids; there was no faculty here to hide from, no one who'd really notice us. We shared a platter of shrimp, tilapia, and chicken with a nicely cooked artichoke and then walked down the salt-encrusted boards to the end of the pier, holding hands all the way. It just felt so right. Huge pelicans and sea birds were still out calling and begging for scraps. A couple passed by with two beautifully groomed standard poodles, one black, one white.

"Do you like dogs?" William asked.

"Sure, but I'm more of a Border collie person."

"I think you might be a wolf person," he said.

"Why?"

"Because when you get your teeth into something, you don't let go."

"Are you glad?"

"Damn glad," he said.

Back at Daudi's, we flung our clothes off. William pushed me up against the bedroom wall and burst into me on the high of my orgasm. I wanted to scream, but houses were packed close on the lane, and I didn't want William to think he had hurt me. It surprised me, his passion seeming to have no bounds. He caressed me as if calming a newborn foal, keeping his mouth ever so gently on mine the whole time. Finally, we had to breathe, but he didn't let go and half-carried me to the bed still inside me. He lay on his back and crushed me against his chest, even harder than earlier that day, sobbing when he came again, burying the sound in my hair, reaching the end of me again and again before slipping away and wrapping me with his arms and the covers. We were overcome with sensations, fiery and pure.

Suddenly, William sat up coughing. I quickly got him a glass of water. He seemed to be unable to catch his breath. He took a swallow of water but couldn't keep it down.

"I guess that was a bad idea," I said.

But just that break in the rhythm of his breathing helped him to recover. He stopped choking and lay back against the pillows. I was on my knees facing him. His eyes were glassy, his body shaking now. I pulled up the blankets we had thrown aside reaching for each other's bare, hot skin. He let me massage his shoulders and kiss his face, his hands, his chest. I gave the kisses not in a sexual way but to soothe him.

"That's what I missed… so much," he finally said. "Not the sex—the kind of touch you give. I so didn't want this to be about sex."

"I think we passed that barrier," I said, relieved that he was talking now.

"I loved it," he said. "I love you, but that's not why I gave you the key."

"I know, William. It was a symbol that there was a place for us… someday. But to be honest, the first thing I thought was *I'm going to have sex with this man I have adored for so long.* But you were giving *me* the choice, when to use the key, if ever. That was so dear, William. I just loved you more. What have I done?"

"Sela… honey, it's not you. I just couldn't breathe for a minute. I panicked. It's not like me."

"Ever the cool, calm professor," I said, trying to lighten the mood.

"Not right then. I felt hot, then freezing, excited, then sick, like I was reborn and then drowning all at once. I've always tried to do everything right, you know? Set an example. Follow the rules."

"You're only human, William," I said softly.

"I just kept thinking, while I was ravishing your lovely body, that I had always said I'd never do this… with a student, with someone vulnerable."

"William, I think you are the vulnerable one here. I should not have gone with you on that Saturday drive. I just couldn't say no. So much for my sensibility."

"Well, my precious, impulsive, brilliant girl, you are going to get a chance to prove your mettle," he said.

"Do you want to go back to LA?"

"No, Sela, no." He paused and took my face in his hands. "I want to marry you."

"Oh… my… God."

"Let's get married, this week, here in Santa Barbara. This secrecy thing, I hate it. You're too good for that."

"Boy, you are full of surprises. Half dead one minute and ready to walk down the aisle the next. What am I going to do with you?"

"Marry me, Sela."

"Well, I guess I can't say no to *that!*"

He hugged me for all he was worth and said, "Thank the good Lord. There'll be no Chalice River for us."

It was a prayer, a recognition of one of my deepest metaphors, and a vow to protect me, even from myself.

7

On Sunday, the relentless tide rolled in against the sea-stained windows. William drove out and found some authentic Mexican breakfast burritos and hot chocolate, and when he came back, we ate with the blankets pulled over us. We decided that for a Christmas gift, we'd get Daudi a better heating system than his tried-and-true method of leaving the stove on. After some very nice hugging and kissing, we dressed in our warmest clothes and pored through the Yellow Pages looking for a minister.

"Here's one: 'Ready to give up your life for God? I will marry you,'" William read.

"Is he kidding?" I said.

Another one said, "I only marry virgins; no gays, no divorcees."

"That lets us out!" William said.

"Oh, wait, listen to this: 'Love God, passion, and the beach (not *you... me!*). You only have to love each other for me to marry you. Call Savanah Longstreet. All denominations and atheists welcome.'"

"Savanah Longstreet? It sounds like we'll be married by a sixties flower child," William said, and he called the number.

He spoke very openly with the woman and laughed several times throughout the conversation. He turned to me once and asked, "Where do you want the ceremony?"

"On the beach," I replied quickly.

He relayed that information and then told her, "We'll write our own vows."

She must have questioned that, because he said, "Well, we're writers."

When he hung up, he said, “Shall we be virgins tonight?”

“Okay, Mr. Self-Control,” I said. “Come on, it’s warming up. Let’s walk on the beach.”

“And find our altar,” William said.

“That too.”

The tide was still high, so we stayed in close to the houses. But there was a place where the sea had created bluffs and caves. We went into the largest one and sat down facing the frolicking waves, shoulders touching.

William said, “Do you want to ask me anything?”

“You mean before I say ‘I do’?”

“Maybe.”

“William, I have known you a long time. I have read everything you have ever written, watched you deal so graciously with students and friends. I regret not knowing Natasha. I worry about your health. But I don’t think you could tell me anything that would keep me from marrying you. Now, you ask me something.”

“Would you tell me about Africa?”

“Oh. I don’t know where to begin,” I said.

“Why did you go?”

“To study, to see the animals, to be as far away from UCLA as I could.”

“There’s an African studies course here,” he said.

“And *you* were here, and the rhinos were in cages,” I explained.

“You wanted something… freer.”

“Yeah, mainly *me*,” I said.

“Tell me what you found there,” he asked.

I began to describe my journey to someone who has not walked in the Indian Ocean; looked in the eyes of a leopard two feet from an open jeep; eaten bananas and avocadoes, mangoes and onions sweet beyond compare from the red earth; or ambled through a Maasai market with lovely black hands imploring him to find what he needs in *their* stalls of jewelry, scarves, ancient goat-bells, ebony bowls, and hand-forged spears.

Of course, he would want to know about Zakariyah, my lover. So I said, "Zak taught me so much. He was gentle. He honored me and was a safe place for a not-so-safe heart."

"Did you love him?" William asked.

"No. I loved you."

William put his arm around me. "Oh, my dear Sela."

I went on. I told him Zak was married but that he honored his wife too, that he had just coveted the girl from America, another gold band on his arm. I admitted that he had said things to me in Swahili that at first I had not understood, that he was a Catholic whose name meant "God remembers." I thought the missionaries had done a good job in Tanzania, which I said with a hint of sarcasm. "Zak would pray for me. He would give me gifts—silver crosses, rosaries of glass beads and tanzanite, and prayer books smudged with charcoal and smelling like roasted corn. It was a beautiful world, an unforgettable world... but you were not in it."

"Maybe I should have gone with you."

"Things were not good for you then?"

"I was so desperate to understand the kind of love Natasha had for Mikeala. Maybe I still am."

"After last night?"

"I don't think I mean the sex," he said. "The sex is as good as the two people, straight or gay. I mean the passion, the bond that kept them together in spite of all odds."

"But it didn't keep them together," I said.

"Maybe they aren't the best example of what I mean." And he spoke emotionally about a good friend, a black colleague who had left UCLA ten years earlier who was now teaching at Southern Oregon University, had some kind of job with OSF, a Shakespearian scholar who was very religious, believed homosexuality was, to be kind, not pleasing to God. But he had fallen in love with a slightly older man, a white man, who was the choir director at their church. "This was about twenty years before I met him. He told me once that they didn't have sex. They slept in the same bed and didn't have sex."

"How can that be pleasing to God?" I said.

"Right," William said. "But they had some kind of love that we will never understand. Not to touch each other for thirty or forty years! I don't think heterosexuals could do that. Why didn't your Zak love you without the sex since he was married and a Catholic? They have rules about adultery, don't they?"

"Yeah… but, William, it's a different culture. I mean, even straight men hold hands in public. It's very sweet, but tourists look at them and think they're gay! Those Africans had traditions and *rules* long before there even was a Catholic Church."

"I guess I've been sheltered by the walls of the English Department, USA."

"But it's why I love you. You ask the great questions. I have to think of the great answers."

A wave crashed and foamed up toward us.

"Sela! We'd better check the tides for tomorrow. We could get married here, in this sea cave," he said brightly.

"Oh, I love that idea," I said. "I think it's about time for Daudi to be coming home. Should we go back?"

Hand in hand, we retraced our footprints, washed and misshapen by the tide. In one place, a piece of sea glass glittered where a foot had sunk in the damp sand. William picked it up and held it in the fog-layered light. "Now this is cerulean and just how your eyes look today," he said.

Daudi greeted us with a warm hug and asked where we had been. William answered, "My friend, we have discovered those caves a ways up the beach."

"Very special place. Nature make for human pleasure."

"Nature indeed made the place… where Sela and I will be married."

"Oh! Oh! God's blessings! God's children! When?" the Tanzanian cried.

"Tomorrow," I said.

"Will you be our witness, Daudi?" William asked.

"Oh, yes, be honored. I bring flowers from zoo, many colors."

"That would be perfect. But, Daudi, do you know the times for the tides? When the cove will be dry?" I asked.

"Oh, yes, driest at 4:20."

"Oh, good. We'll have time to buy the rings and Sela's dress," William said.

"Dress?" I said. "You mean jeans aren't more appropriate in a sea cave?"

William said, "You are going to be a bride in white, with a veil, and... well, you might have to go barefoot."

I thought I had never seen William so animated. It was as if he had found his place in the world and was engraving his name on it.

"You rest. I fix delicious meal," Daudi said. He began to unload sacks of vegetables and meats.

William and I flopped on the couch and studied the Yellow Pages again for bridal shops and jewelers and directions to the courthouse. Wonderful smells began floating toward us, and Daudi was humming some African melody.

"What is that music, Daudi?" I asked.

"Is wedding song," he replied.

Soon we were eating, and William practiced his Swahili with Daudi between bites of lamb, mango risotto, and slender green beans with avocado and onion sauce. I was not sure I was in the real world. Daudi had lit candles because it got dark so early now. The burners on the stove flared away, stabbing at the cold. The Tanzanian told us he had totally tamed the zebra filly and that one of the white rhinos was pregnant.

"Imagine," he said, "born in America. Little zebras and now rhino. Parents be immigrants, babies all American. So proud. You come see."

We promised we would and then retreated to the white bed in the white room. The next morning, we got blood tests and a marriage license. Then we went to a store called A Wedding to Live For and had great fun choosing and hiding our wedding clothes from each other. We had a light lunch at a sidewalk café, really not eating much. Down the street was a jewelry store, and I let William pick the rings without me, although I tried on a few just to figure the right size. He was so happy. I felt my short story muse having a heart attack.

We met Savanah Longstreet at a small chapel covered with wisteria and morning glories.

"I thought you liked the beach," William said.

"Well, I certainly like *you*!" she said to him and then, turning to me, "My dear, how long did it take you to land this gorgeous man?"

"Eight years and a few months," I said seriously.

"Oh my, I hope I didn't overstep," she said apologetically.

"Not at all, Miss Longstreet," William said. "It is I who found the treasure."

"A romantic too!" she cried. Then she said to me, "And you golden-haired creature with the eyes of... of... my goodness, I don't think there's a color... wait a minute! You are an ultramarine! I don't think I've ever married an ultramarine. Mr. Langley, you should not have made her wait so long!"

"It's complicated," he said.

"I don't suppose I'll know you long enough to learn the whole story, but I am happy to join you in holy matrimony. And you've chosen the beach for the ceremony. How lovely. You've checked the tides?"

"Yes, ma'am," William assured her.

"Do you want prayer?"

"Our witness is a Tanzanian and will pray in Swahili," I said.

"Well, this just gets better and better," she said and smiled genuinely. "Tell me where to go."

"The end of Oceanside Lane, at four thirty," William said.

"We've written our vows," I told her, "and I can see that we don't have to worry about a fundamental sermon."

"I *can* do that, but my hope is that the couple will make their own rules, spiritual and otherwise. When I read the Bible, I am overwhelmed by its beauty, its power, its lessons, but others may find guidance in poetry or music. I only ask, will you be good to each other? Will you be good to others? Will you be faithful to and thankful for the love that brought you together?"

We nodded yes to each question. This Savanah Longstreet was one of a kind. You just never knew what you'd find in the Yellow Pages. We said good-bye and drove back to Daudi's, where we rested for a couple of hours, William on the porch couch and me on the bed. At three thirty, we embraced in the doorway between rooms but didn't speak.

It was hard to get ready without seeing each other in that little house, but we managed. It felt so right to be marrying William. A vast weight was lifted from my being, and, I imagined, his too—his loneliness and sadness about Natasha, my unquenchable ache that had been my dream of William for most of my adult life.

Soon, Daudi came in with Reverend Longstreet and handed me a bouquet of baby's breath, orchids, and day lilies, blooms with splashes of lavender and burgundy and yellow. I waited in the bedroom in my strapless knee-length silk and organza creation, a ripple of lace around the waist falling in a wide wave almost to the floor behind me, and a sheer veil attached to a narrow crown of rhinestone hearts. When I walked out, my breath caught in my throat at the sight of William in a white tux with one day lily matching one of mine pinned on his lapel. I threw my shoes on the porch, and we all began a slow walk to the cove. William held my hand, and Savanah Longstreet stayed beside Daudi, asking how to say this and that in Swahili and wanting to know if she could visit him in her pastoral rounds—*but not for preaching,* she assured him.

We drew near the cave. It looked like a Langley painting against the cloud-etched sky that was barely bluer than the sea it fell into. The tide had receded as promised, and sea glass sparkled in all directions like stars. The sounds of our little procession mingled with the cries of gulls and the soft boom of waves breaking farther out. William led me through the opening, Daudi stood behind us, and the reverend was in front with her back to the ocean. Through my veil I could see William's tears forming, and I squeezed his hands as he took both of mine.

Savanah Longstreet said, "In this hall of a thousand storms, the groom may speak to the bride."

William said, “I, William Langley, lift you, Sela Hart, forever out of the Chalice River, with my love, my strength, my honor, all my worldly goods, my promise of fidelity and friendship, and the best my heart can give.”

The reverend said, “In this sanctuary of the blessed, the bride may speak to the groom.”

I said, “I, Sela Hart, lift you, William Langley, off the endangered list, with my love, my spirit, my dreams, my poetry, and my trust. I promise to you the very whole of my heart, never to leave you or let you suffer without my care. I will honor everything you are—eyes and lips and hands and voice and ideas and spirit—always.”

William put a platinum band inscribed with the words “What is rare is now protected” on my finger. It fit into a ring with a deep blue diamond set on a curved S of white diamonds. William whispered, “The S is for *Sela*, the blue for your eyes.”

“The best poem you ever wrote,” I said.

Daudi spoke his benediction in Swahili and then in English.

“Mungu muumba was vyote uliyewaumbaba william na sela kuwa kitu kimoja daima, waepushe na mabaya. Wapende wangali wakosefu. Watukuze wangali watakatifu, na uwachukue mbinguni pamoja nawe siku ya mwisho. Baraka nyingi kwao kutoka Africa, nakutoka kwa mlinzi mwaminifu na rafiki pia. God of everything who created this William and this Sela to be one forever, guard them from harm. Love them if not perfect, glorify them if pure, and take them with you into heaven, wherever that be in the end. Many blessings on them from Africa and from faithful watchman and friend, Daudi Fahja.”

“You may kiss the bride!” Savanah said.

William lifted the veil and pressed his lips into mine.

“And now, ladies and gentlemen, seagulls and sandpipers, may I present Mr. and Mrs. William Langley,” Savanah said, and she threw a handful of tiny white shells over us.

We went out through the front of the cave into the world of the sea that we felt more a part of than ever before. The tide drew us into its cerulean arms. Daudi and Savanah were walking back to Daudi’s beach house. William and I just stood and looked at each other in the afternoon light, surprise and revelation in each other's eyes. I had perhaps carried us here with my invincible longing for this man, but he would carry us on, finding peace and comfort and joy that he had long forgotten, if ever known, and tell me all his deepest secrets and desires, the things I could not have named eight years ago.

Then, we kissed again where no one could see our divine connection, only the gulls overhead crying their haunting cry and the ancient waves breaking, forever breaking, on the resilient shore.

Savanah stayed for dinner; Daudi had to go next door to borrow a chair. Then, he fixed a superb meal, and no one said a word as we began to taste the food on our plates. Finally, Miss Longstreet said, "Now that I've married you, I want to know your story."

William and I smiled at that and then explained how "story" itself was the way we met.

"A literature professor and his student. Oh my, what have I done!" she said good-naturedly. "How much older are you, Mr. Langley?"

"Thirteen years, but it doesn't feel like it," William answered.

She sighed. "It never does in the bloom of love. I have a good feeling about you two, though."

"Thank you, Miss Longstreet," I said.

"Oh, call me Savanah, dears. What *is* this I'm eating?" she continued.

Daudi described the sea mussels with mango-ginger sauce, corn-quinoa cakes with local honey, and the freshest kale he could find cut with onions he'd had to soak in sugar to get them as sweet as Tanzanian onions.

"Oh my," she said again. "I'm afraid to ask what's for dessert."

"Just white cake… for wedding. Had to buy, no time to make. Store let me taste. Much cream cheese and butter. I put pansies from zoo. You can eat them," Daudi said proudly.

"*You* can eat them," she said waving her hand over us.

We all laughed. William grabbed my hand under the table. The tide that had come back by then swirled against the porch in a melodious rush. We ate cake with pansies and ice cream and toasted each other with Vernor's ginger ale. Savanah told us she lived to do weddings like ours and that she had another one tomorrow that would pale by comparison.

"Oh, forgive me. I should not be so judgmental. I'll go now and rest so I can do my best for them," the Reverend Longstreet said.

She gave Daudi a hug and then wrapped her arms around us as we stood to say good-bye.

"My new lovers, go with God. I'll remember you. I surely will."

William walked her out to her car and handed her a very modest check, I thought, considering how much time and support she had given us, but she just said to give an equal amount to a school for children at risk she had founded, another place for endangered beings. When he came back inside, he told Daudi that we could go back to Malibu.

"No, no, too late. I sleep on porch. Have done much times. I like sea air. You stay long as need to."

"Daudi, you are an angel," I said.

"You the angel, Sela. Mr. William bring angel to us all."

When we finally got to bed, William said, "I think we've already had our wedding night."

"And Daudi's right outside the window," I reminded him.

"Can I just hold you, Mrs. Langley?"

"I'd be very glad for that, Mr. Langley."

His kiss almost changed my mind.

"Oh, you wonderful girl," he said. "Can I have a rain check on the rest?"

"I'm happy just to lie next to you legally," I said.

"Curl up behind me then, and don't let go."

Daudi fixed breakfast for us before he left for the zoo. He said, "I hope you use key still. I hope you come see how zebra filly so tame. I hope William learn more Swahili!"

"Yes to everything, Daudi," I assured him. "This house is very special to us, as you are."

"*Asante sana, mama.*"

"*Asante sana, baba.*"

"Don't be surprised if we're still here when you get home today," William said. "But we will take you to dinner. Do you like the cafés on the pier?"

"Oh, yes, very good!"

Daudi headed off on his bicycle to his job, and we sat out on the porch watching the sea birds begin their morning patrols. In the distance, the caves were rising out of the fog, and I looked at the blue diamond on my finger. My eyes, yes, and the ocean and the sky and the Chalice River and so many things we could not know.

We stayed two more days in Santa Barbara, wandering the shoreline, collecting glass and oddly shaped shells, dancing in the sand to the music of the sea. We didn't talk about school or world news or Natasha or Zak. We went into the zebra pen with Daudi and ran our hands all over the filly. We sat at the rhino exhibit and remembered the first time we had touched.

"I knew that day, I was not going to be able to live without you," William said.

Some nights we didn't make love but just held onto each other's warmth and kissed eyes and lips and hands and didn't say anything, not even "I love you." The words could never match the feelings, so we let them linger in our voices unspoken. I had imagined many scenes with William Langley, clung to images of wild sex and trauma that would bind us, but never this quiet sharing of silent space, of being one without words.

Finally, in the middle of the week, we hugged Daudi, promising we'd be back soon, packed up the gold Mustang, and headed south on 101. We talked about selling the Malibu house and moving closer to the university.

"But I haven't even seen it yet," I said.

"I guess I'm thinking if we didn't have that drive every day, we could have more time for writing, reading, dancing longer than ten minutes before bed, spending more time with friends. And it was Natasha's house."

"William, wherever you are, I want to be," I said.

As we got closer to LA, I began to worry about all the consequences of our being married. Would it affect William's career, my graduate status, my relationship with my friends and my other teachers? Miss La Monde would surely have a fit.

"Shall we tell Melissa about us?" William asked.

"I hope she's not home. I really want to tell my folks before we're the talk of Southern California."

He picked up my hand with the gorgeous ring, the line from my story hidden under the wedding band. "You had a rather short engagement, my lovely Sela," he said.

"I loved every minute of it," I said.

We exited at Moorpark.

"Here we go, babe," William said.

But Melissa's car wasn't there, so I didn't even go to the door, just got in my car and followed William to Malibu. He never let me out of his sight. I knew it must be bothering him for me to be following in another car. In about twenty-five minutes, we turned off the freeway into the canyon.

The country was spectacular that time of year, the hills submerged in green grass, yellow field oats, patches of wild iris and Indian paintbrush. *I could live here*, I thought. But I knew William would never be free of the memory of Natasha not making it home that night and constantly seeing her shadow in the house. I dreaded being there as much as I imagined the pleasure of it. *I could have a horse!* I thought suddenly. The road was lined with miles of white fencing, fancy ranch-style homes nestled in the mountain curves, evidence of old fires sprouting new growth, and once in a while a veritable mansion with barns and pastures and arenas full of jumps.

William braked and drove into one of these entrances! There was just one recently built six-stall barn and one outdoor arena—no jumps, but the house was sprawling, the driveway and one side of the house lined with tall eucalyptus, a pond in the front, and the entire yard landscaped with chaparral and desert plants, a nice ecologically conservative touch, and bougainvillea draped over retaining walls along the back bank. I pulled up next to William. It didn't seem possible that he could be my husband here.

We went in through a side door to a spacious kitchen with plants in the sunny windows and on gold-flecked, gray granite counters. There were spotless, stainless steel appliances and an island with an indoor grill and butcher block. William led me into the living room. Natasha was everywhere. Her colors, her materials, her choice of art on the white walls—not even one William Langley print—her white Italian leather sofas, polished cherry wood end tables, one with a photo of her clearing a four foot fence on a huge black horse.

"Natasha was a horsewoman?"

"Yes, when we first lived here, before tennis. We sold the horses and the jumps many years ago," he explained.

"Horses? Not just this one?"

"We had three. Her jumper, a Dutch warmblood gelding; her trail horse, a tireless pinto; and my grey quarter horse mare. I couldn't manage them when she lost interest. They were gone before the fire, thank God, but I liked having a barn on the property, so I rebuilt it. I boarded horses for friends and enjoyed the look of it."

"William, I can't stay here," I said.

"There's a guest wing off of my study where she never went. We'll make it ours," he offered.

"It's not because of Natasha. It's because I've dreamed of horses and a luxurious barn and miles of trails and a hot tub to soak in after hours of riding, and here it is, but it can't ever be mine. I didn't earn it. I didn't work for it."

He went on as though he hadn't heard me. "I'll buy a couple of horses. I'll ride with you."

"William. I don't think you want to bring another woman into this space, especially me. It's lovely. Who wouldn't want to live here. I just can't have Natasha's husband and her home too. Don't you see?"

"Sela, *she* left *me*. She made her own life choices. She isn't here. I left the one picture because it was from the days when things were good for us."

"I love you so much, but standing in this beautiful room, I feel the Chalice River flooding in."

I think I actually fainted into his arms. I found myself on one of the expensive sofas. He'd put a pillow under my head and was feeling for my pulse. I just cried, and I didn't even know why.

William said, "Sela, I know what would help. Can you stand up?"

"I think so."

He supported me with an arm around my waist, and we went through three more lavish rooms until we reached a carved oak door. On it were horses of all sizes and shapes, a collage of his favorite animals. He opened it, and we entered a room in which Natasha had never been—his study. I noticed shelves full of books and DVDs, mostly PBS nature specials and lectures in his field, bronze statues on tables stacked with short stories and some poetry, writers' magazines, some published pieces, anthologies, and even a couple of rejection letters. The window to the west had a view of the pond. Another doorway led to a screened-in porch with tables on which to write or eat. He said he had spent a lot of time there when Natasha was playing tennis and coming home later and later. Then we went back through the study and into a small, comfortable bedroom with windows facing east for the morning light to filter through. He had picked the drapes himself—masculine, patterned squares of lace that invited the day's first rays.

"I can guarantee you that Natasha has never been in this part of the house," he said seriously.

"Here I could make love to my husband without jumping out of my skin," I said.

"Maybe I'll hold you to that later," he said.

We carried our things in from our cars, which included papers he needed to grade and my story assignments. He fixed us a tasty lunch without my having to go to the kitchen. I sat at an extra desk he had stored in the garage and brought in that afternoon after spending an hour sanding and polishing it.

"Oh, William, thank you," I'd said when I saw the beautiful finished product.

"And tonight you can wear that black dress to dinner… and maybe later one of those frilly night things."

"I can't wait," I said, my discomfort fading with each hour in William's personal domain. He made room in his closet for the few clothes I had with me and hung around me for a while until I got started to work on my African story. Then he went over to his desk and began sorting student assignments and lecture invitations and Christmas cards that had arrived while we were in Santa Barbara.

"There's a faculty Christmas party Friday night, I just remembered," he said.

"Do we dare?" I asked.

"I think it's the perfect time," he answered.

Later, I offered to get us something to drink.

"I have some of that great ginger ale in the fridge. Do you mind?"

"I'll get it," I said.

This time when I walked through the living room, Natasha's picture was gone.

We worked at our projects until six, and then William came over to my desk and swung the chair toward him. I put my arms around his waist and my head against his heart. My heart started racing. And in a moment I will never forget, I felt the blessing of Natasha Langley.

"William, I think I'd like to save my black dress for the faculty party."

"Okay, sweetie. We'll go to dinner like this. Down on the coast is a wonderful place, but it's casual."

"Might we see someone?"

"Thursday night? Probably not."

He was right about the restaurant. It was dimly lit and uncrowded. We could sit close together, talk softly, and still hear each other. William caught my hand and turned my wedding ring this way and that to catch the slightest gleam from the fisherman's lantern over our table. The large diamond turned ultramarine; the smaller white diamonds sent their own radiance into the room.

William smiled. "No more beautiful than you," he said.

But if a man can be beautiful, I was astounded anew at the gentleness and humor, mystery and confidence, passion and vulnerability that showed all at once on his face. I wanted to tell him this. I wanted to say that I had seen all those things when I was sixteen. The ring said we were married. My heart said I had carried the beauty of him in my heart all these years.

A waiter stood over us. "You want the special?"

"Yes," William said. "Whatever it is, surprise us."

He looked at me suddenly with a startled expression. "Sela, I remember you now. I remember you in that high school English class. You were the only one who got that poem 'Webs' and challenged everyone, even me. I thought, *That girl is going to break someone's heart. Thank God it won't be mine.* It won't be mine, will it?"

"Never."

"You are a heart mender, with your words, your touch. I steeled myself for so long against the loss of my marriage, my partner, and then, I had to steel myself against grief. Sometimes I don't know how to believe in what you are, even though I do, somewhere deep inside."

"You're still grieving, William, and I should honor that."

"I guess I'm grieving for the part I don't understand, but when I look at you, it fades a little. The grief, I mean."

"That's your own strength, William, shining through."

He kissed me lightly on the cheek and said, "I guess we make a good pair then, don't we?"

"Like William and Angela," I said.

"Just like that."

Even after we ate the savory meal, we didn't know for sure what it was. We left the restaurant arm in arm, laughing and at ease. The whole world could see us now.

When we got home from the coast, he carried me into his bedroom as over a threshold with a new bride and was less rushed than he had been in our first hours of lovemaking, which had seemed to resemble the turbulent sea outside Daudi's window. The room smelled only of William, his clothes, his books, and the Christmas cactus he had chosen for himself, "because it's hard to kill them," he had explained.

After we were quite satisfied, I slipped back into my multilayered night dress from Victoria's Secret that William had so sweetly removed piece by piece. The negligee was the color of my ring and the color of my eyes, he said, different again from my eyes in the daylight or next to the ocean at Santa Barbara or when I read him my stories.

The night was quiet and safe. A coyote howled on the back hill, and something scurried along the edge of the house. "We always have raccoons in the winter," he told me. "Usually I put out some cat food or something during the coldest months." Then, we slept back to back. We preferred lying on opposite sides, and his strong back felt like a living dyke over which the Chalice River would never fall.

8

Then, it was Friday. We decided to box up my things from my off-campus apartment and get ready for the faculty party there. My roommates were still with families or boyfriends, so we had the place to ourselves. William went out about one thirty and got us some Kentucky Fried Chicken and coleslaw. We ate in my tiny breakfast nook and watched nuthatches and California jays and yellow finches at the bird feeder. Sometimes kestrels flew in and scared the smaller birds away.

"I'll have to fill it before we leave. I don't think anyone will be back this week."

"I used to feed the birds, but honestly, the last few months, I haven't thought of them. You are bringing me back to life, Sela Langley."

We sat and read for a while and then showered and changed. My shower was large enough for two! I let William slide my black dress over my shoulders and could barely keep from kissing him as he shaped it to my waist. He took some deep breaths.

"William, what is it?"

"I just didn't think it was possible to love someone so much."

And then, I did kiss him.

The party was at Randall Hall's home. Several professors were standing on the lawn with drinks in hand, and a few student waiters wandered around with trays of hors d'oeuvres. Lois La Monde made her way through the crowd, which was beginning to notice us.

"Bill, how could you bring *her*?"

"Maybe you'd better sit down, Lois," William said in a meaningful voice.

Another lit teacher interrupted to admire my dress, and there was Professor Hall, his eyes wide and disbelieving. "What do we have here?" he cried.

William answered with obvious glee, "Mr. and Mrs. William Langley."

William's faculty friends broke out in a cheer and raised their glasses to us. Someone put champagne flutes in our hands.

Lois said, "This is disgraceful."

Randall slapped William on the back and said, "Oh my god, Bill! You don't fool around. Well, congratulations, man! Drink up." He paused to swallow half a glass of liquor. "Where did this surprising wedding take place?"

"On the beach at Santa Barbara," William answered.

"I'll be damned," he replied, looking at me as though he'd never seen me. "You clean up good, little girl."

"Is that a compliment?" I asked.

"The best one I know how to give. Come on. There are more folks in the house. This is spectacular news!" Randall said.

William took my hand, and we followed our host into his renovated thirties home. We met his wife and some of the new faculty members we didn't know. I heard someone say, "She's one of his *students*," and another guest commented, "I guess this is closure for him."

We set our glasses down. Neither of us had had a sip of the very pricey alcohol. Blake Adams passed by with a platter of stuffed mushrooms. "Hey, Mr. Langley, Sela. You guys got married?"

"We did, son," William said.

"Well, heck. I was thinkin' of askin' her out," Blake said. "I guess she'll be gettin' straight A's from now on."

"Probably," William said.

"Well, congratulations, sir," Blake said and moved off through the gathering.

"I think it's shameful," Lois La Monde said when she was sure we could hear.

"I think I'd rather be at the zoo," William said.

I smiled, reached up, and kissed his cheek. There was a slight reaction in those nearby, but it seemed favorable to me.

"There goes one fine bachelor down the drain," another female colleague noted.

William kissed me back and whispered, "Did I tell you how terrific you look?"

"Several times, my dear," I said, "but don't stop."

We stayed about an hour. We struggled with the snide comments and felt relieved when someone sincerely wished us well. The university chaplain gave us his blessing. It seemed a good time to leave.

When we started back for Malibu, I said, "Now, we just have my family to face."

"I'm more nervous about that," William said.

"They'll love you. They can't help but love you."

"They might like me but not really understand why you married me."

"It might take a little time, but they'll know a good thing when they see it," I assured him. But I was not so sure myself. My father would not like that he didn't get to give me away. He would not like our age difference. He would not like that I was living in the house in which William had lived with his now-deceased, gay wife. My father did not like surprises or situations that strayed from the norm. My mother would be okay because she would see how happy I was and what a wonderful man William was.

I moved over and put my head on his shoulder. "I'm glad we're going to the canyon. It feels like home already."

"Good." William rested one hand on my knee. "Tomorrow we'll go look at some horses."

"Can we sleep in a little bit?" I asked.

"As long as you want. It's your vacation too."

I woke up about nine in the morning. William brought me scrambled eggs, an English muffin, and orange juice on a silver tray. "Don't get used to this," he quipped. "When school's back in session, we'll be grateful for a bite of toast on the way out the door."

"You're very sweet to do this… and let me sleep. I didn't even hear you get up."

"About six, I couldn't stand not finding out about the horses. I read sale ads until eight and then made a few calls. Put your cowgirl clothes on. We have a full day ahead."

"We're really going riding? Right now?"

"You bet."

It was stormy when we went out. The eucalyptus bent across the driveway in the wind.

"Good test for a horse anyway," William said.

"Good test for us too," I reminded him.

The first horse was so lame I couldn't believe the people had advertised him.

"He goes fine on some Bute," the woman said.

"Are you kidding me?" I said. *Pain killers?*

Down the road were a couple of nice quarter horses, ages eight and nine, both buckskins. Their trots were choppy, and one carried his head so low that I felt like I was constantly being thrown forward, but both were calm and pretty. A huge plastic tarp was flapping on a haystack, but it didn't bother either of them. We told the folks we might be back.

"William, are there any Arabians or part Arabs on your list?"

"I think there are four or five at a breeder's up near Calabasas. They're young, but the guy said they had a lot of trail experience."

So we went to the Golden Heart Arabian Farm next. The horses they brought out were clipped and groomed. One was definitely too small for either of us. Another had to be ridden with a tie-down to keep him from constantly tossing his head. Then they showed us a more strongly built, 15.2 hand, dark dappled grey gelding. He didn't stand quietly when I mounted, but that was fairly easy to fix. His gaits were smooth, and he responded well to cues. William said he didn't think he was a competent enough rider for this one, but I liked him a lot.

The last two were bays. The mare had a bright, almost red, coat with a black mane and tail; the other was a dark brown gelding who had the most beautiful head and eyes I had seen in a long time. William cantered him around in a large outdoor arena. Banners announcing the next event were slapping against the fence, but the horse didn't react. He was quiet on the bit and would go on a loose rein. He had a big, confident walk. William was crazy about him, and I had to agree they looked great together. Of course, that gelding was the most expensive horse we'd seen, but William gave the owner a deposit pending a favorable vet check. He asked if the vet could check out the grey too but said that we had a few more places to go.

We grabbed a bite to eat at a Mexican restaurant and then drove out toward Thousand Oaks and Moorpark. "Do you want to stop by Melissa's?" William asked.

"Oh, let's do. I think she'll keep it to herself at least one day, until we see my folks tomorrow."

We tried out a couple of horses along the way, a Morgan mare who would only canter to the right, signaling some physical problem, and a Thoroughbred off the track who was a nice jumper and fairly quiet but who'd had a minimum of trail time. We passed on those two.

Melissa's car was in her driveway. She ran out when she saw William's Mustang pull up to the curb. "Sela! Mr. Langley! What are you guys doing out here?" she cried. She hugged me and then William too.

"We have a surprise for you," I said and held out my hand with the dazzling blue diamond.

"Sela!" she screeched, holding my hand out to the light and then closer to her eyes. "You got married?"

"We got married last Monday on the beach at Santa Barbara," William said.

"Oh, Lord, nobody could have written a story like this. Oh, I'm so happy for you. Shocked, but happy. Jealous too, maybe. There are hearts that will be broken, Mr. Langley."

"Oh, I doubt that," he said.

"How 'bout Miss La Monde?" Melissa asked.

"She was never in the picture. I was polite to her. I never *kissed* her, for heaven's sake."

"Poor woman. I'm sure she was waiting for that," Melissa said. "But really, who knows about this?"

"We went to the faculty Christmas party last night," I told her.

"That must have been something."

"It was interesting," I said.

"So what are you doing out here?"

William spoke up. "We're horse hunting."

"Really? Wow. You've got to go to Aiken's place. I'm sure he's selling some trail horses, or do you want show horses?"

"Just good, sound horses. Pretty would be nice," I said.

"I'll call Aiken right now," she said and flipped open her cell phone. While she waited for someone to answer, she said, "You two—honestly, I can't believe it. You're going to shake that campus up. The student-teacher-not-dating rule is going to fly out the window!"

She closed her phone. "I guess he's out with the horses. Let's just go over there."

Melissa came with us, asking more questions about our wedding, delighted with the enigmatic Savanah Longstreet, saying that if she ever got the proposal of a lifetime, that's who she would want to do the ceremony. When we reached Aiken's stable, she raced on ahead to find the owner, whose business of renting horses seemed to be failing. Several animals were tied to a long hitching post.

"Those are the sale ones," Aiken told us when he and Melissa found us walking down the fence line.

I recognized the liver chestnut I had ridden the day William and I drove to Daudi's with our keys. "Why are you giving him up?" I asked Mr. Aiken.

"So few people can ride him, and he needs a job. Gets too high-strung and then has to stand around until someone comes along who can handle him. He's only ten. He's miserable here. I don't have enough stalls to shelter all of them in the winter, and he gets pushed away from the hay pile. Could use some weight, I think."

"Oh, William, I love this horse. And I've ridden him enough to know his gaits and his temperament."

"And you're lucky too," Aiken said. "Some guy had a vet check on him yesterday, and he passed just fine, X-rays and all. I'll show it to you. But the guy called back and said he'd found a younger, cheaper horse, so this one's back on the market."

"Shall I get my checkbook, Sela?" William asked me.

"It would be a dream to own this horse," I told him.

"Mr. Aiken, we can't have him for about a week. My wife and I will be out of town. I could call you when we return."

"Oh, I don't mind bringin' him to you when you're ready. I'm truly glad this fine horse can have a home with someone like Miss Hart," Mr. Aiken said. "I'll pretty him up and stall him with extra feed."

"That will be so kind of you, Mr. Aiken," I added. I stroked the big gelding's neck, and he rubbed his face on my shoulder. I could hardly stand not to take him home that minute. Most of Aiken's other horses didn't appeal to William. He said he couldn't stop thinking about the chocolate bay Arab back in Calabasas.

"I might be up to seeing a few more, but this is hard. So many of them need attention. We surely can't handle more than two."

"I like that bay Arab," I said. "Let's see how his vet check goes."

We stopped at two more places. We tried out gaited horses, but even though they were smooth and sure-footed, the bobbing of their heads was not comfortable for me. Melissa liked a palomino Morgan, but the mare had only had thirty days' training and no trail riding at all. Finally, we collapsed in the Mustang and agreed to call it a day. It was about four thirty.

"You girls need some food?"

"Yeah," Melissa and I both said at once.

"Something about riding just makes you hungry," she added.

We sat in T.G.I. Friday's and split an order of appetizers. Melissa asked William if she could write her point-of-view story from the horse's mouth. He laughed and said then he'd know who wrote that one.

"Right," she said. "Sela, have you finished yours?"

"Not quite, but I have a good start, and I know the ending."

"I'll bet Mr. Langley will guess yours."

"Probably, but only for a very obvious reason. I'm not really trying to fool him with mine."

"I guess you don't have to fool him about anything anymore," she said.

"I don't think I ever fooled him, did I, William?"

"Not from the first story on," he said.

It had been such a marvelous day, and I was glad we had included Melissa. When William went ahead to open the car, she said, "Oh my Lord, Sela. Are you just madly in love or what?"

"Madly," I answered, putting my arm around her.

As we drove back to Melissa's, William said, "So Miss Wells, how long did you keep Sela's secret?"

"Oh, almost three years," she said. "She told me when she came back from Africa. I thought maybe she'd get over you after that, but no, there she was standing in line for your class the first day of her junior year. I had worked, like Lee, for a couple of years, so I was a freshman. I almost told you about her. One day I saw Miss La Monde hanging on you. And you were still… I mean, your wife was alive,… I mean…"

"It's okay, Miss Wells. I don't mind talking about Natasha."

"Well, here's what I knew. Sela cared about you enough to stay away from you when you were married, and there was that awful woman making a big play for you for all to see. I thought it was so unfair."

"Do you think you might find a story in that situation, a point of view unusual for you?" William asked her.

"Oh, wow, yes. I see it now, but you'll know it's my writing. Whatever character I choose, I'll still have to assume a lot."

"But it's fiction. You can assume anything you want. It doesn't have to be believed, just given a real life in the story. Life is just a story anyway. Some things we'll never know may be deep in the writer's heart and thus in the character's as well," he told her.

"You are an inspiration, Mr. Langley," she said seriously as we stopped in front of her house.

"I believe my students have the inspiration. I just guide them in freeing it," he said. "Hey, come ride with Sela next week after we get the horses home."

"Oh, I'd love that," she said.

"William tells me there are so many beautiful trails in Malibu Canyon. We can write a short story to end all stories," I told her.

"I can't wait," she said. "And thanks, Mr. Langley, for including me today. I feel like you didn't take Sela away from me but added me to your life. I love you both."

She blew us a kiss and went up her walkway.

We had only driven a few miles when William said, "Sela Hart, life with you is going to be such a joy."

The next day, Christmas Day, we arrived at my grandmother's early. My folks were already there. I'd hoped to let my grandma have some time with William. I knew it wouldn't take long before she'd be completely enthralled by him and reassure my father that I had chosen the best path for my future. She and I were pretty close, always had been, but when my folks were in the room, she didn't express her opinion as freely unless she had taken a strong stand in her mind—like about my taking three years off from university to live in Africa. For weeks, I had explained every detail of my plans to my grandmother, shown her stacks of photos and articles about Tanzania, and told her that I would be getting college credit for several projects there. By the time I laid the plane tickets down in front of my parents, I didn't have to say a thing. Grandma totally pleaded my case while my folks sat there with their mouths open.

"You always rush into things," my mother said.

"How do you think I paid for these tickets? I've been saving money for three years!"

"And look," my grandmother said, "here are all the places she'll visit, all the people she'll meet. And she's even been learning Swahili!"

"Well, I'll be damned," my father said, leafing through maps and project outlines and photographs.

So today, I thought I had little chance of Grandma's support. William and I walked up the old, cracked sidewalk. Grandma's roses bloomed sweetly in the winter air. Some were pruned and mulched, but she nursed the hardiest ones along through the cold season. Those lined the edge of the front porch. My grandmother opened the door, and William said with enthusiasm, "Mrs. Ellis, I particularly like your Queen Elizabeth and your Mr. Lincoln."

He knows the names of her roses?

"Grandma, this is my husband, William Langley."

"Well, come in, come in, darlings," she said. "Mr. Langley, those are my two very favorite roses."

"Then that's why they're so beautiful," he said.

My father got up from the couch and came over hastily. "William Langley. Aren't you a poet or something, teach at UCLA?"

"Yes to both. I mostly publish short stories these days and teach creative writing and some of the graduate programs," William answered.

Then my mother was holding onto my dad's arm looking at me. "Isn't this that professor whose class you always wanted to be in?" she asked.

"Yes, Mom. I got in his class this year… and now I'm married to him."

Grandma spoke up, "He knows about roses. Isn't that something?"

"Well, he doesn't know about Sela's family. We don't elope in this family."

"There's always a first, Daddy," I said. "William, my father, Thomas Hart, and my mom, Clara."

"Are you joking? You really married this man?"

Grandma came to the rescue. "It's Christmas, loves. Let's be peaceful. I'll need some help in the kitchen, Clara. Mr. Langley, would you like to see some of my catalogs? You can help me decide what to order."

"Do you think there might be a rose the color of Sela's eyes?" William asked.

"I don't know. There are so many new ones. That would be a special rose," she replied.

William and I sat in separate chairs, afraid to touch. My father questioned him mercilessly.

"How long have you been at UCLA? You tenured yet? Didn't you just lose your wife awhile back? Drunk, wasn't she?"

"Dad!"

"I have to know about the man who seduced my daughter. Where do you live?"

"Malibu Canyon, sir."

"Out with a bunch of hippies."

"Hardly, sir."

"Daddy, if you don't stop this, we're leaving. If there was any seducing, I seduced him. I've wanted this man just to look at me since I was nineteen years old!"

"Oh, right, just like one of your stories," he said.

"Sir," William said very calmly, "I love your daughter. I'm sorry we got married on the spur of the moment. Frankly, I would have waited until she finished her graduate program, but that would have put her in a terrible position at school, having to lie, meet me in secret, and giving her anxiety about my losing my job. I didn't want that for Sela. So I asked her to marry me last weekend. We were married on a beach at Santa Barbara by a lovely Christian minister. I think you need to consider your daughter's feelings."

"You telling me how to relate to my daughter?"

"Yes, sir, I am."

My dad thought for a moment and then said, "Well, I give it six months. These things don't last. A younger one will come along, and my daughter will be so much grist for the mill." Then he got up, wandered off to the den, and turned on the TV.

William stood up slowly. "I think I'm going to be sick," he said.

"Oh, no, sweetheart, come here." I encircled him carefully in my arms. "Think of us standing in the sunlight saying our vows. Think of the sea-blue sky and..."

"And your eyes," he whispered.

My grandmother came over to us just then. "Everything all right?"

"My father was pretty hard on William, asking him such personal questions. I couldn't stop Dad from just being a jerk," I told her.

"It's not his fault, Mrs. Ellis," William said. "I've not been feeling well all day."

"Please call me Edna, dear. I'll fix you some ginger-peach tea. My tea has been known to stave off many a crisis. Just you wait and see." And she hurried back to the kitchen.

"I'm sorry, Sela. I really wanted your folks to see how much I love you."

"*I* see how much you love me. Grandma sees it."

"I love your grandmother," William said.

Soon we were drinking her elixir. William paged through another catalog full of incredible roses but couldn't find a blue one. The TV blasted the unfamiliar football jargon, and my mom kept her husband supplied with chips and beer.

"Go be nice to the young people," we heard her say once.

"The game's almost over. I thought they'd want some privacy—newlyweds, you know," my father said.

"I think they want us to approve of them."

"That I will not do," he said decisively.

"Oh, Tom, what's wrong with you? This is our daughter. Can't you let her be happy without it always being what *you* want?" my mom begged.

"Not this time, Clara. He's not right for her."

"Do you have a crystal ball or something?"

"I know things," he countered.

"What things? What do you know?"

"Things about that wife who died."

"Thomas! That is none of our business." She had lowered her voice, but we both heard it.

"Your mother is cut more in the mold of her mother," William said. "Let's go outside."

We stood on the porch overlooking the few blooming roses. William reached down and bent one close enough to smell. "Now there's a tonic for all ills," he said.

A man who takes pleasure in the smell of a rose, I thought. *Someone my father will never be.*

Grandmother called us all to the table. She took William's hand and said, "Now you sit right by me, young man. Sela, your husband is so handsome. I can see why you ran off with him. You have my blessing. You know, Grandpa and I eloped. Those days no one had money for a big wedding. Did you have a white gown?"

"I did, Grandma. I'll show it to you one day."

"Pass the dressing," my dad said.

"Who married you?" Mother asked.

"A woman who's a pastor of an interdenominational church," I answered. I couldn't bring myself to say her name, afraid of what my father would do with that.

"And your witness? Who was that?" she went on.

"That's a little harder to explain," I said.

"Well, try. Your mother asked you a question," my father ordered.

"It was a Tanzanian gentleman we met at the Santa Barbara Zoo."

"How bizarre," my father said.

"Oh, Thomas, what a wonderful thing for Sela!" my grandmother said, and then she turned to me. "Did you speak to him in Swahili?"

"Yes, Grandma, I did. He was so thrilled. He'd come from Africa with two pregnant zebras, and William and I got to go in the stalls with their new foals. One of them touched our hands. It was the most exquisite creature."

"And what did you think, Mr. Langley?" my mother asked William to include him in the conversation.

"It was the best day I'd had in a long time. It was the day I fell in love with your daughter."

"How nice for you," my father said.

"Thomas, would you come help me with something in the kitchen," my astute grandmother said.

"Mr. Langley, I do apologize for my husband. Sela was always his special girl. He was never the same after she went to Africa. I think you must be a fine man. Sela has good instincts."

"Thank you, Mrs. Hart. I would never want to come between Sela and her family."

"It was just such sudden news, Mr. Langley. Sela has always been headstrong, and her father is especially protective of her."

"I will protect her now, ma'am."

"I'm sure you will try. How old are you?" she dared to ask.

"I just turned forty," he said.

"Sela's only twenty-seven."

"I know," William said. "But she and I see the world the same way. We can't imagine a life without each other."

Tom Hart came back to the table only slightly more subdued.

"Edna," William said. "This is probably the best Christmas dinner I've ever had."

"Your wife didn't cook?" my father asked.

"Food was not high on her list," William said.

My grandmother shot my father a warning look. I tried to get William's attention. He seemed to be willing to take my father on, which was a bad idea. No one ever trumped my dad in a confrontation. Grandma, bless her, brought out her famous peach pie. "From Grandpa's and my trees!" she announced.

William helped her dish up the fragrant, hot dessert.

"So you must be a drinker," my father continued.

"Do you see a wine glass by my plate?" William asked.

"Maybe you're just trying to impress us with your abstinence today."

"Mr. Hart, I don't believe it would be possible to impress you," my husband said humorously.

"I'll drink to that," Daddy said. He handed William a glass of Chablis.

"Mr. Hart, it would only take three swallows of this to make me sick as a dog," William said. He set the glass down.

"Now that would be impressive," my father said heartily.

"You know, Edna, peach pie is my absolute favorite," William said, deflecting my father again.

"I'll send some jars of peaches home with you. Sela used to help me make the pie, so she can make it for you whenever you need it."

"That will be wonderful," he said.

Grandma hugged him, reaching around the back of his chair to place her hands on his chest, a touch I knew he loved, so I was not surprised to see tears in his eyes. He said, "I lost my grandmother about twenty years ago. She always gave me books at Christmas—poetry, classic literature in gold bindings, and sometimes her best-loved short story collections. She'd say, 'One day we'll see your name on the cover.' She never did. Will you adopt me?"

"I certainly will," Grandma exclaimed.

"Boy, you're good. I'll give you that," Father said. "So what are you going to do after Sela goes back to New York with us tomorrow?"

"I'm going to work in the garden with Edna. I noticed a few weeds out there."

Grandma clapped her hands. "Oh, Mr. Langley, I'm so embarrassed by those. When Grandpa was alive, we kept everything so tidy."

"It's hard to manage alone. I know, Edna, and I've only been alone a few months. Sometimes you just need that partner so badly… and please call me William."

"William Langley, the love of Sela Hart, who came into my life on Christmas Day," she mused.

My mother finally decided to find out my plans. "You *are* still going to New York aren't you, dear?"

"I'm sorry, Mom. Working in the garden is much more appealing to me at this point."

"I figured you'd disappoint us when you sashayed in with Mr. Langley," my father said.

"Daddy, William and I only have one more week before we go back to school. It's kind of our honeymoon. I'll pay you for the tickets."

"That won't be necessary. Well, Clara, have you had enough Christmas?" Dad was reaching for his coat and thanking my grandmother for the "excellent meal."

My mom hugged me and whispered in my ear, "I want to hear all about your wedding someday."

"Okay, Mom, I promise."

And then they were gone.

I stood at the sink with my grandmother and rinsed the dishes as she handed them to me. Our shoulders touched, and the evening breeze brought the scent of roses through the partially open window. I told her what William had said when he breathed in the fragrance of her Memorium.

"What a lovely thought," Grandma said. "He is beautiful inside and out. I can see that you treasure him deeply, but Sela… you didn't *have* to get married, did you?"

"Oh, no, Grandma, no."

"Because sometimes marriages like that don't turn out so well."

I clutched the sink so hard a glass broke in my hand.

"Oh, darling," she said as she began to clean up my wound. "I thought you knew, I truly did."

I glanced into the living room. I didn't want William to know why I had cut my hand. He had some papers spread out, class exercises and short stories, and—I had to smile through my pain—rose catalogs.

My grandmother was saying, "I think it's just a scratch. You'll have to wear gloves tomorrow. You'll stay with me tonight? I fixed up the guest room for you, extra pillows and towels. You know I take my hearing aids out at night."

"Grandma!"

"I was young once. Go be with your husband. I'll finish up."

I went out gratefully and sat on the coffee table with my knees against William's.

"Hey, what happened?" he asked taking my hand with the bandage.

"A glass broke. It's superficial."

He leaned over and held my head up so he could look into my eyes. "I will find that rose, the color of your eyes in your grandmother's evening light."

"You are a poet," I said.

"You are my poem."

Grandma came in and sat down next to William. "Can an old lady join the conversation?"

"Anytime," William said. He gathered up a few catalogs and opened them to the pages he'd turned down. "I like these," he said.

"Oh, I have that one, Angel Face, and those, Peace and Sunset. I'll show them to you tomorrow," Grandma said with delight.

"But Sela's eyes I have not found," he said.

"Oh, I'm sure there are a couple that would do," Grandma said. She pulled out another stack of magazines William hadn't noticed. One was called *New Roses for a New Millennium.* We turned the pages hopefully. There, on page sixty-two, was the only blue rose in the world. It had been genetically engineered by Japanese rose-growers just three years earlier using blues from the pansy. It ranged in color from lavender to violet to aqua to cerulean to, yes, ultramarine.

William held the page up next to my face. "That's the one," he said.

The rose's name was Applause.

"Do you have a place for another rose, Edna?" William asked.

"For that one, I surely do."

"It will be my Christmas gift to you," he said.

"Oh, you dear man," Grandma said and kissed his cheek. "Now don't stay up too late, you two. We have a day's work ahead of us." She went back to her bedroom.

We turned a few more pages of indescribable roses. We didn't speak of my father's callous behavior. He'd had a tough childhood with foster homes, school failures, and, I now knew, an unexpected need to marry sooner than he had wanted, although he had run a large and successful advertising company for most of his adult life. He was used to being in control, *needed* to be in control. He might love my mother but expected her to shape herself to the world according to Thomas Hart.

I didn't blame him for that. My mother made her own choices. But to cause such discomfort to my husband, that was almost unforgiveable. William seemed to have let it go.

"Are you feeling all right?" I asked him.

"Yeah. You'd think I'd have a tougher skin, dealing with all those administrative types and publisher rejections, but I don't care about those people. I wanted your parents to *like* me."

"First, they have to like themselves. I think they're still working on that."

"I had a nice surprise to share with everyone, but there didn't seem to be a time to say it," he said.

"Can you say it to me?"

"Oh, most definitely. You won the short story contest."

"Oh, William. Oh, wow. Really?"

"You got all the votes."

"I can't believe it," I said.

"I can," he said. "Most of the stories were overwritten. Yours was understated and powerful. I still think of William Hathaway sitting all night in his living room chair after hearing the news of the girl who was lost in the Chalice River, unable to understand what it meant for his life but feeling something shift in his being, and then going to the Santa Barbara Zoo with his daughters—endangered indeed."

"You weren't a judge, were you?"

"No. I was relieved of that duty."

"The honor of the award is for William Hathaway anyway, not me," I said.

"You really believe in your characters, don't you?"

"I do. They never leave me."

"I don't want the stories of William and Angela to end," he said. "Darn that quantum theory anyway."

"When I wrote the last story, I didn't know it would be the last one, but there was no one left to speak. And the stories made sense no matter what order I put them in. Time nor space nor dimension changes the love story."

"Like someone else's love story I know," he said.

"Maybe I was writing our story and didn't know it," I said.

"You are such a romantic," I told William later lying in bed, "buying Grandma a rose the color of my eyes. Well, at least the color they were at eight o'clock on Christmas night in La Puente."

"It meant a lot to her, didn't it?" he said.

"You know it did. And since when do you enjoy pulling weeds?" I asked playfully.

"It'll be good for me and help someone to not be so alone. When she looks at her neat rows of vegetables, she'll think of us, out there in the dirt."

"Us? I have homework, Professor Langley."

"I'll give you some homework, young lady. Come here."

So started a honeymoon embrace that lasted late into the night.

My grandmother knocked timidly on the door in the morning.

"Come in, Edna," William called.

"I have your breakfast, darlings," she said as she brought us a big tray with omelets and toast spread with her homemade plum jam. "I didn't know if you'd want coffee."

"How 'bout hot chocolate, Grandma?" I asked.

"Oh, I can do that," she said and scurried out.

"I think she's trying to make up for my father's rudeness."

"I think she's trying to energize us for yard work!" William suggested.

"Or homework," I reminded him.

I was anxious to start on another short story, and I had a risky idea—risky because the theme would be too close to home, risky because he'd never think I would write it and maybe be hurt when he found out.

We ate leisurely, letting Grandma spoil us, and then got up and put on some semblance of work clothes. We had not thought to bring actual gardening clothes. "I wonder if people ever raked and tilled on their honeymoon?" I said.

"Probably your grandma and her husband," he said.

William went into the bathroom to shave, and I searched through my duffel for my oldest pair of jeans. I glanced at my husband, bare from the waist up, and got a lump in my throat. But then I saw him grip the sides of the sink and lean his forehead against the mirror.

"Sela," he called, "is the world going around?"

"God, I hope so!" I said. When I reached him, I put my hand on his back. It was sweaty though the room was quite cool.

"William, what's wrong?"

"I don't know. I was so dizzy for a minute. It's better now... really."

He kissed my cheek and picked up his razor. "Maybe too much sugar so early, you know, jam and chocolate."

"Maybe," I said, but I felt a spark of fear in my gut.

In a little while, the three of us began on the garden. I weeded the rose beds while Grandma started in on the rows of chard and beets. Later we'd all thin the carrots together, a back-breaking and sad job, in my opinion. It always seemed to me like killing puppies, choosing which tiny vegetables would live or die. William was cutting the tall, dead cornstalks and stacking them by the compost pile. Meadowlarks and crows made a raucous harmony around us, and a neighbor's dog barked ferociously when we got too near his fence.

William stopped once and came to my place in the roses. He embraced me tightly and said, "I love you, Mrs. Langley." Then he moved back to the rows of onions and knelt down in the damp earth.

Grandma told him not to put any weeds in the compost but that dried-up vegetables or flowers could go. He stood up with an armload of dead material and headed—slowly, I thought—toward the oversized bin Grandfather had built years ago. When he reached it, he grabbed the top rail and nearly collapsed against it. I got there as he sank to his knees.

"God, I feel terrible. I don't know if I'm going to throw up or pass out."

Grandma was there too, patting him on the shoulder. "Let's go in. I think you just got too much sun, dear."

"I'm okay, Edna. Don't you worry about me," William said. He took some deep breaths.

"Well, I need a break. Come on. I'll fix you some of that magic tea," she said.

We sat at the kitchen nook and drank the ginger-peach tea with extra bits of ginger. "Just swallow that right down, son," Grandma said, and he did as she said but didn't touch the shortbread cookies or say anything for a while.

I told Grandma about our wedding day in the sea cave and the flamboyant Savanah Longstreet.

"How did you ever find her?" Grandma asked.

"In the Yellow Pages," I said.

We all laughed, even William, who now had more color in his face and was breathing more normally. He said, "I guess I'm ready for those weeds now."

"Oh, no, son. You lie down a piece. No rush on the weeds."

"Okay, Edna." He didn't protest.

"I need to work on a story anyway," I said.

"And I need to do some mending. We'll tackle that garden later when it cools off," Grandma said. She looked at William with such tenderness and caressed his hand where he had set his cup down and was still holding it.

He said, "I have never felt so loved."

William lay on the living room floor with a couch pillow under his head. I curled up in a corner of the couch with my pen and paper and wrote the words I thought he would never recognize. Grandma sat in the big chair under the reading lamp with a pile of torn pants and shirts, not her own.

"Grandma, why do you still mend those old clothes of Grandpa's? It's been three years." I said.

"My dear, look over there at your beautiful William. Think how you love him. Think how, if one day—years from now, God willing—he was gone, and you found your favorite shirt of his with a missing button. What would you do?"

"I'd sew it on in a hot minute," I said.

"Of course you would. In your heart he would still be alive. He would still need you. You would still love him."

I couldn't stop the tears from coming. She was so right. I had then the clearest understanding of my reason for taking over his last two classes that day when he was struggling with his emotions. If he had been in an accident and never come back, I would have taught his classes as long as they'd let me.

"You are so wise, Grandma," I said.

"And you, my child, for choosing that man," she said. She tipped her head toward my husband, curled up slightly and still. She got up and spread a light blanket over him. Then, she said something I thought no one, except Melissa, knew. "You have loved him for a long time."

"Grandma, how did you..."

She held up her hand. "Darling, I saw you plenty of times with one of his books in your hands. I read your short stories about an actor named William, and I remember you wanting so badly to be in one of William Langley's classes. I thought you were headed for a broken heart, but here you are with his ring on your finger. This old grandma knows the real thing when she sees it."

William turned over. "Are you gals talking about me?"

"Ears burning, young man?" Grandma said. "Just talking about Sela's stories. Your name might have come up. Now, how 'bout some lunch, you two?"

"I think I could handle that," William said.

We ate cold turkey on Grandma's homemade bread, some more ginger tea, and peach pie. William asked about my grandfather.

"Would you believe his middle name was William? James William Ellis," Grandma said. "He was the most generous man, helped all the neighbors no questions asked, even the ones with petty grudges. We used to have milk cows. They'd get out and damage someone's lawn. Jim would be down there the next day sowing grass seed. He bought a pony for Sela when she was about eight, even though we couldn't afford it. Couldn't stand for her not to have her heart's desire."

William smiled and put his hand over mine on the table.

"Funny thing is," Grandma went on, "it's what got him killed."

And she began the story I'd heard a hundred times and always found something sad but healing in it. She told William about the new family, the Garcias, who had moved into their neighborhood several years ago, how some folks got uppity about people who were different lowering property values or some such nonsense. Jim had gone right over to welcome them. They were poor and needed to raise their own chickens and vegetables. They bought a couple of cows after a while, but one was a hard milker, kicked pails and stuff to high heaven. One day, Jim thought he'd try to get some milk for them out of that cow.

"She kicked him right in the head. Jim never woke up, died a few days later. The Garcias lit candles for Jim down at St. Michael's, gave me their other cow, and moved away, but you can see I don't have any milk cows anymore."

William looked stricken.

"Oh, young man, I didn't mean to make you feel bad all over again. Jim and I had fifty-four wonderful years together. He's still with me in many ways. Come on, let's go pull some of those weeds for Jim. He hated a messy garden."

We spent the afternoon in the rows of winter lettuce, cabbage, and potatoes. William pruned some fruit trees and thinned the pampas grass that threatened to block the sun from the roses. William and I rested from time to time with our backs against the peach tree while Grandma fixed us all lemonade, from her lemons, of course.

"There's nothing as healing as working in a garden," I said.

"I think you're right," William said. "Maybe we can make a small plot back in the canyon. I know a place where the sun shines most of the day."

We stayed through Wednesday morning and had the farm up to Grandpa's standards. Grandma gave us enough fresh vegetables, canned fruit and jam, and pie to fill the entire refrigerator and called out, "Don't stay away too long," as we backed out of the driveway.

A few blocks away, William stopped the car and handed me the keys. He didn't say anything. When I wasn't shifting gears, I grabbed his hand. We made love that night in that same silence, and William didn't get up afterward as he usually did. I hooked my arm around him and pressed my body against his back.

"Hold on, Sela," he whispered as though I could keep him from spinning off the face of the earth before he fell asleep.

The next day, we stayed in. William read class papers, and I worked on my two stories. I typed the Africa one on my laptop in the same font I usually used. Then, I changed fonts, margins, spacing, and even threw in some punctuation and dialogue errors to further elude him. But finally I had to correct those, perfectionist that I was. Later I asked him if he wanted me to follow the assignment as his student or give him *my* voice as his wife.

He looked up from a story he was destroying with his red pen and said, "I don't know, Sela. I love that you're my wife, that there is a truth between us that can't be shaken, but I can't change that you are my student, so do the assignment as best you can."

I put titles on the two short stories and slipped them into my backpack.

Later that day, Mr. Aiken brought both of our new horses to the ranch. We spent a couple of hours in the barn grooming the geldings and letting them touch noses before turning them out together in about sixteen acres of grassy field that had a seasonal creek bubbling with clear water. We watched them from a huge, flat rock that had fallen from the cliffs behind the property and come to rest at the south end of the pasture years before William and Natasha had bought the place.

"I always wanted to be out here with the horses grazing peacefully, maybe some red tails swooping around overhead on the air currents. Natasha always locked the horses up in their stalls so they wouldn't get scruffy with dirt or burrs in their manes. I have not been on this rock for twenty years. I did whack down all those burr weeds and plant pasture grass especially formulated for equines, but Natasha said, 'That's nice, Bill, but my horses are not going out there!' I didn't hold it against her then. I was too involved in academia to pay much attention to them, but I think I do hold it against her now. Look at those happy horses."

The geldings were loping up from the creek tossing their heads at each other and grabbing mouthfuls of timothy. Chisholm had put on some weight at Aiken's, and his coat glistened. William's glossy brown Arabian gelding, Malibu, seemed to be the boss, but when my chestnut fell behind climbing a hill, Malibu stopped and waited for him.

William said, "Tomorrow we'll ride up the canyon this rock tumbled out of. The trail may be overgrown, but the view from the top is awesome." He lifted me up from our granite slab and said, "We only have a few days until we go back to school. It'll be an adjustment for both of us."

"William, can you treat me like you would any other student?"

"I doubt it. You were never just 'any other student' anyway," he said, hugging me.

We rode for several hours on Friday and Saturday, picking our way over downed trees and tumbleweeds and rivulets of rainwater draining out of the hills. At the top of the first climb, we dismounted and surveyed the green vistas stretching across the Santa Monica Mountains toward the Pacific, where a layer of fog threatened to roll in. One day, he said my eyes were the color of the lupine still struggling in the winter air and the next that they matched the friendly jays that flitted around our lunch site. God, how I loved him.

"Should I be worried about you?" I asked once when we stopped to let the horses catch their breath.

"No, babe. Right now I feel the best I've felt in a long time," he said, and, as if to prove it, he leaned over and gave me the best kiss he'd given me in a long time.

On Monday, when we walked onto the campus at UCLA, we were mobbed. Even students who didn't know us personally went along with us clapping and taking pictures with their phones. We felt like celebrities. William certainly qualified, being the bright star of the English Department, but who was I? Aspiring writer, older than most of my classmates, and my husband's pupil. Kids called me Mrs. Langley with shy smiles, and faculty members greeted us with hugs, minus Lois La Monde.

I had told the story so many times that, by fifth period, I was ready to go home. William and I went in together after the bell rang. Everyone cheered and threw confetti on us. "That better not be your homework!" William said. Someone had made a wedding cake. It had to be Melissa since she was the only one in all of William's classes, except for Blake Adams, who would never make a cake, who knew about us. She was cutting pieces and passing them out. William let the girls hug him who had never dared to touch him before. Finally some semblance of quiet ensued, and William said, "I guess I don't need to read you *this* story."

Lee asked if we'd gotten married on the Santa Barbara beach by the zoo from my story "Survivors."

"Yes, we did, Mr. Henderson."

Blake raised his hand. "Mr. Langley, would you guys do the part where the minister says, 'You may kiss the bride'?"

I was already at my desk, but William held out his hand to me. When I reached him, he made a pretend motion as if lifting a veil and gave me another of his best kisses. There was a roar of approval. Then William said, "I think you have an assignment to turn in."

I separated my two in the group of stories that were passed up my row and watched them disappear into the larger stack piling up on William's desk. When they were all assembled, he asked, "Now, who had a hard time with this?"

I raised my hand with most of the class. He smiled.

"Well, that was part of the lesson. How can you write what you don't know, especially in someone else's voice? There are, I'm sure, some good stories here, but are they 'real,' as Ms. Oates suggested? We're going to study them carefully and decide if rewriting them in the author's true voice would make them any better."

Risa said, "I don't think it will be possible to rewrite them. Once you are looking at life from someone else's point of view, something changes inside you. A new you emerges in the new voice."

"Aha," William said. "Maybe there is more than one angle to this assignment. I'll choose one now at random and read it."

"Can we try to guess who wrote it?" Leticia Martinez asked.

"Maybe," he said. He reached into the middle of the stack. "Running Springs," he read.

Oh God, it was one of mine, the one I was sure he wouldn't know I wrote.

Running Springs

On a mountain morning sometime in the fifties, a fifteen-year-old stands in the hard dirt yard by the sign Livingston Stables. She has wanted to be here her whole life. She waits for the animals to be brought out and tied to half-chewed hitching posts, the pintos and bays, palominos, and dappled greys, the beasts of dreams. A couple of wild-looking dogs run up growling. "Git to that trailer!" the man yells and then, "Hey, I'm Cal. You wanna ride?" A woman appears from the dusty corrals leading three thin horses. "This here's Sue," Cal says, nodding his head at the slight figure in frayed jeans and sleeveless white shirt. She's a dark-eyed beauty (a line the girl remembers from a Randolph Scott movie). The woman is smiling, handing her the reins. The horse is made for her, excites her with his prancy stride, his satin black coat. She always asks for him after that, sits straight in the saddle, circles him smartly, for the woman, Sue. She knows Cal kisses her in the tack room and doesn't want to know what else they do. The summer passes. She's part of them. Cal lets her catch the rent string, canter in the rye grass meadow. Sue braids her hair in the soft afternoon light. "Hey, kid, I missed you yesterday," she says once, her arm around Cal's waist. The girl feels everything.

The smell of rain on hot flesh. Santa Ana wind in the old pines. Cal watching from the broken window. The coyote-dogs sniffing around (they're used to her now). Sue's hand touching hers for a heartbeat over the back of the horse. The ache that won't go away.

That has never gone away.

At the last sentence, William's hand was shaking, and he looked stunned. There was dead silence in the room. The bell rang. I put my arms around him on my way out.

"That is just damn brilliant," he said. "There's no one in this class that could write a story like that, except"—something in his eyes changed—"you."

"William," I said nearly crying now, "please forgive me."

"It *is* yours," he said, "but nothing to forgive. I love it. Don't you get it? You wrote with Natasha's voice. You wrote about a part of her I never understood, 'the ache that has never gone away.' It's what she had her whole life. Even alcohol couldn't kill that ache. Oh, my dear, this is a gift. I love you for it. Don't cry."

Of all his reactions that I had imagined, this was not one. His last-period students were coming in. They gave us a "thumbs up," and I left the room with William holding my story.

On the way home, William said, "Well, we made the first day, sweetheart."

"Yeah, we did. Everyone was so nice. Are you tired?"

"Hmm, not too tired for you-know-what," he hinted.

We stopped at our favorite Mexican restaurant so I wouldn't have to cook that night. He had two briefcases full of stories to grade, and I had the horses to feed and my own assignments from classes besides his. We headed to our niches in William's study. After about an hour, he came over to my chair. "Sela," he said seriously, "why did you write two stories?" He put my Tanzanian story, Kiiku's words that didn't fool him for a second, in my hands.

"Because I knew you'd know I wrote this one, the voice of a warrior's son from Africa. I wanted to speak in a voice you wouldn't recognize, to see if I could do the assignment. I didn't want to hurt you," I said.

"But it's a blessing, my dear Sela. I can let a lot of stuff go now." He put "Running Springs" on top of "Found History—Tanzania, 1985."

"This first one is really a prose poem, you know," he added.

"Not my field of expertise," I said.

"Nor mine. But there's some growing popular appeal for it. I might do a unit on it next semester. What do you think?"

"I think whatever you teach is genius."

He kissed me and returned to his desk. I couldn't work for a while. I thought how I loved being his wife, having him trust me, touch me in places I had never been touched, and treat me as an equal. My fantasy of him had never ventured into those areas. But there was something else I couldn't name, a love I felt for him sitting in his classroom, listening to him read, helping his students find their voices, creating an atmosphere of genuine care. He was an artist and a healer; his medium was words.

At about ten, William handed me a single sheet of paper with a short poem.

You Are

eyes that take the color
of the sea
or winter skies or diamonds
buried hot and blue in Africa
for a million years

lips that touch my lips
and moving shape the words
no one will ever hear
that Angela spoke to William
on the beach where we were wed

hands that linger where the heart beats
that hold foreshadowed pain at bay
and voice that's not afraid to say
I love you

It was signed, "your loving husband." I couldn't do a thing after that but follow him into the bedroom and love him in the room that had always been his alone.

A few nights later, William said, "What do you think about going to Laguna Beach for the metaphor workshop?"

"Not Santa Barbara?"

"Too personal for me, love. I don't want to share it."

"I know how you feel. I wish we could go to the Indian Ocean. It's so wild, indigo blue far out and transparent aquamarine where the tide rises against the shore. The history too is just heart-wrenching—spice galleons, slave ships, pirates, British and other colonists invading the ports, a metaphor for man's inhumanity to man. Laguna Beach makes me think of surfing and volleyball."

"You're right, Sela, and I… I just don't feel up to a week with thirty kids at a resort."

"William! What if we did the workshop right in your classroom! We could use paintings, Langleys and Monets. We could use videos even. Remember that series *The Blue Planet*? Things like that. We'll hang art or watch a video, something different each day. We could ask Daudi to come one day to tell us about his crossing the Atlantic with the zebras! It'll be easier for everyone, not the expense or the distraction of being at the actual waterfront. I'll find the art for you. You can do the lesson plans. I think it could work."

"Boy, that is tempting, Sela. Let's run it by the kids tomorrow. Maybe we could include more students that way."

We each began with renewed vigor to outline the workshop that meant so much to both of us. "Sela, what's your unique perspective on this? I know you have one," William asked.

"This is what Miss La Monde didn't know. I wanted to do a graduate project on the metaphors that have arisen in the last fifty years or so that reflect climate change in the oceans. Maybe there's a poem about catastrophic glacier calving that parallels the poet's life catastrophes, deaths, depressions, or failures. I could have written about how each year that I didn't reach you in your class line, a piece of the glacier field of my life broke off, sailed away, melted, never to be seen again."

"Your imagination is one of the things I cherish most about you," he said.

"Oh, that wasn't so hard," I said, "but creating those metaphors and *finding* them in the literature are two different things."

"Whatever help you give me on the workshop will earn you some credits for sure."

"Credits or no, I'll help you."

"Still my anchor, huh?"

"Speaking of *sea* metaphors," I said. Then I had another idea. "William, we could do the workshop every Saturday for six weeks instead of cramming it all into six days and exhausting ourselves."

"The definition of workshop *is* exhausting, but then it's over. What about this—I'll finish all my classes the week before the semester ends and then hold the workshop that last week. It'll be a nice transition into semester two's Writing the Modern Poem. You and I could stay in town that week to save the daily round trip to Malibu Canyon. There's the Foothill Trails Bed and Breakfast in Sierra Madre with an equestrian center close by if we wanted to take the horses and be able to ride some in the evening. They have an indoor arena with lights."

"That sounds great. I guess I should listen to my teacher," I said.

"And I guess I shouldn't treat my wife like a student!"

"Well, I am still that, anyway."

"Come here, you. I'll teach you something you'll never forget."

That January, William had us all writing overtime to finish the short story unit a week early. Melissa, Lee, Marcella, and Riley ganged up on him to ask me to read my eleventh Quantum Crossing story, but I shied away from doing it. I don't know why I was so reluctant about reading "The Ending." I felt as if I were saving it for a clearer purpose than satisfying everyone's curiosity.

I noticed that the girls still hung around William and flirted, even with me sitting right in the classroom. I didn't mind. He was dreamy-looking and generous. He lifted everyone a level above expected capabilities. He gave praise and criticism with the same supporting words. I loved watching him light up just doing his job, knowing he would bring that same light into our private world and sweep me away on some powerful tide.

I would be ready for that workshop.

9

Winter edged away. The longer evenings gave William and me time to have a brief gallop down the newly completed bridle path that wound along one side of our property. The horses were so matched stride for stride that we could clasp hands as we flew down the trail. One time William said as we groomed the geldings afterward, "I keep wondering if *this* kind of riding could have saved Natasha. It always seemed to me that jumping carried a lot of stress with it and competition in general."

"It's such a pleasure for us because we don't have an addiction driving us," I said.

"And I wonder what would have happened if she had met Mikeala before she met me."

"William, when are you going to stop blaming yourself?"

"I don't know," he said, resting his head on Malibu's dark brown neck. "I understand Natasha's part in what happened. I just don't know if I understand my part."

"Your part was to stay loyal and loving, which I'm sure you did," I told him.

"Do you think it would be okay to contact Mikeala? To find out exactly what was going on that night?"

"I don't know, William. That seems like asking for trouble."

"I know this is so trite, but I think I understand now why people want *closure*."

"Well, I love that title for a short story," I said, "but I'm not sure that's what you'll get. It could make you feel worse."

"But at least I'd know the whole truth," he said.

"Maybe. Do we ever know the whole truth? Besides, she has alcohol on her side. That may bend the truth a little."

He took a deep breath and almost collapsed. I helped him down on a bale of hay nearby. He put his head between his knees.

"William, you're scaring me, really."

"I think it's just vertigo. My mom and her dad both had it as they got older."

"You sit there. I'm turning the horses out," I said.

When I came back, he was arranging the saddles and bridles in the tack room. He said, "Sela, will you do something for me?"

"Anything."

"Will you call Mikeala? You'll know what to say. I'd just mess it up."

"Oh, William. Are you sure you want to do this?"

"I'm sure," he said.

We went in and had a light supper. After that, he searched through Natasha's things, still unsorted in their bedroom. He found a number on a notepad with the letter *M* after it. The letter had a heart drawn around it in red. It was about eight p.m. by then. I dialed the number reluctantly.

"Hello," a female voice said after the first ring.

"Mikeala?"

"Yes?"

"Please don't hang up. This is Mrs. William Langley."

There was a brief silence and then, "Oh, the *new* Mrs. Langley. The student. Boy, he sure knows how to pick 'em, doesn't he?"

"Is this a bad time to talk?"

"That depends on what you want to talk about."

"Well, I think you know," I said as calmly as I could.

"I expected Bill to call long before this. Tell him he can stop beating himself up. It was really simple. Natasha and I loved each other madly. But I wanted her to get sober, and she didn't. I had to save myself. I didn't mean for her to *die* over it. I would have stuck by her if she'd just gone to rehab. And oh, she loved Bill too, just not the sex part. She doesn't—didn't blame him for anything. Now see if you can tell him this without hurting him, and don't call again." She hung up.

"Was she angry?" William asked.

"No."

"Was she drunk?"

"No, that's why they broke up. Mikeala went into treatment. Natasha wouldn't go. But she said they really loved each other, and Natasha still loved you. That's not so bad, is it?"

"I don't know. If she'd found the love of her life and still had me to be her very public husband, give her everything she asked for, and accept her as a gay woman, why would she go on drinking?"

"There's no way to find that out. Maybe Natasha didn't even know. Can't you let it go now?"

"I'll try."

"I just think you need some more time. It hasn't even been a year. Maybe we shouldn't have gotten married so soon."

"No, Sela, I need you, and the best thing is that you need me. I couldn't live without that—a woman who thinks I hung the stars, or whatever that old cliché is. You make me feel whole and real, just like what Angela did for William Hathaway."

"That is a fine compliment, Professor Langley. Now, can you back that up?"

And he did.

A week before the metaphor workshop, William had everyone read another student's best story, looking for weaknesses. "Who can name some potential problems?" he asked.

A dozen hands went up.

"Dialogue tags!"

"Using the passive voice!"

"Background information in dialogue!"

"Mixed point of view!"

"I guess you have been listening," my husband said.

There were more questions. I tuned them out. I looked at William as though seeing him for the first time. Was he thinner? Did he sit down a little more often? Did he seem relieved when the bell rang? I got a hint of an answer when we met at the car at the end of the day. He handed me the keys. Then he hugged me hard right there in the parking lot.

Professor Hall walked by clearing his throat. "Take it home, kids. Take it home!"

William waved him away. "I'd like to take it clear to Santa Barbara and Daudi's white room," he said.

"What do you need, William? Tell me and I'll do it."

"I don't know, sweetheart. But I was sitting at my desk during third period grading a paper, and when I looked up, I didn't know where I was. I couldn't have named one student at that moment. Then at lunch, I looked for you, missed you..."

"I had promised Melissa and Anne I'd listen in on their interviews for another housemate."

"Oh. Well, anyway, I had a grilled cheese sandwich and some fruit salad. After I'd eaten a few bites, I had to stop. I didn't feel sick, just totally disinterested, as if I'd forgotten why I was eating. It was so strange. Even now, I'm not sure if I know how to get home."

"I think we should go over to the medical center right now," I said.

"Right now I just want to go home."

"Okay, love."

I tried not to show how scared I was as I pulled onto the freeway. I told him I'd fix some of that African soup Daudi had taught me how to make. He said that sounded good, leaned against the window, and fell asleep. When we started down the canyon, he woke up after the first winding mile and said, "These curves are bothering me, Sela. I'd better drive."

"You sure?"

"Pretty sure, babe."

I found a turnout and stopped. We were still a few miles from our driveway. William drove slowly and carefully. He seemed to be looking for familiar landmarks. He turned the radio off, and Elton John's voice was cut abruptly out of the air. William said, "The sound was disturbing me. There, I see the barn and the eucalyptus trees. I'll be glad to lie down."

"How I love you, William," I said as he turned into our sanctuary.

"Do you mind feeding the horses?" he asked.

"Of course not."

I gave the geldings their oats mixed with molasses and carrots and closed the big gate to the pasture. They had the choice of a stall in bad weather or a large run but would be safe from the coyotes, who had been harassing them in the field. The horses could usually outplay them at their taunting game, but I preferred that they didn't have to.

When I got back to the house, I couldn't find William. His coat and briefcase were in his study, but he was not in our bedroom or bathroom. I called his name, trying to stay calm. There was no answer. Finally, I was drawn to a place I swore I'd never go—Natasha's bedroom. And there he was, lying on top of the covers, his eyes open.

"William, what are you doing in here?"

"Oh, Sela, did I come to the wrong room?"

"It's all right, but do you feel like sitting in the kitchen while I make us some dinner? I don't like you in here by yourself."

"Sure. I'll come with you," he said. "I know I'm struggling. The only thing that seems real is you. I would be so lost without you, especially today."

"Why today, love?"

"Because I think I wandered into another dimension. I'm just grateful you're there too," he said.

"Do you want some ginger-peach tea while I fix the soup?"

"That would be nice."

I said, "Keep talking to me, sweetheart, okay? Tell me about your classes today."

"The ones I can remember, you mean?"

"Anything."

"I read some of your stories to kids who hadn't heard them."

"Really? How did that go?"

"Everyone loves your stories. I had a hard time keeping back my own tears a couple of times."

"Which stories?" I wanted to know.

"'Survivors,' of course, and this time 'The Beginning.' It's so demanding of the reader to put that story into context. But it's beautiful and mysterious. I must hear 'The Ending' soon. I believe it will mean something profound for my life."

After a few more minutes, the soup was ready. I let it stand to cool a bit and allow the flavors to blend. I sat across from William at the granite-topped bar. He took my hands and put them against his lips. "My angel," he said, and then more softly, "My Angela."

"William, are you in pain?" I asked as he moved my hands from his lips to his head.

"Maybe a little. Nothing serious."

I disentangled my fingers from his reluctantly and picked up the bowls of soup. When I set his down in front of him, he said, "I'm not hungry."

"William, you need the nourishment. It will take the edge off of your confusion, give you strength. Trust me."

"I'll try to eat. For you, Sela." And he took small sips of the delicious African meal until he had finished it all. "That was so good, Sela. I did need it. You always know what I need."

"I hope I always will," I said.

"Let's go to bed," he said. "I don't think I can make love to you like I want to tonight. Maybe tomorrow?"

"William, we have a whole lifetime to make love," I answered, knowing that lifetimes can be cut short in an instant.

For several days, I drove us to UCLA and back home. William gave his classes some reading assignments so he wouldn't have to lecture. In my class once, he went into the inner office and closed the door. Everyone looked at me for an explanation, and I just told them he wasn't sleeping well.

Just before metaphor workshop week, William seemed to recover. It was as if he had awakened from a bad dream. He called out students' names joyfully at remembering them. At lunch, he commented on how good the food tasted, even the not-so-authentic chili rellenos. Our rain checks for sex were spent like there was no tomorrow.

"I haven't been myself for a while, have I?" he asked one day while driving in to the campus.

"The only thing you knew was me," I answered.

"I think I went into the Chalice River," he said with a strange expression.

"Promise me you'll get help if it happens again," I said.

"Promise me you'll tell me," he said.

"William, you don't remember anything?"

"I remember feeling sick in the canyon one afternoon going home. I remember sitting in a faculty meeting and not knowing anyone's name. I've lost weight, and I don't know why."

We parked in his campus space but didn't get out of the car right away.

"I'm looking forward to being in Sierra Madre with the horses next week. The snow on the San Gabriels, having a nice breakfast together that we didn't have to fix, riding every afternoon—it will be a welcome change," he said.

"Sleeping in fresh sheets I didn't have to wash," I added.

He leaned over and kissed me. "See you fifth period. I've got a faculty meeting at noon," he said.

"Okay, *Mr. Langley*," I said.

It was the final day of the semester for William's students. He thanked them for not making a fuss about his "lapses of memory," and in fifth period he announced proudly that each of us had received an A for a final grade. "You listened, you learned, but most of all you *cared* about language and what you were committing to paper. You cared about me during one of the most difficult times of my life. Those of you in the metaphor workshop, I'll see next week. The rest of you enjoy your break and be ready to write poetry, to write your hearts out. It's going to be a grand semester two!"

I joined in the applause for Professor William Langley.

We moved ourselves and the horses to Sierra Madre that Saturday. The bed and breakfast room had a Jacuzzi, and we relaxed in the swirling water with Gabrieli on the satellite radio or danced in the quiet, spacious suite to Celine Dion's poignant love songs. On Sunday, William wanted to go to church. This was new—I didn't say no. We sat, slightly awkwardly, in the back of the Episcopal church, not understanding the ritual but feeling safe and serene.

The priest found us after the service still sitting in the pew.

"Hello, folks," he said as he reached his hands out to us.

"We're just visiting here in Sierra Madre," William said, "so you may not see us again."

"Well, I'm glad you worshipped with us today," the tall man in the flowing robes said sincerely.

"We may not exactly have done that," I said.

"You are holding hands," he observed. "A form of prayer, no?"

"We're newlyweds," William explained.

"Ah… a true prayer then," the priest said. He wandered off to greet others.

"Not a Savanah Longstreet but maybe someone we would like," William said.

"Are you thinking of questions to ask him?"

"That I am, my darling. That I am."

Monday morning, more than fifty of us gathered in an expanded classroom. William had written in large letters on the chalkboard: "METAPHOR WORKSHOP #8 The Sea? You Tell Me." He had decided to open up the theme but started out by reading my poem "Resurgence" just to get the idea of metaphors in our heads.

I ride the horse that almost died
into the autumn sea,
galloping breakers, breathing the light,
the salt streams that saved him for me,
for once he fed on saline fields
drifting his tidal days,

now loosed in plankton, dangling shells,
in the source of waves to graze,
where furrows carved by dripping hooves
close in and disappear
like scars that used to bleed, like pain
that drowns in the dancing here.

I ride him off the edge of earth
where once he fell in a storm,
swam the surgeon's element
with torn and silent form.
He reaches now for that churning dark,
that ocean in his eyes,
as if remembering from what depth
his broken limbs can rise.

Some kids wanted to know the story, but my husband said, "The story is right here, but it is drenched in metaphoric language. Let's talk about that."

Lee said in an excited voice, "I see metaphoric language in every line!"

Marcella agreed but said, "Some is so strong you can't avoid it, like 'swam the surgeon's element.' I love that."

"I like 'furrows carved by dripping hooves,'" Leticia commented.

"This is going to be a fantastic workshop," Professor Langley noted.

The next day, I hung some William Langley prints on the wall. We wrote poems with lines like "sand castles / the rooms of my heart" and "color me that ultramarine / that beyond-the-sea hue / where what I live for abides / where life began" and "if the sky is why I fly / the sea is why I swim / though human caught in both worlds / trying to flee creation."

Oh, we had such fun that week. We had class for two and a half hours in the morning and a long lunch, and then we wrote and discussed the personal metaphors of our work. William would tell us not to worry about the language of the entire poem at first. “Find the metaphor; the words will follow,” he'd repeat like a mantra.

Daudi was able to come one afternoon and draw everyone into his story of the little zebras and their dams coming by ship to a new world. “I try understand this *metaphor*,” he said.

Calisha told him to just talk about everything that happened, that our job was to discover the metaphors.

So he closed his eyes for a moment and then said, “When sea rough, zebras very calm, loved rolling of waves, darkness in pens. When sea smooth, zebras very excited, unsure. They leap and cry when sun flashes through bars. This behavior strange, no? Can find poems there?”

“Surprise and revelation,” Lee said softly.

Even though our esteemed professor had encouraged all metaphors, many writers called on the enticing faces of the sea. I felt so vindicated one day when Lois La Monde walked in and Marcella had just started reading her latest poem.

Crossing

I take my horse to the sea.

Above the waterline sand is safe.

Farther out
riptide pulls great chunks
of self
and sends them tumbling
to the darker heart.

I rein my horse
toward that deep
where something gallops

tossing its unchained head
at me,
rearing in breakers
against my beach
untruth.

I take my horse out to sea,
diving with my old dreams
tied to him
like bottom stones,
drowning in the purest fathoms
we never learned to ride.

I was just blown away.

Marcella said, "Sela, I apologize for using your horse metaphor, but I didn't know how to get into the poem, and it was something I *had* to do."

"It's even better than mine, Marcella. You took the horse and the sea and turned my metaphor a hundred and eighty degrees. The last two lines are just... genius. How many ways can we interpret 'purest'? Or 'drowning'? Or 'never learned to ride'? I wish I had written it."

"But *you* wouldn't have needed to," she said very quietly.

Later, William and I talked about how brave it had been of Marcella to read that poem to everyone. Of course, the irony was lost on Lois that the girl was coming out of the closet, "crossing," as it were, from the safe shore to the deepest fathoms of her true self. There's no finality to it, just a hint of what she has "never learned to ride." I supposed maybe only the gay kids got it, really. William wisely didn't discuss the poem in depth, in case Marcella wasn't quite ready for that, but told Marcella she had marvelous insight and that he appreciated the uniqueness of her metaphor.

After Marcella had finished, Miss La Monde had asked, "May I sit in for a while, Bill?"

"Certainly, Lois," he had said politely.

"Well, that was a surprise," William said at home that night.

"You know what I think?" I said.

"I can't imagine, my dear."

"I think she can't deny the power of language, that she will humble herself to hear poetry that cries to be heard, and that words will open her up to the whole world," I said.

"It's why I put my pen to the page," he concurred.

"Me too," I said.

We rode a couple of early evenings at the equestrian center but mostly lounged around in our room in our pajamas sipping Grandma's ginger-peach tea or jotting down lines that may draw us into a poem. We made love as softly as a new tide on a shallow beach, reaching, reaching, reaching for its line in the sand.

In workshop the final day, all fifty-five of us, and Lois La Monde, stood and clapped for a solid ten minutes until tears were rolling down William's cheeks.

We returned to Malibu Canyon and prepared for the routine of regular classes, graduate studies, and the long commute. I felt as though I'd been William's partner the entire eight years of my secret alliance, fulfilled and blessed.

William began his second-semester classes by reading the best of the metaphor workshop poems. He didn't give the names of the writers because of the personal nature of some of them. But those personal ones got the oohs and aahs of astonishment and appreciation. This is the order in which he read them, the first one eliciting talk for days:

song at six hundred feet

down in the dream
i still cling to him
trailing his black robes
through fathoms
sea star coming home

he opens his mouth to the
water
i cry out
there is silence
where i used to sing
i try to make sounds
allelu alleluia

alleluia the tide takes away

down in the dream
he calls boys sweet and
dark
wants their bodies
as close as their breath
to his face
wants his hands on their skin
floating softly

there is no place for me

down in the dream
i am holding his music
my last chance to hold him
he turns with his rosewood baton
in the darkness expects
alleluia
soft on my lips

that can never stop saying
i love you
i love you
to eyes looking through
the light that i am

Lake Powell: Surfaces

I remember to hold my breath
as the river-that's-been-dammed
closes over me
to open my eyes before landing
on Anasazi watery streets
I see myself stoop
by a meager fire
roasting meat
small flames making shadows
on sandstone
Half-coyote pup rolls
in the twilight dust
with dark-eyed children
not mine
I have no children
My name is Woman-Who-Drowns-In-Sorrow
I am ghost in this backed-up water
singing about corn
washing clay pots by a clear stream

The Color of History

You live in white-washed
Air
Breathe where
Someone fell far from home
Holding a curl of honey-colored hair
A bayonet
Bent and red

You think it's quiet now
On the southern front

Applause

There are no more grandmothers
Who remember
Swarms of blue and gray
Gunbursts
The sound of a single horseman
Bearing the news

You might walk there
Accidentally
Might brush up against
A ghost mingling with bee drones
On a spring day
Feel the sting
Before death

But even if you never see
A crimson shell
Hear the name Antietam
There will always be
Soldiers circling overhead
Dripping pollen
On some scarlet field

tide to a kill

I come up
from ages of silent water
spread my silver cumbersome secrets
to light

kisses dangle
in the passage—
questionable bait

rapture grazes my arm—
fin to be sliced
and sent to the deep—
still
bones and eyes
press for the open sea

my truth tries to breathe
someone worthy of it
someone who thrills at its breaching
the waves
lets it surge close
lets it gasp
cannot in the end
bear the heart of it

and is quick to slay
like a shark hunter
who has to make the first shot count
firing a crazed and stinging bullet
into my love

Turning Point (Camp Pendleton, California)

The horse runs
where the land meets the sea.
For seven miles he runs
straight as an ancient tide.
The ocean sings in our ears.
If there is another life
I can barely summon it.
Beside us & around us Marines dig trenches
in yellow dunes
& dolphins lope the silver swells
& the domes of San Onofre
threaten annihilation
of all.

A marker looms in the sand.
It means TURN,
fling yourself to a new element
where marsh grass tangles your limbs
and ascents can suffocate hope.
I pull on wet reins
and lunge into the fierce hills.
I've been here before
in a land of traps,
racing racing to be wanted
to be held,
again & again veering
into the wilderness,
taking the blows.

But in the end I remember being carried.
I remember that in the darkest crossing
the horse could see,
the horse could fly.

Learning to Breathe

I spent a long time looking down the shaft
where through the shadows Kathy Fiscus fell,
and summers after when I sailed my raft
from Father's sight, the terror of that well
went out across the water, pulled me in.
I thought his ropes, his dark cries from the ledge
would never rescue anything again,
would even suffocate me at the edge.
But then he caught me midstream with a wave
of Merced River plunging at my throat
and tore death back and proved one arm could save,
could drive me down or teach me how to float.
I stayed as deep in Kathy's grave to dare
my father's anguish to be rich as air.

The Horse Who Ate Stones

They caught her on the Utah plains
whirling
mane to her knees.

They pulled her last wild gulp
of sagebrush
tossed it half-chewed
with all her mare dreams
away
away from desperate
mouth.

Applause

They gave her pipe fence with four corners
aluminum roof
wanted her to be real.
She kept looking for a way
out
lived on images of mesquite seas
breast-stroking the pale days.

What would they believe?

She ate stones
gathered them into herself
like talismen
swallowed them with hope.

At last
she showed them pain.

They tried to mend her
put her on cool steel
sheets
under the sign Equine Surgery
lifted out those rocks
those last pieces of her desert
sewing carefully with nylon thread
the holes that gaped in her flesh
like open gates.

To Sir Martin Rees

just six

in his hands
the bright equations
blazing down the dark-time scars

in his mind
a quantum burning
racing back to all beginning's
cold and incandescent black

in his heart
a kindled longing
turning in the fires of space

days and hours
the white-hot paper
feels the ardour
in his face

in his dreams
a turbulence soaring
to the source of wind and song
still roaring

in his eyes, the stars

The last was mine. We had read Sir Martin Rees's *Just Six Numbers* in my quantum physics class, and I was totally drawn to the man and his words. On a whim, I had emailed the poem to the incredible Sir Martin, the Queen of England's royal astronomer, and I had received a reply in about five minutes! It was almost better than getting an A on the work from my equally incredible husband. But William did not reveal my private correspondence with the physicist.

March brought us clear, windy days and longer evenings. We tried to ride after school, but it was still fairly cold, and homework and papers to grade piled up. William seemed to need more light at his desk to read and took breaks from his tasks to move around the room with his hand pressed to his forehead. I knew something was troubling him, but he never complained.

We talked about Natasha and Mikeala, but he had calmed down considerably on that subject and, in fact, said he wished we had some really close gay friends. One night, he called his black, gay colleague up in Ashland, Oregon, and they were on the phone at least an hour. Then he came out of his study and sat down next to me on the living room couch.

"Arlan's partner died last year, about the same time as Natasha," William said.

"Oh, no," I said.

"And something else—he knew Natasha was gay before I did. He wanted her to tell me, to make a clean break, but as far as I can figure that was about three years before I saw your face in Ransom Creek, the day she finally told me about Mikeala."

"William, don't let someone open up old wounds," I said, and I put my hand against his chest where he liked to feel a slight pressure.

"Some wounds never heal," he said. "Arlan and John got married a couple of years ago, and then John got liver cancer."

I thought of William Hathaway waiting beside the Chalice River.

"It doesn't seem fair," I said. "Two men who tried to honor what they believed was God's Word and then were broken apart."

"I didn't ask if they'd ever had sex, but I'll bet after the diagnosis, they did," William said.

"I hope they did, William, truly," I said.

"So how brave is Marcella, writing all those poems now about her homosexuality?"

"I think without poetry, she would never have come out."

"Language wins again," he said. "And maybe a little straight sex now and then." He pushed my hand down until my fingertips barely slipped under the waist of his jeans. "Now I could not live without that, just that hint of where your hand might go... oh, God, I think I'm going to have to have more."

We went to bed early that night.

And so, our lives went soaring along between poems and lovemaking, riding the horses and walking on the beach at Malibu on weekends. Our sea glass pile grew along with William's blue-color vocabulary. The sand- and storm-blasted piece we found one day at the beginning of April was called "Aegir blue" after the Norse god of the sea. William said it had to be very old to have that hue.

We started making plans for spring break. Daudi had been begging us to come see him. Of course, the beach at Santa Barbara wouldn't be as isolated as it had been the day we got married, but we thought we could take the horses and ride along the coast where it was allowed at Hope Ranch. William's mother had some friends with an empty two-stall barn and easy access to groomed trails that led to the sea.

At school, William collected poems and gave out notes about each student's work. Then they were all hugging him and telling him their Easter week plans. I always waited in the background and let him have the adoration. Really, I had never known a professor so loved.

Lee came over and kissed my cheek. "I miss you these days, my friend."

"I know. I miss you too. Time seems to get away from me."

"You are so in love," he said.

"I am so in love."

William and I walked to his Mustang arm in arm. It was a blustery day. Birches along our path bowed with new green leaves, and Ransom Creek was beginning to swell. We didn't talk—just let ourselves be filled with the joy of spring. Ahead of us, Lois La Monde stopped and pushed some branches off the trail. We caught up then, and she turned, a little off guard.

"I just want you to know that I deeply admire the both of you. I'm truly sorry if any of my behavior troubled you. I hope we can be friends."

William said, I imagined a little off guard himself, "I always knew you had a good heart, Lois. I'm sorry if I hurt you."

"Well, that is a great relief," she said. "And you, Sela?"

"I always thought that poetry would bring you to a better place," I said.

"Oh, but not just any poetry! Those metaphors that you finally made me see. They were the life changers."

And we went along together toward the parking lot.

10

Even though we were tired that night, we loaded the horse trailer with saddles, bridles, hay, stable blankets, extra water buckets, and grooming equipment. Then we packed our personal things, and William carried it all to the truck while I made a supper of leftovers and food that wouldn't keep while we were gone.

William came into the kitchen and rubbed my shoulders and kissed the back of my neck. I couldn't *not* turn around and kiss his lips, revealing my always deep hunger for the rest of him.

"Do we have to eat?" he asked.

"Yes, we have to eat."

After dinner, I cleaned up while William got ready for bed. When I finally slipped under the covers, he was sound asleep.

In the morning, we loaded the horses into the black and silver trailer hitched to William's silver truck, drove up the canyon, and turned north onto 101 about nine o'clock. William wanted to get to Santa Barbara in time for a short ride before we met Daudi at the zoo at four. We were taking him to dinner at the Opal Restaurant and Bar, which offered delectable fare, a place where the African had never gone as he was always saving his money for his family. It would be a long day, and I wondered if William was up to it.

"I feel okay," he said, but as we passed the crash site on Conejo Grade, he gripped the steering wheel so hard that his hands turned white.

"Do you want me to drive?" I offered.

"No, babe, I'm fine," he said.

Soon we were beside the ocean. There were surfers along the Rincon, some suiting up and others already paddling out toward the swelling waves. Traffic was heavy. There was an art show in Montecito and an all-breed Equine Exhibition at the Earl Warren Showgrounds. We decided we might check out both of those.

"Oh, there's a car auction some place in town—renovated older cars like mine. I thought it might be fun to have matching Mustangs, except yours could be blue. We could easily sell your Prius if you wanted to."

"It would be fun to *look* anyway, kind of like horse-hunting," I said.

We took the exit to Hope Ranch and drove into a lovely area of meticulously landscaped properties. There were already horses on the bridle path. The early morning fog had lifted, and the sun illuminated the colors of the bougainvillea, day lilies, and beds of pansies and roses along the way. In about a mile, we came to the Hilliards' Hide-Away, a modest but well-maintained home on about three acres. Grace Hilliard appeared at the top of the drive, directing us to a turnaround and welcoming us as we climbed out of the truck.

"William! I've known your mother for years and never met her handsome son! Of course, I've seen pictures, but how wonderful to meet you! And this is your new bride!" She gave me a quick hug.

"Grace, this is Sela, Sela Hart Langley."

"And you got married right here in Santa Barbara?"

"We did," William said.

"Have you seen your folks lately?" she asked him.

"You know they are still traveling for that international NGO. I'm not even sure what country they're in at the moment."

I didn't know too much about them, but William had shared several letters they'd sent from such exotic places as Malaysia, Sao Paulo, and Bangladesh. Apparently William's father had devised an easy-to-set-up, safe housing system for orphans. The building could be used as a school or a temporary shelter during storms. William didn't talk much about his parents. I learned that they had never wanted him to be "just a teacher" or "just a writer." Lucky for me, that was his heart's desire.

Grace showed us the way to the small barn and how to reach the most direct trail to the beach. Some wind had come up, and the horses were excited when they backed out of the trailer and looked around at the unfamiliar scene.

"Did you bring hay?" Grace was asking.

"Yes, we did," William told her.

"Use the pallets in the room left of the stalls. There's a tack room on the right, but it's pretty messy. Haven't had time to clean it out. Gabriel's in a wheelchair now, but come in and say hello."

"Grace, we'd like to give the horses some water and take a short ride," William explained. "Could we meet your husband after we put the horses away for the day?"

"That would be fine, William," she said.

I had already filled a couple of buckets, and the geldings were sucking the water down. William got out some brushes, and in about fifteen minutes we were saddled up and leading the horses down the paved driveway to the shredded bark trail. We mounted and followed the signs, meeting two women who were riding to the beach. They called, "Follow us!" and went off at a swift pace, more like a running walk. We broke into a lope and tried to keep up with them.

"Those must be gaited horses," William said after the trail widened and he moved up beside me.

"Yeah, let's walk," I said, a bit winded.

"This is beautiful country. I want to enjoy it, not race past it," William said.

We could hear the ocean now, its mysterious voice echoing against the cliffs as we filed through a narrow gap and came out on the sand. A teenager was riding toward us, and he yelled, "Tide's comin' in! Don't go down that way too far. Try again in the morning."

"Thanks, young man," William called to him, and the boy continued on the trail away from the beach.

The horses danced and fretted as the lip of each wave reached farther inland. We stayed next to the cliffs and talked to them soothingly. Whenever the water retreated, they relaxed. Riding with the tide going out would definitely be better. But we trotted north along a section that didn't have any high tide marks and then turned around after about twenty minutes.

We didn't talk much on the beach, concentrating on controlling our mounts and taking in the vast and thrilling sight of the Pacific trying to swallow us up. What could be in the minds of our sensitive animals? We sidestepped toward the surf until it rose up over their fetlocks and then moved directly back into the dry sand. It was enough for the first day, and it was already past two o'clock. When we rode up onto the bridle path, William said, "Is that not a healing place?"

"I could move here, I think," I answered.

"Can you wait twenty years?" he asked.

"As long as I'm with you, I could live anywhere," I said.

"Bangladesh?"

"That's pushing it, mister!"

We cantered some and walked over the quaint wooden bridges, the horses shying at the tumbling water below. We reached the Hilliards' fairly quickly, the horses already seeming to know where "home" was. We rinsed the salt off of the horses' legs and turned them out in the Hilliards' paddock, throwing some hay into the feeders and making sure the automatic waterers worked. Grace was standing on the back porch beckoning us in. We removed our damp, sandy boots and went into the living room, where Gabriel was reading on the couch.

"Sorry I can't get up. Not paralyzed, you know, just weakened by MS."

"Oh, please don't worry about that," I said. I reached for his outstretched hand, "I'm Sela."

"Gabriel Hilliard," he said. "And you are William." He kept holding my hand and held out his other for my husband. "This is such a pleasure for us to meet you at last," he continued. "We just love your folks, have had some memorable times together. You know we were with them in Haiti after the earthquake. We still had horses then, but I was beginning to have trouble riding. I'm so happy to have horses in the barn again. Wish you'd stay longer."

"We wish we could. We loved the beach—met some friendly people and some horses we couldn't keep up with!" William told them.

"Oh, you must have seen Mae and Dorothy. They have Tennessee Walkers and leave everybody behind! We like the gals, but some in the neighborhood don't approve of them."

We looked blank.

"They're partners," Gabriel said.

"Oh, well that certainly doesn't bother us," I said.

"Are you planning to go to Earl Warren?" Grace asked.

"Yes, Mrs. Hilliard. And to our favorite place—the Santa Barbara Zoo," William said.

"Oh, that's nice. Haven't been there in years," Gabriel said. "Too busy and then too infirm."

"Maybe we could take you," I said. "They have African exhibits now, some endangered animals, and a caretaker from Tanzania who has become a good friend of ours."

"That sounds intriguing. Is the place wheelchair accessible?" Grace asked.

"I believe it is," I said.

"And how did you two end up at that zoo together?" Gabriel asked.

His wife motioned to him. "Gabe, I think we should let the young people get on with their day."

"No," William said. "I love to tell that story. Sela turned in a short story..."

"She was in one of your classes?" Gabriel asked.

"Yes. Still is. Anyway, in her story an actor who has been estranged from his daughters takes them to the Santa Barbara Zoo to see the white rhinos. It's a special and rare moment for the three. Sela has a way of pulling you right into her characters' lives. I decided to surprise her one Saturday and drive up here. The rest is history, as they say."

"Well, that is just better than any fiction I've read in a while," Gabriel exclaimed.

"I'm trying to get my students to be as real as possible, but Sela rearranged my own reality in a big way. I had a troubled marriage, as you may know."

"William, your folks were very discreet. We understood you were having some problems. We prayed for you, didn't we, Gabe," Grace said.

"Such as my prayers are worth," Gabriel said.

"Gabe didn't stay with the church as I did," Grace explained.

"Well, you and Sela seem entirely suited to each other. If God had a hand in it, then so be it," Gabriel said.

We thanked them again for boarding our horses and said we'd feed them, that they didn't have to do a thing. Grace asked if she could help us groom them before our rides, and we agreed that would be nice.

"Oh, what are their names?" she asked.

William answered, "Chisholm and Malibu."

"Lovely," she said.

William unhitched the trailer, and we drove out in the soft afternoon light that flickered through eucalyptus, cedars, and jacarandas, purple blossoms falling on lawns and roadways like violet snowflakes. We drove to the zoo, picked up a snack from the vendor's cart, and sat by the white rhinos waiting for Daudi. William put his arm around me, and then, after a long while, whispered, "I love you more than I can ever say."

Daudi saw us and hurried over. "Come see zebra babies!" They'd been weaned and were together in an enclosure separated from the mares. They had grown a lot in six months. "I name them W and S for William and Sela," the Tanzanian said.

We went in the back gate as we had the first time, and the youngsters galloped right over as if they recognized us. They pushed us with their noses and tossed their pretty striped heads in the sea-scented air.

"I play with them every day. I catch S but not W. He very smart. Girl baby like me."

The female stayed closer to us and nickered when we finally left. Daudi had about forty minutes left to finish feeding his section of the zoo, so William and I walked out to the truck and listened to music on our favorite CDs. "Natasha and I never did this," he said after a few minutes.

"What, babe?"

"Just sit and enjoy music or the feel of the air in spring. She always had to be busy. 'Let's visit so and so, let's play tennis, let's work on my jump courses or repave the driveway or paint fences'—you name it. She was not comfortable with just being with me, with silence, with touching."

"I'm so sorry, William. Can I tell you that that was the first thing I wanted all those years ago? To sit next to you on a bench in the quad and feed the birds, for heaven's sake. To feel your shoulder next to mine. To write a poem with you watching my hand move on the paper. I thought I would never be good enough for you with such simple desires."

"I tried so hard with Natasha, and I was never enough. You would have been glad to have me look into your enigmatic blue eyes."

"Even I don't understand why I felt the way I did last September when I got to the front of the line and waited to hear your question."

"You loved me."

"That I surely did," I said.

Daudi soon joined us, and we put his bicycle in the back of the truck and headed for his beach house. Again, he had flowers in every room and our favorite ginger ale on ice. We told him about our Christmas at my grandmother's, working in the garden, about my winning the short story contest with "Survivors," and then some of the things William had suffered lately.

Daudi looked concerned. He asked questions, touched William's head, and said, "In here, something not right."

"Well, I've never been called crazy," my husband said.

Daudi did not smile. "You see doctor." It was not a question.

"No, my friend. I'm better now. Sela takes good care of me."

"I will speak to her about this 'taking care,'" he said.

I gave the African a hug, trying not to cry.

We all changed one at a time in Daudi's room. I put on my black dress that I had worn to the faculty party last year. It was William's favorite. William had chosen the Opal Restaurant and Bar on State Street. He knew the manager, Carrie Prelas, who hugged my husband when we walked in and murmured something about Natasha. Carrie gave a warm welcome to Daudi, who bowed shyly. We were seated at a table near the front windows. The light was perfect, the conversation around us politely quiet, and we all relaxed.

Daudi was the only black man in the restaurant or on the street outside, but it didn't seem to bother him. I still feared the racism that he might experience here, a color bar that didn't exist in his country.

"Daudi, are you treated well at the zoo?" I asked him.

"Oh, yes, mama. I have nice room there if need to stay, very good money, my house on beach..."

"I mean, do people respect you—your boss, white visitors?"

"Not to worry, Sela. People happy I do my job. Some give tips, some ignore," he said.

"You don't mind that?" I asked.

"Not mind. I have animals. I have you and Mr. William." He smiled.

William had ordered for us. We shared an appetizer he thought would be unique for the Tanzanian—grilled eggplant and portabella mushroom salad with gourmet greens, goat cheese pesto crostinis and a fresh cilantro-infused extra virgin olive oil. Daudi said maybe he had had goat cheese but not fixed *this way!* The main course was a lemon grass–crusted fresh salmon filet with a Thai curry sauce, sauteed julienne vegetables, and a caramelized apple and orange zest basmati rice.

"I not believe this American food!" Daudi exclaimed. "What is?"

Even I could not interpret the exotic-sounding dishes. One of William and Natasha's favorite chefs, Felipe Barajas, had created a special dessert as a late wedding gift for William and me, a cranberry cheesecake with a fresh berry coulis sauce, and he served it to us personally, greeting the three of us with unreserved pleasure. The world seemed perfect at that moment.

After dinner, we wandered along State Street looking in shops for presents for Daudi's children. We bought books, art and school supplies, a used flute, stuffed "American" animals, photographs of Santa Barbara hills and beaches, and some fine yards of material for Daudi's wife, Sara, to fashion clothes for everyone. There were purple silks and red cottons and washed linens the colors of the sea.

"What need most is shoes for work in fields, but don't know sizes anymore," the Tanzanian said sadly.

"We can send money for those," William offered.

"No, not safe," Daudi replied.

"Daudi, I have friends in Tanzania." I thought of Zakariyah, his high standards, the respect for him in his community. He would never steal from the Fahja family. "We can send money to them to give Sara."

"Bless you, mama Sela," Daudi said.

We walked on carrying our packages. The streets and alleys were lined with planters and hanging baskets overflowing with geraniums, petunias, lobelia, snapdragons, portulaca, fuchsias, dahlias, pansies, and other spring beauties, a heaven for painters and photographers.

"Santa Barbara like coast of East Africa," Daudi said. "Flowers everywhere in streets and markets. People playing music and taking hands. Santa Barbara like second home. Never forget."

William drove slowly down Oceanside Lane, not wanting the day to end.

We slept in Daudi's white bed after the quietest sex we'd ever had while Daudi lay outside on the old couch. Fog rolled in during the night, and William wrapped us in a down comforter we'd brought from home. I could not think beyond the warmth of my husband's arms. I could not think of Daudi's fears about William or the odd symptoms that had plagued him for months. When he kissed me good morning, there was only the enrapturing feeling of his mouth on mine.

We rode the horses again that day and visited with Grace and Gabriel. They promised they would befriend Daudi, and we made plans to get Gabe to the zoo the next day. We went back to Oceanside Lane and walked on the beach barefoot searching for shells and sea glass to add to Daudi's decorative collection. We decided to keep one piece each as a memento of spring break. William asked me if placing those keepsakes around the Malibu house would make it easier for me to live there. I told him having our own horses in the barn and bringing things we bought or found together into the rooms he had shared with Natasha meant a lot to me. At that moment, William reached down and pulled a smooth aqua blue piece of glass out of the sand and held it up to my face.

"Amazing," he said. "Sela with the aqua eyes."

Later we drove to Montecito to the art show and purchased a small watercolor of the high tide against the cliffs at Hope Ranch and a charcoal sketch of two Arab-looking horses hooking necks over a fence. I couldn't wait to hang them on the living room walls in Malibu Canyon.

Daudi fixed dinner that night, and we talked about taking the Hilliards to the zoo. Daudi wanted to push Gabriel's wheelchair and maybe roll him in with the zebra babies. "I don't know," William cautioned. "He could get kicked. The wheelchair might scare the little ones."

"They not afraid of manure cart or man with leaf blower," Daudi said.

"Well, it would be fantastic if it would work," William said.

We all went to bed early. I stared for a long time in the light of a full moon at the sculptured pile of shells, sand dollars, and glass, trying to see where our fragile selves might fit. William kissed every sensitive place on my body he could find, and we went down that known path to its very familiar and exquisite end.

Daudi went to work in the morning dressed in the clothes he had worn out to dinner on Saturday night, not his regular zoo uniform. William and I headed for Hope Ranch and the Hilliards'. Their car was set up for Gabe's wheelchair, so they followed us back to the zoo. There in the parking lot, Daudi stood proudly directing Grace to a convenient handicapped space and meeting Gabriel as he opened the side door and emerged on a lift that brought him to the ground.

"Hello, Daudi," Gabriel said. "I've heard wonderful things about you! This is my wife, Grace."

"Mama Grace, *karibu*, welcome."

"Oh, is that Swahili? What a beautiful word."

Daudi clapped his hands. "*Asante sana!*"

"Thank you very much," I translated.

We began the tour. Grace was glad to have Daudi handle the wheelchair. The zoo had installed ramps, so we had no trouble getting to all the pens. At the white rhino enclosure, Gabriel motioned for Daudi to stop, and then he turned to me. Grace and William sat on the bench, and Gabriel handed me a copy of my story.

"Will you read it to me, Sela?"

I was startled.

"I was going to read it last night," he said, "and then I thought how amazing it would be to hear you speak the words right here."

I began, "Survivors." A small group of tourists had gathered to see what was going on. A writer has to get used to doing readings. This would be one for the record books. Even the white rhinos edged closer to the double fence. After I read the last line, Gabriel said, "My dear, that just takes my breath away. It's so simple yet so moving. You must let me read the rest of the stories."

William said, "I only gave him that one."

I promised to send him the rest of them, except for the last one, which no one had heard.

"Not even your husband?" Gabe asked.

"Not even him."

A woman in the crowd came forward anxiously. "Oh, young lady, may I have that copy autographed? Apparently, you know this gentleman and could send him another copy. I may never see you again."

I hesitated, but William said, "Do it, Sela. This is how you become known."

I signed it, "Protect what you love, Sela Hart Langley" and gave the stranger a piece of my heart. Later I said to William, "Maybe I don't want to be *known*."

"You would deny the world your talent?"

"Maybe," I said.

"As your teacher, I'm telling you, you did the right thing."

"Okay, professor, I submit," I said.

We passed many exhibits and had hot dogs along the way to W and S. Grace kept asking, "What on earth is W and S?"

"I think it means William and Sela," Gabriel suggested.

"Yes, but not good names for zebras!" Daudi confirmed. And there they were, acting like little horses, dancing on their tiny back hooves.

"They feel good," Daudi said. He decided that just he and Mr. Hilliard should go in the pen. "Too many people might frighten."

We were silent as the two men entered the zebras' space. The youngsters trotted right over to Daudi, but when they saw the wheelchair, they spun around in mock terror. Soon they were back when they realized the metal thing wasn't chasing them and when they heard a human voice coming out of it. Daudi gave Gabe a pan of grain. The zebras stretched their necks out and nibbled the oats. Gabriel told them how beautiful they were and how glad he was they had come all the way from the Serengeti to see him. They never made contact with Mr. Hilliard, but he was thrilled to watch their dark lips picking at the feed and their dark eyes looking back at him. The zebra mothers paced around in the next pen feeling left out. It was time to go.

On the way back to the van, the Hilliards asked Daudi a lot of questions about Africa. They learned that Daudi had a wife and five children, three boys and two girls, that the oldest two boys and one girl were in school, the others waiting until he saved enough money. I saw Grace glance at Gabriel, and I knew good things would come of this crossing of cultures.

William and I stayed around Daudi's the next day. Grace said she'd be happy to feed the horses for us. We read and meandered down the beach and danced to some slow songs on Daudi's radio. We rested on the fresh white bed with the ocean crashing a few feet from the open window. William slept, but I lay with an uneasiness in my heart, a restlessness that matched the rolling waves. That day I felt, more than any other since I had walked into William's classroom, the calm before a storm.

On Wednesday, we saddled the geldings early to ride with the ebbing tide. The horses were getting used to the sounds of waves breaking and the sight of joggers appearing on the edge of the surf. The sky was gray that day, but light broke through a shifting patchwork of blues and greens across the expanse of the Pacific.

"There's a heaven here," William said after we had loped on the hard sand a ways and then slowed to a walk where driftwood and stones from the cliffs above were strewn. Malibu, who was a little braver than Chisholm, went first around a small point of land that narrowed the trail to a single file passage, so William was the first to see them. Mae and Dorothy were standing on the beach, reins in one hand and an arm around each other. They were kissing. They stopped when they heard the horses.

"Excuse us, ladies," William said graciously. "Didn't mean to interrupt."

"That's okay," one of them said. "We don't own the place. I'm Mae, and this is Dorothy. We've seen you two before."

"Yes, we've admired your horses," William said. "We're glad to know someone here, maybe to ride with, show us the trails. This is my wife, Sela, and I'm—"

"I know who you are," Dorothy said abruptly. "You're Professor Langley. William Langley."

"Have we met?" William asked.

"No," she said. "I was a friend of Natasha's… and Mikeala's."

"Small world," William said.

"Perhaps you want to rethink connecting with us," Dorothy said defensively.

"Not at all. I always wished Natasha would introduce me to her friends."

"You're younger," Dorothy said, looking at me.

"Not much," I said, "but here's a truth that might shock you. I was in love with William while Natasha was with Mikeala."

They both gasped.

"It's not what you think. William didn't know it."

"You're one of his students, right?" Dorothy asked. Mae seemed unable to find her voice.

"I'm doing graduate studies, and I'm in his short story and poetry classes, yes," I answered.

"I was at the funeral, Mr. Langley," she said, turning back to him.

"I was a mess. I don't remember anyone. I'm sorry," William said

"That's okay. We all knew you were very good to Natasha. It was a terrible thing, that accident. Maybe you can have some closure now," she said.

There was that word again—the word I didn't believe in.

"We need to get back," Mae said. "We've got an appointment."

They tightened their girths and began to mount their horses. Why was everyone so damn wary? I couldn't let it go.

"Dorothy, Mae. I wrote a poem once about two women embracing on the beach. I don't know where it came from because I just saw it now for the first time. Would you like to have it?" I asked.

"I think that would be very nice," Mae said. "Who are you staying with?"

"Our horses are at the Hilliards' place," I said.

"Oh, yes, great people. I'll call Grace and give her our address. You can mail the poem. It's very kind of you to offer."

"Thank you, Sela," Dorothy said. "And thank you for taking care of Mr. Langley. We all cried for him too."

They restrained their Walkers through the rough section, and then, by the time we had picked our way around the point, they were a good distance away, their dark horses flying in a running walk, the women's hair whipped by the stormy air and incredible pace. Chisholm and Malibu bunched up for the canter, but William grabbed my hand.

"I need to slow down, honey," he said. He put a hand to his eyes.

"What is it? What is it?" I pleaded.

"I can't see... just shapes and colors. Which side of us is the ocean on? The sound is everywhere."

"Oh, God, William, will you please let me get you some help?"

"Hang on… I see you now—the ocean, the storm on the horizon. I'll be okay," he said, but he didn't let go of my hand for a mile or so.

The tide had turned, and the geldings pranced a bit. The beach was deserted, the air gusty and chilling. We put our windbreakers on and trotted toward the break in the cliffs where the trail led back into Hope Ranch. When we got to the Hilliards', Grace had tea ready for us. The warm liquid revived us, but William asked if there was someplace he could lie down.

"Oh, goodness, you're not ill?" Grace asked.

"No, no, I just got a little dizzy on the beach."

"Well, stay right there. I'll put a pillow on Sela's lap, and you can lie right there on the couch. I think we should keep an eye on you."

After William was comfortable, assuring me he was really all right, I told the Hilliards about meeting Mae and Dorothy at the point on the beach, how they had surprised us by talking about Natasha, and that I had written a poem some years ago that I wanted to give them.

"Oh, I love good poetry," Gabriel exclaimed. "Could we hear it?"

"I don't memorize my poems, and I don't have it with me. I'll send you a copy," I promised.

"But I'd love to hear you read it," Gabe said.

"It's kind of a *gay* poem," I said.

"Good poetry is good poetry. Do you like it?"

"Very much. To see the women almost as if they *were* the poem was quite remarkable," I told him. "I knew next to nothing about that kind of love when I wrote it, so it surprised me. It was a strange point of view for me, something Professor Langley here always encourages."

"I like my students to get inside somebody else's head," William said quietly. Then he sat up slowly.

"Better, dear?" Grace asked.

"I think so. I hope so because I wanted to look at some cars at the auction today," William answered.

"What are you looking for?" Gabriel wanted to know.

"I'd like to find another '78 Mustang, something Sela would like," he said.

"I don't really need a car, but I like the Mustang," I said.

"Can you drive it?" Grace asked.

"I can. I've driven William's several times. It's not that hard."

"Well, it would be hard for me!" Grace joked. "I can feed for you again tonight so you can get on with your plans," she offered.

"We appreciate that so much, Grace," I said, and we got ready to leave.

"Do you think you'll have time to check out the horses at Earl Warren? Or the booths?" Grace asked. "You know, Gabe and I always spent about a thousand dollars there every year!"

"If we buy a car, we won't have much left for horse stuff," William said. "I should let Sela choose."

"Oh, I'd take the horse stuff!" Grace admitted.

"And I'd take the car!" Gabriel exclaimed.

We hugged them and promised to see them again that week. William hesitated at the truck as if he were going to give me the keys, but he didn't. We headed out of Hope Ranch for the auction lot wondering what was waiting for us there.

We saw the one we wanted before we'd gone down the first row. It was a Mustang—didn't know the year yet—but it was a muted blue-green, the exact color of the wild ocean that day. When we stood next to it, William said, "Today your eyes are that shade, I swear." It was a '78 stick-shift, V-6, newly painted. The seat covers were white like William's, and there was extra chrome in attractive places. The hood had a metallic ornament of a running horse. It was quite beautiful.

"Oh, William, you should have this one! I'll take yours," I offered.

"No, this suits you, sweetheart, really."

The seller stood close by, listening. He said, "Take it for a drive, why don't you? Just leave me your truck keys."

"Come on, Sela. We'll drive out to the zoo and show Daudi."

We got in, and it felt like ours. After a few blocks, William mentioned that the gears were sluggish and that he had noticed some scratches in the paint. But he said he could deal with those things. He'd drive it home if I could handle the truck and trailer with the horses. I guaranteed

I could. We picked Daudi up for a quick drive on his break. He made a big fuss, saying most people in his country rode motor scooters or bicycles—sometimes work trucks, sometimes ox carts, but rarely anything as fancy as the Mustang. William told him it was about thirty-five years old.

"Still beautiful," Daudi said. He ran his hand along the sea-blue hood. "And for a beautiful girl."

Back at the lot, William got the price down considering the status of the engine and the paint scratches. He let me drive it back to Daudi's while he drove the truck.

Daudi treated us to deep-fried tilapia rolled in maize, fresh lima beans with dill, and a lemon pudding that was just right. Then the three of us sat on the dilapidated couch that Daudi had brought in earlier. It creaked under our weight but held up. The storm was still far out to sea but threatening and secretive as if saving its power until just the right moment, refusing to show its true colors.

Daudi laid his hands on William's closed eyes and said, "There is problem."

William said, "Some pressure, an odd pain, not like a headache but annoying. If I move too fast, I get dizzy and my vision goes haywire. I hate feeling so ill."

"There is something that does not belong," Daudi said gently. "Something for shaman or doctor to heal."

"Your hands are enough, Daudi," William said, letting the African caress his head and murmur some words I could not translate.

"You are liking horses on beach?" Daudi asked me.

"We are a part of the elements, a part of the horses, in a kind of heaven," I tried to explain.

"Ah… I know this about you. Even storm has place for you," he said.

"I think so," I answered.

And the storm came on shore. The little house rattled, and the wind whistled through the cracks in the siding. Daudi brought us cups of Vernor's warmed a bit with fresh mint stirred in. *A healer for a healer,* I thought, looking at the two most important men in my life.

Then, William and I went to the white room that Daudi always gave to us with freshly laundered white sheets and blankets and, tonight, a white rose on each pillow. We lay talking softly for a while, wondering at the coincidence of meeting Natasha's friends on the beach and whether we'd ever see Dorothy and Mae again.

"What's the name of that poem you're sending them?"

"Out and Back," I said.

"Like the tides."

"Yes."

"Like Natasha," William whispered.

"You're pretty smart, professor," I said.

"But how could you know what to write? How could you speak in Natasha's voice?"

"I was only an observer, but strangely, it could be Natasha's voice," I told him. "Those gals will hear her voice anyway. But I was only imagining it, not feeling it."

"I can't wait to hear it," he said and then paused as if trying to decide if he wanted to go on with this. "I've got to tell you something. It's not easy."

"I'm listening."

"At first, I was hurt when Natasha told me about Mikeala. Then, I wanted to know what that kind of love was like," he said.

"William, I think love is love."

"No, I mean the *sex*."

"Oh."

"She would come home just high with… joy. She'd say, 'Oh, Bill, thank you, thank you for letting me be who I am.' I'd say, 'Tell me who you are—no, *show* me.' She'd say, 'Bill, I can have sex with you if you want, but it won't be the same!' It was like getting punched in the gut."

"William, I'll give you what you want."

"Can you give me *gay* sex?"

"I can give you gay, straight, crooked, kinky, you name it," I whispered.

"But have you ever felt *that way* about a woman?" he asked.

"When I was twelve, I had a crush on my flute teacher who was a stunning woman that I suspected was gay but never knew for sure."

He didn't say anything.

"Then when I was nineteen, I had a crush on you. That certainly defined *my* life, sexual and otherwise," I said. "Have you ever been attracted to a man?"

"No, never."

"Then, William, I don't think you're missing anything."

"I just think Natasha and Mikeala had something I will never know, something my wife died wanting."

"I think that was alcohol, sweetheart, not gay sex."

He shuddered.

"Oh, William, come here. Let me love these demons out of your head."

He kissed me gratefully, quietly, and yet famished for something he didn't understand. After we made love, I said, "Isn't *that* orgasm enough?"

"At the moment, it is everything, but when I saw Mae and Dorothy on the beach, I wanted more."

"William Langley, you are a complicated man, and I love you with all my heart."

"I love you. You are everything to me."

"Don't you think there are some things we are not meant to know?"

"Probably… yes, I think so."

We fell asleep holding onto the only love we knew, the only marvelous bodies that fit like gloves, that made us ache again and again for the orgasms we were born for.

We went fairly early to Earl Warren Showgrounds in my blue Mustang. It made an odd sound between second and third gears, so William was determined not to let me drive it home. I told him that was fine but that I wasn't going to drive very fast with the horses. He agreed to keep me in sight. I got a chill when he said that.

We wandered around the arenas and vendors' stalls. William bought me a gorgeous *mercate*, a parachute cord rope of pure white with a horse hair tassel at one end the color of Chisholm's chestnut coat. We looked for snaffle bits. There were so many, but we settled on a handmade ring snaffle with copper on the mouthpiece.

We watched a "round pen" demonstration and a beautiful six-hitch dressage test around obstacles, the driver handling horses and carriage with precision and style. We bought some authentic quesadillas with guacamole and sat down to eat under a canopied table. Then we saw Dorothy and Mae coming toward us. William waved them over.

"Hi, ladies," he said warmly. "Come eat with us."

"Oh, we've already had a bite," Dorothy said, "but we'll sit for a minute."

"Let's see what you bought," Mae said excitedly, noticing my package.

I showed her the bit and rope rein, matching headstall and slobber straps, and tried to show her how it would go together. She loved the whole thing but said that Walkers' gaits developed better with a curb bit. William and Dorothy were talking about Natasha. *Damn.*

"You protected her. You gave her freedom. You accepted her. You should be proud of yourself. It's more than most men would do," she was saying.

"You two need to let Natasha lie in peace," Mae said.

"So how am I supposed to get *my* peace?" he asked them both.

"By holding onto this heavenly creature right here beside you," Dorothy said. "Come on, Mae. Looking forward to that poem, Sela."

And they faded into the crowd.

"That didn't go too well, I guess," William said. He'd only eaten half his quesadilla.

"You feel all right?"

"I've felt better," he said.

"Let's go back to Daudi's while he's not there. I'll make you forget everything but me."

"It's a deal," he said.

Oh, Lord, he couldn't get enough that day. The storm had passed, and the room was full of light. It poured right into us entangled on the white bed, our heads just above the water with every leap from the river of disconsolation coursing from the unknown.

I left William asleep and went out to greet Daudi when he came home from the zoo with his bicycle basket filled with flowers and fresh fruit. He wanted to make dinner for us on our last night in Santa Barbara. The African and I stood together in his little kitchen peeling mangoes and avocadoes and crumbling crackers to bread fish. We didn't talk, but once I glanced over, and tears were running down Daudi's face.

"Baba?"

"Cannot lose Mr. William," he said. "Cannot."

"Me either," I said.

We fixed the meal in silence.

"Something smells good," William said from the doorway.

"Many healing things, my brother. You eat," Daudi said.

"*Asante sana, rafiki.* I will surely need it," William said.

We all sat at the round table and clasped hands for a moment.

"Is it dark?" my husband asked.

"Almost," I answered, and I kissed his eyes that seemed to see another world.

Later, we fell asleep again to a tide drawing away from the beach house on its own dark journey.

It was hard to say good-bye. Daudi embraced William as if he never wanted to let go and said to me softly, "Mama Sela, if you need me, I come."

"*Asante sana, baba, asante sana.*"

William took the Mustang and I the truck up to the Hilliards' to pick up the horses. Grace and Gabriel hugged us too, saying we had brought a peace into their lives and to please come back soon. Grace gave me Dorothy and Mae's address and reminded me to send some of my poetry to them too. Chisholm and Malibu seemed glad to jump into the trailer. It was a hazy Friday morning and vacation traffic would be starting to build up, so we were anxious to be on our way.

William and I arranged some signals we'd use if either of us needed to stop and we couldn't reach each other by phone. We got gas in Montecito and a couple of Vernor's ginger ales. My husband put his arms around me, rested his cheek on mine, and said, "See you in Malibu Canyon."

11

Then, we were on our way. We passed the nearly deserted beaches at Summerland and the Rincon. I wondered how long it would be before we had our feet again in the sand of the Pacific Coast, searching for sea glass and breathing the salty air. Another horse transporter went by me, and Chisholm nickered. I slowed down. The Ventura freeway was packed. It wasn't much better through Oxnard and Camarillo. I dreaded the thought of Conejo Grade, but there it was winding its course through a patch of fog that hadn't yet dissipated from its morning hover over the scene. *God, just let us get over this mountain.*

The hill steepened. My heart was in my throat. We made it by the place where Natasha had careened over the divider. I breathed a little easier. I couldn't imagine what William was feeling. I pulled over into the truck lane and lost sight of the blue Mustang. The horses shifted around as a truck geared down right beside us. God, it was noisy. The hill seemed to go on forever. The fog thickened. *Where is the Mustang? Is William all right? Why can't I see him?*

I glanced over at my purse. *Should I get my cell phone? No, too dangerous.* I reached for it anyway. Then I looked up. The blue car, already somehow ruined and unrecognizable, was veering wildly off the shoulder. Directly ahead of where William would have been driving was a big rig that was totally stopped in its lane. Behind that was another semi still screeching to a stop and twisting slowly, dream-like, into an odd angle half out of the road, his emergency lights flashing. *What was happening?*

"No! No! Oh, God, no!" I cried, trying to make sense of the scene.

Brake lights flared. I just had time to pull the truck and trailer off into a wide turnout, screaming all the way. One hand was on my phone and the other on the door handle. I got out about a hundred yards from where the crumpled Mustang lay upside-down. A highway patrolman rushed up beside me shouting out the window, "I already called it in, lady. Keep moving! Get that rig back on the highway. You're just in the way!"

I shook my head. "That's my husband in that car!"

"Oh my God. Okay, stay here for a minute!"

The truck drivers were trying to help. I heard one of them say, "You'll need the jaws of life. I think he's still breathing, but he's trapped."

I just knelt on the ground. I couldn't move. The horses stamped in the trailer. Traffic had slowed to look, and sirens wailed in the distance. The Chalice River flowed over me with a vengeance. I was drowning.

Then someone touched my shoulder. It was Lee Henderson. "Sela! What the hell's going on?"

"Lee, it's William. William is in that car!"

"Stay here! I'll go up there!"

He came back in a few minutes. "He's alive, Sela, but he's pinned behind the wheel. No air bags in those damn old cars."

"I have to see him."

"No, Sela. They're getting to him. They called for Life Flight. Just pray this fog clears out. There's nothing else you can do. Come on, give me your hand. Hang onto me," Lee said calmly.

Then he told me that he'd been visiting his mom in Ventura and decided to go back to school a couple of days early. I sobbed while he talked. I could hardly take in the scene before me. Finally, an officer approached us. "Ma'am, you'll need to get your vehicle out of here. Visibility's better. The helicopter needs to land. It will scare your horses. Is there a place you'd like your husband to go?"

"UCLA Medical Center," I answered immediately.

"Good choice. Okay, can you get your horses home and yourself out to UCLA?"

"No, I don't think I can drive," I said feeling my strength fading away.

"But I can, officer. I'm a friend. I can drive her all the way, but I'll have to leave my car here."

"Okay, son, but pull off the road as far as you can. I'll make sure it's not ticketed."

"I'll get someone to bring me out tomorrow to pick it up," Lee promised. "Sela, trust me. I had horses in high school, remember? I can help you."

"Lee, I have to touch him. I have to."

But the helicopter was coming in, and the horses were screaming. I let Lee carry me to the truck, and he went around to the driver's side. Soon we were in a lane moving slowly past the place where William had lain in the wrecked car, the blue car the color of my eyes.

Lee drove carefully and kept asking me questions so that I'd have to talk instead of cry. It was so hard to leave William on the Conejo Grade even though I saw the helicopter land and a stretcher carrying him toward it. I banged my fists on the dashboard of the truck until they bled. I remembered him saying, "See you in Malibu Canyon." Were those the last words he'd ever say to me?

"Sela, Sela, tell me about your week," Lee begged.

I started describing the times we rode on the beach, but that only made it worse.

"Did you stay with that African guy who came to Langley's class?"

"Yes. Oh, I have to reach Daudi! I have to tell him!"

"First, I'm taking you to your husband," Lee said as though that was all that mattered, whether he was dead or alive.

We fell into an anguished silence. The horses stomped and fretted in the trailer, but Lee kept a steady hand on the wheel, and we left the grade behind. For a while, I hardly recognized where we were, but suddenly I was startled to see an exit sign for Hidden Hills.

"Lee, you just missed the turnoff!" I cried.

"I'm going to Griffith Park. It's closer to the campus and the medical center. You can't leave your horses alone at Malibu. You don't know when you'll be back there. I have it figured out. I'll drop you at the hospital first, settle your horses at the stable, stay with them if I have to..."

"They're not used to being stalled. They need a run or something," I broke in.

"I'll take care of it," he said.

"Lee, thank you. You are a gift."

"Hey, girl, what are friends for? I'm just glad I was on the grade when you needed someone. Besides, you and Mr. Langley are just about my favorite people in the world. After I get all this stuff done, I'm coming straight to the medical center. I can make some calls for you," he said. "Oh, God, Sela, I'm so sorry."

"Did you know that I have had William Langley in my heart for more than eight years?"

"Really? No, I didn't know that. But he was married… and older."

"He didn't notice me until I got in his writing class and his wife was dead," I said.

"Damn."

"He's forty, and I'm twenty-seven. Not so much difference," I told him.

"I don't think your ages matter, Sela. But you didn't date anyone all these years?"

"I had a lover in Africa. He was married. I had to learn about life somehow. When I came back to the States for my junior year, I passed Mr. Langley in the hallway going to my seventeenth-century lit class, and I thought I was going to faint. I leaned against the wall. He caught my shoulder and said, 'Miss, are you all right?' I looked right in his eyes and said, 'I didn't have time for breakfast.' He said, 'You kids should take better care of yourselves.' I was so nothing to him, just one of the *kids*. The funny thing is William doesn't remember that. I remember thinking that day, *Someday I will touch you when you least expect.* I didn't mean with my stories, but that's what it took to get to his heart."

"But, Sela, now your touch means everything to him. You can go into his room, wherever they've taken him, and touch his wounds and *love* him back to you."

"Do you really believe that, Lee?"

"I do. It's kind of like believing in God," he said.

"That I'm not so sure of," I said.

"Things that are equal to the same things are equal to each other," he quoted. "If God is love and you love Langley, then you love God."

"There have been moments..." I started to say.

"Sela, you've got to believe in the divine moments. Anything else is giving up."

"I'll try, Lee."

"Oh, here we are. Look, I can't park. Get what you need. I'll be back."

I grabbed my duffel. At least I'd have a change of clothes. I watched Lee maneuver out of the congestion that always seems to peak at hospitals. Then, I ran in the front door and over to the first official-looking person I saw, a young woman behind a sign that said "Information."

"My husband's been brought here on Life Flight. Can you help me?"

"Name?"

"William Langley."

"Oh. The Conejo Grade incident. Yes, he's here. I'll get an attending for you. You can wait in the ER visitor's lounge," she said. "Down that hall and to your right."

There I was told to wait again. I thought to take a long drink of water from a fountain in the corner. I had to be my best for William, but I was out of my mind with fear. Then someone was calling my name.

"Mrs. William Langley?"

I got up slowly, dragging my duffel.

"No, young lady, we're looking for Mr. Langley's wife," an orderly said. I tried to stay calm.

"I *am* his wife," I said. "Please let me see him."

"I don't think you can see him, but I'll get his doctor. Come this way."

And then I was in another room. There was only one other person in it, for which I was very grateful, an older lady who began talking immediately. "My grandson fell off his horse," she exclaimed.

"Oh, I'm sorry," I said. I watched the door for any sign of movement.

"And you?" she asked.

"My husband was in a car accident."

"Oh, dear, is he all right?"

"I have no idea. I had to leave the scene. I was in the way of the helicopter," I said.

"Oh, dear," she said again.

A tall, bald-headed man came in. "Mrs. Wilson, you can see your grandson now. Just a broken collarbone. He'll be in some pain but should be fine. These young people heal quickly."

"He'll want to know when he can ride," the grandmother insisted.

"I would say six weeks at a minimum," the doctor said.

"Oh, dear."

That seemed to be her favorite expression. A broken collarbone—William should be so lucky. They went out toward a row of curtained partitions. *Is William in there? Is he conscious? Does he know I'm right here?* It was almost harder being alone. I knew how Angela felt standing on the edge of the Chalice River. How could I have ever written that story without knowing how *this* felt, this utter, dark, cold emptiness?

I was so tired. What had Lee said? *Believe in the divine moments. Anything else is giving up.* I barely noticed when another white-coated man appeared in the room.

"Mrs. Langley? I'm Dr. Salieri," he said holding out his right hand.

"Like the composer?"

"Yes." He had to smile that I would ask such a question. "We are assessing and stabilizing Mr. Langley. He suffered a broken leg and some internal bleeding. We're doing a head CT to rule out any brain trauma."

"I can tell you there's something wrong," I said.

"Really."

"In the last few months, he has had some dizziness and vision problems, as well as memory loss and vague feelings of not being well," I told him.

"That could be significant. We'll look carefully at the brain scan. I may call the chief of neurosurgery and alert her of possible complications. In the meantime, we'll make your husband as comfortable as we can. He is still unconscious and on a ventilator."

I had to grab the arm of the chair and sit down. "May I see him?"

The doctor hesitated. "Let me get back to you. I promise not to make you wait too long. Are you injured?"

"No, I was in a separate car," I said.

"You witnessed the accident then?"

"Yes, sir."

"I am truly sorry, Mrs. Langley. But may I ask you something?"

I nodded.

"Could Mr. Langley have passed out and lost control of his car?"

"That I can absolutely tell you did not happen. A semitruck had come to a complete stop in his lane. There was a truck beside him and one behind him. He had no place to go!" The sight of the blue car flashed through my mind again, the way it flew out from between those huge trucks. I didn't know why I was so desperate to have the exact facts known.

"I'll take you to him as soon as I can," Dr. Salieri said and returned the way he had come.

In about twenty minutes, a nurse led me down another hallway to a double door marked ICU. "You'll have to clean up a little, dear, and put on this gown and slippers. We can't take any unsterile matter into that environment."

"Of course." I went into a bathroom and washed my hands and face and as much of my hair as I could. I put on the white suit and white boots and tucked my hair into a white bonnet. I thought, *If William wakes up, he won't recognize me*. The nurse then took me to William's bedside. I couldn't believe what I saw. I was not prepared. There was a breathing tube taped to his mouth. His face was terribly bruised. His right leg was splinted and held by some kind of traction device. He had a catheter and an IV dripping God knows what into his veins. And he was so still.

The nurse was saying, "Ten minutes is all you have this time, Mrs. Langley. He probably can't hear you, but you may talk to him."

"Why can't he wake up?" I asked her.

"We don't always know the full extent of someone's injuries immediately. We're giving him some drugs to reduce the swelling in his brain and bring his vital signs under control. Things should look better in a few days," she said.

"A few *days*," I said, losing my composure.

"I'm sorry there isn't something more definite to report. I believe Dr. Salieri called the chief of neurosurgery to look in on this case."

"A surgeon?" Now I was really becoming alarmed.

"There was a mass of some kind on the CT scan. The attending would like Dr. Hastings's opinion."

I put my hand on William's heart. There was heavy bandaging.

"He has some broken ribs," the nurse explained. "Now, say to him what you will. Your time is almost up."

I rested one hand over his eyes as Daudi had done. I repeated my wedding vows. I told him I would not let him die. I told him the Chalice River was not real, do not go there. I begged him to stay with me, to open his eyes. He did not move. Machines were breathing for him, giving him fluids, and taking them away. For all I knew he could already be at the bottom of the Chalice River and never find his way out.

Soon I was taken back to the waiting room. I saw that I had enough power on my cell phone for one or two calls. First, I called my grandmother.

"Oh, my darling," she said at once, "it's on the news. They didn't give his name yet, but you told me you were coming home today and that William had bought you an old blue Mustang. I didn't know who was driving the car, but they kept saying 'a male, no passengers.' Even then I didn't want to believe it. Tell me."

"It's not good, Grandma. He's not awake yet."

"Shall I come there?" she asked.

"No... maybe later. My phone's dying. I just wanted to hear your voice."

"You tell him I love him, okay?"

"Okay, Grandma."

Then I called Melissa.

"God, Sela, what happened? Are you all right?"

"Not really."

"Listen. I'm taking Lee to get his car, and then we're coming to the hospital."

"Okay... I can't do this alone. I can't lose him."

"Hang on. We'll be there in about..."

My phone went dead. I dug around in my duffel and found the charger. I plugged it into the wall and lay down on a small couch on one side of the room. No one came in. The last thing I saw before I fell asleep was a blue car swerving over a bridge railing into a raging river. My eyes would never be that particular blue again.

In the middle of the night I heard whispering. I turned over and looked at Lee and Melissa sitting in chairs close by. "I can't talk. I can't feel," I told them.

"You don't have to do anything. Lee has a friend on staff here. He's going to try to get as much information as he can. But Sela, Mr. Langley is still alive. There's always hope," Melissa said.

"Half alive," I said.

"We have to have faith," she said. "Lee and I are going to take care of your horses. I can make phone calls for you."

"Daudi! The Hilliards!" I said quickly. "See if my phone's charged!"

Lee handed me my cell phone. Grace answered on the first ring. I confirmed their fears about the accident they had seen on TV. No one had mentioned Natasha's death on that hill yet, thank God.

"We're coming right there," Grace was saying. Then she put Gabriel on.

"Darling girl, what can we do?" he asked.

"Bring Daudi," I answered. "Just bring Daudi."

"Done," he said.

In the morning, William's condition was the same. By then, the waiting room was filled with his friends, students, colleagues, and my unusual contingent of the Hilliards and the Tanzanian. Melissa and Daudi tried to keep everyone away from me, but I had to tell the story over and over until I couldn't say another word. When the reporters finally found me, I was a wreck. Daudi stood between them and me and began to speak in Swahili in a firm voice. Of course, I knew what he said but they didn't, and they fell silent. Later that day, someone handed me a news clipping, a photo of the African standing over me. The caption read: "Sela Langley's personal guardian needed no English to quell growing crowd of journalists!"

I got to spend five minutes with my husband. If anything, his bruises were darker, and he was still in a coma. Daudi paced outside the ICU. He pleaded with every doctor or nurse who came in or out of the unit to be able to see William, but they told him politely, "Family only." Finally, that evening, I grabbed an attending's arm and said, "This African is my husband's brother, his *true* brother. Do you understand me? I will give up my time with my husband so he can be with him for a few moments." The man could not resist such a plea, and soon Daudi was garbed in white and walking toward William's bed.

There was no magic that could be seen or recorded, but Daudi said when we were finally alone, "He squeeze my hand, mama. He know we're here." A divine moment? You bet.

The Hilliards reserved hotel rooms for themselves and for Daudi such that they could return to Santa Barbara so Daudi wouldn't lose his job and they could rest a little but still come to LA at a moment's notice. Just before they left the first time, Grace took me aside from the crowd that still gathered every day for news of William.

"Honey," she said, "Gabriel and I thought we should call William's folks. They're in India and won't be able to get here for a week with plane schedules and all. They were very upset, of course. We didn't even get a chance to tell them about you. I don't know how they'll take it. I just hope it doesn't cause you any more anxiety."

"What else can hurt me?" I said.

A nurse stepped in. "Mrs. Langley, could you come with me?"

"Shall we wait?" Grace asked.

"No. I'll call you later. Stay close to Daudi, will you?"

"We will, dear."

I was taken to an office not far from the ICU. When I entered, a striking, green-eyed woman got up from a desk, reached out her hand,

and said, "Mrs. Langley? I'm Sonya Hastings, Chief of Neurosurgery. I was very grieved to learn of your husband's accident. I've known him for many years and, of course, his wife Natasha. Lovely people. You are newly married to Bill?"

"Yes. We got married the week before Christmas."

"Well, I won't pry into why he married one of his students, but let me assure you I will do everything possible for him."

"Thank you, Dr. Hastings."

"Normally I'm not called in so early in a case. We wait for the patient to be more stable, awake and breathing on his own, but because I know him and because Dr. Salieri saw something questionable on Dr. Langley's head CT, I thought I should take a look. There appears to be a mass of some kind in his brain, not related to the accident. We are doing further tests and hoping he will do a little better physically, but could you tell me of any recent health issues Bill may have had?"

I repeated what I had told Dr. Salieri about William's vertigo, vision problems, and mental confusion that had plagued him since before our winter break in Santa Barbara, and I mentioned that he was allergic to alcohol. Then I added, I don't know why, "Did you know the accident was only a few hundred yards from where Natasha was killed?"

"No, I did not. That just stops my heart for a moment, and I am not a very emotional woman," she admitted.

"I didn't mean to shock you. I just thought you should know. He... was not really over *that* accident."

"And I can see now that you have *two* accidents to deal with," she said.

"You might say that."

"Mrs. Langley, why don't you go home and get some rest. I'll call you if there is any change. You must be exhausted," she said kindly.

"Dr. Hastings, I am exhausted, but I live in Malibu Canyon, I have no car and a barely charged cell phone, my parents are in New York, some of my best friends are in Santa Barbara, and I love that man probably more than I can say, except maybe in a poem."

"You're a poet?"

"Among other things," I said. "And my name is Sela."

"Sela, I'm going to get you a private room as close to your husband as possible. It's against regulations, but I am called to make an exception. We're going to wait a few more days and then remove the ventilator. If Bill breathes on his own, that will be a very good sign. I'll arrange for you to have more time with him. What do you think?"

"I think that's the nicest thing anyone that I've only known for twenty minutes has done for me. Thank you. *Asante sana*."

"Oh, yes, I heard there was an African prowling the halls," she said, not in an unfriendly way. "I have been in Africa many times. I love the people, but I never learned Swahili. Now, at least, I know 'thank you.' *Asante sana*. I'll remember that."

And, believe it or not, she gave me a hug.

So I had a place to go when the crush of well-wishers became too much for me. As school started, there were fewer and fewer during the day—once in a while the friends and relatives of other ICU patients, but they would come and go as their loved ones were transferred to other rooms or the rehabilitation floor. I stayed. Usually Lee and Melissa, sometimes Marcella or Anne, would come over for a couple of hours. They said it was a quiet place to do their homework and that they didn't mind keeping me company.

In the first week, William showed some signs of restlessness, which Dr. Hastings said was meaningful. "He's trying to find his way back," she said. But when I was with him, he was still as stone. Daudi had given me a piece of sea glass he had found the day of the accident. It was a mosaic triangle, probably out of someone's Tiffany lamp, that had the colors of the sea, our amber horses, the white of the tide foam, and the green of the gardens in Hope Ranch. I put it in William's hand every day and closed his fingers around it, but I knew it would take more than that to arouse him.

One afternoon, I found myself alone in the ICU lounge. I was trying to write but not having much luck. My professors were letting me turn in assignments as I could and were very generous in allowing me to stay with William. I noticed a tall, immaculately dressed woman enter the room. She even had gloves on, and I thought, *Now there's a class act.* She came toward me, a little uncertainly.

"I'm sorry to bother you, but I'm looking for someone who might know about Dr. William Langley."

I held out my hand and said, "Well, you don't have to look far. I'm his wife, Sela Hart Langley."

She took my hand but stiffened a little when she heard my name.

"Oh, please forgive me. I didn't know he had remarried. You seem quite young."

"I'm a bit over ten years younger than William, but I have adored him, from a distance, for almost that long," I told this perfect stranger who still had a grip on my hand.

"I am Marjorie Skinner," she said.

"Natasha's mother! Oh, please sit down. Talk to me," I said, amazed at meeting her like this.

"I wouldn't have intruded. This must be a terrible time for you. But Bill always said I was like a mother to him. His was always out of the country, doing good works for sure, but he missed her. Are they here?" she asked.

"No, not yet. It'll be a few days. They're traveling from India."

"And Mikeala?"

"I... don't know. I don't know what she looks like. I've only spoken with her one time on the phone."

"Well, you're just thrown right in the middle of it, aren't you?"

I didn't know what to say to that. She continued, not missing a beat, "When did you marry Bill?"

"Just before Christmas, in Santa Barbara."

"You are a beautiful young lady. How did you meet?"

"I'm one of his students," I said, expecting some reaction, but she just smiled.

"You're a writer. You loved him. He wouldn't have had a chance," she said and then added quickly, "Oh, I only mean that in a nice way!"

"Mrs. Skinner, you wouldn't believe what's been said about me. And here you are still holding my hand."

"Oh, call me Marjorie, but may I ask… how did you and Bill get past the thing with Natasha?"

"I'm not sure William is… past it," I told her.

"Does he blame himself? For her drinking? For her… death?"

"In a way."

She sighed. "I blame myself too. Oh, not that she was gay, heavens! She was a bright and generous soul. She was good to everyone. But she should not have married that lovely man."

An attending leaned in the doorway. "Mrs. Langley, Dr. Hastings would like to see you."

"Oh, Marjorie, I think she wants to take William off the ventilator."

"I'll be glad to wait, if you'd like me to," she said.

"I'd like that very much," I said.

I went into the ICU with my sterile white outfit and saw Dr. Hastings by William's bed.

"Here we go," she said.

It was not easy to watch. But William did not struggle. He was too deep in the River. The tube came out swiftly, and William went on breathing, a bit raggedly at first and then as quietly as a penitent at prayer. He was asking to live, taking those redeeming breaths on his own.

"Good job, Bill," Dr. Hastings said. "Good job."

I told her Natasha's mother was in the waiting room.

"Oh, I'll come out and speak with her. Maybe you can sit with Bill in an hour or two. We should let him rest now, and then we have to discuss a feeding tube. For an extended period of recovery, his metabolic requirements go up."

I could not fathom these medical routines. I didn't know much beyond the value of ginger-peach tea. I returned to the lounge.

"He's breathing on his own, Marjorie."

"Oh, thank the good Lord," she said. "Now Sela, I am here for you. The first thing I'm going to do is bring you some clothes. Are you about a size four or a six?"

"Somewhere in there," I said. "All I had with me were beach and riding clothes when my friend Lee dropped me off at the hospital the day of the accident. I must look pretty frayed."

"May I surprise you, dear?"

"A surprise would be very welcome," I said. And she went off on her errand of mercy.

Later, I sat in Sonya Hastings's office in a well-cut pair of charcoal linen pants, a high-necked charcoal silk blouse dotted with tiny white hearts, and a white cashmere three-quarter sleeved sweater with an attractively angled bottom hem. Around my neck was a sterling silver band on which hung a small silver heart, and Marjorie had found some nice, dark gray mary jane flats that were the right size and very comfortable. It helped my appearance but did not make me feel any closer to my husband. I knew he liked me in jeans and a sweatshirt. But I also knew that Marjorie Skinner had felt like a mother again, buying this outfit and a few more packages of things I had not yet seen.

Dr. Hastings commented on how nice I looked and then hit me with the news that she wanted to operate on William in a few days. She had ordered an MRI that more definitively outlined a growth in William's brain.

"It needs to come out," she said. "We won't know what kind of tumor it might be until we can remove it and have it biopsied. Can you sign the release for the surgery?"

"I can," I said, trying to take in this new information. "But what are the risks?"

"More risky to leave the tumor there. It appears to be growing. It could further damage his brain function. He could wake up and not know you. On the other hand, in his condition, he could die on the table."

"Have you done this before?" I asked her.

"Operated on the brain of a person in a coma? A few times."

"And?"

"They all died. I'm sorry. But they all had more severe medical conditions. I think I can save your husband. It's his only chance of a normal life, if he is to have a life at all," she said.

I signed the paper.

"I'll do my very best," Dr. Hastings said.

The day of the surgery, William's parents walked into the ICU lounge. I didn't know who they were at first because I heard a nurse say, "One moment, Mr. and Mrs. Ward." They paced around the room until Dr. Hastings came in and told them she was on her way to the operating room and they'd have to wait until Mr. Langley's procedure was completed before they could see him.

"You're operating on Bill?" the woman asked.

"Yes. He has a large mass in his brain that may kill him if we don't remove it," she informed them.

"Don't we have to sign some papers or something?" the man said.

Then I knew. Ward was William's real last name.

"Not in this case," Dr. Hastings was saying. "His wife has signed permission for surgery."

"His wife?" they both said at once.

Dr. Hastings pointed at me and left quickly.

"There must be some mistake," Mrs. Ward said, grabbing her husband's arm.

"There's no mistake," I said. "Forgive me if I don't get up, but the doctor has given me a tranquilizer."

"But how could you be his wife?" Mr. Ward asked.

"Would you like to see our marriage license?" I asked.

"Yes, I think I would," the man said.

"Remember, Richard, we tried to call Bill around Christmas but he never answered his Malibu number," Mrs. Ward said, still holding onto his arm.

"William and I were married during Christmas break. I'm sorry you didn't know," I said.

"You made quite the move on him, young lady, only a few months after he lost his precious Natasha," Richard said.

They don't know, I thought. *They don't know she was gay.*

"You don't understand..."

"No, we certainly don't. But there's still time for an annulment," he said.

"Are you crazy, sir? Richard? Mr. Ward? Whoever you are? Your son is the love of my life. I wouldn't give him up for anything, not anything!" I almost screamed. The tranquilizer was not doing its job. But then, in a *divine* turn of events, the Hilliards came into the room.

"Donna, Richard, please don't traumatize Sela any further! You have been out of touch. William is quite in love with this girl!" Gabriel said immediately.

"*Girl* is right, Gabe! What is she, all of twenty?"

Grace was whispering to Donna, and the woman seemed to be calming down. Gabriel pushed himself up out of the wheelchair, which I knew was quite difficult for him, and stood eye to eye with his friend. "You should be on your knees thanking God for this *girl*, and I'm not much for the religious side of things!"

"Oh, Gabe, for heaven's sake, sit down. If she's here for Bill, then, for the time being, I'll let it go," Mr. Ward said.

The four of them went off in a huddle. Lee and Melissa and Daudi found me in the farthest corner of the room and held onto me. Mr. Ward shook his head when he saw that but didn't say anything. He reminded me so much of *my* father.

Two hours, then three hours passed. An attending came in and said, "Mr. Langley is doing well. Dr. Hastings is pleased so far. From her, that is a positive sign."

Lee brought me a sandwich and some juice. "You guys, what about your classes?" I asked.

"Miss La Monde took over some of Mr. Langley's. She's giving us credit for writing notes to Professor Langley and thought you might like to read them to your husband during his recovery. One time she said, 'Contrary to popular belief, I love *both* of them,'" Melissa told me.

"I'll be damned," I said.

By the fifth hour, I was left with Daudi and the Wards.

"Who are people?" Daudi asked.

"William's mother and father," I said.

"Oh, mama, you not speak to them?"

"Yes, Daudi, we've met, but they didn't know about me. They're just in shock."

"I fix," he said and got up before I could stop him.

Mr. Ward glanced up at the beautiful African, who bowed and said, in Swahili, *"Hujambo, baba*?"

And Richard Ward said as clear as a bell, "*Sijambo! Unaitwa nani?"*

"*Naitwa Daudi.*"

"*Unatoka wapi?"*

"*Natokea Tanzania.*"

And I said for the second time that day, "I'll be damned."

"How do you know our son, Daudi?" Mrs. Ward asked.

"William and Sela come to zoo in Santa Barbara where I have job. We friends right away. Miss Sela speak Swahili to me. We have memories from beach, many fine dinner, many kind word. Your son, brother to me. Love Sela very much. She his life."

By the time Dr. Hastings came in after more than nine hours, we were all sitting together, weary, but past the wall of suspicion and doubt by the grace of another language.

"I have good news, but Bill is not out of the woods yet," she stated. "The surgery went very well, and I believe I was able to remove all of the tumor. It was large and fairly inaccessible." She sighed and continued, "That's why it took me so long. But it's being biopsied at this time. We should know more later today. In the recovery room, Bill did open and close his hands several times, but that may or may not be significant. He doesn't respond to stimulus."

She paused again as if searching for words that would give me hope. "There don't appear to be any complications with the injuries from the accident itself," she said. "I'll have someone come get you, Sela, when he's back in his room. Bill is lucky to have so many people who care about him. Don't give up."

"When can we see him?" Donna Ward asked.

"The first person in the room will be Sela. After that we will take one day at a time, one visitor at a time," she said.

I looked over to the door just as Marjorie Skinner turned and started back down the hall. I caught up with her at the elevator. "Marjorie! Wait. You are always welcome to be in there with the people who love William," I said.

"But aren't those his parents?" she asked.

"Yes…"

"They'll ask too many questions. I just wanted to know how Bill's surgery went."

"Dr. Hastings said he might have shown some signs of waking up," I told her.

She touched my face. "That is all I need to hear right now. I'll come back tomorrow," she said and pressed the down button.

Oh, how long could a week be? Daudi and the Hilliards went back to their hotel, and I said good night to the Wards and returned to my private room a little ways from the ICU. About this time last week, we had been driving the blue Mustang out of the auction lot. I felt some relief that Lee and Melissa were looking after the horses but wondered how I'd feel if I were left with Chisholm and Malibu and no William. Then I had another horrible thought. If he didn't come out of the coma, would I have to make some kind of an end-of-life decision? I knew so little about this. William and I had never talked about it. I fell asleep thinking about the only way I could possibly find out more about William's wishes.

In the morning, I found the note Grace had given me with Dorothy and Mae's address and phone numbers. The poem I promised them was back in Malibu Canyon on my laptop. I'd have to ask Lee or someone I trusted to go get it for me. Lee would be the best person, but he and Melissa were already doing so much for me that I hated to ask for more.

I put Dorothy's number in my phone and pressed send, but I only got her voice mail. "Dorothy, this is Sela. I need your help," I said simply and left my number.

About an hour later, she called back. "What can we do, Sela? We're all praying for Langley," she said.

"I haven't been able to retrieve that poem from my computer that I promised you."

"Oh, don't worry about that! How is Bill doing?"

"Not too great. That's the other thing. I need to see Mikeala. I can't do this on the phone."

"I don't think she'll come to the hospital," Dorothy said. "Is there a place you could meet her?"

"On a bench in the quad?"

"That she'll do. I'll call her right now and get back to you."

But Mikeala herself called a few minutes later. "I'll be near the university later today. I could meet you on the quad. Let's say three o'clock? And Sela, this is just devastating news about Bill. I'm sorry I was so harsh with you before. Of course, if I can help Langley, I will."

"Thank you, Mikeala. 'Til three then?"

"Yes."

She was there when I walked over from the medical center in a short pearl-white leather skirt with black tights, black fashion cowboy boots, a black turtleneck, and a strand of crushed fresh-water pearls. It was cool out, so I slipped into a sleeveless white and charcoal-black knitted feathery vest.

"You look terrific," Mikeala said.

"Natasha's mom is buying my clothes. She has good taste," I said. "I probably feel worse than I look."

"Marjorie has been to the hospital?" she asked with some surprise.

"Almost every day. She avoids William's folks for some reason, but she has been very sweet to me."

"She's a special lady."

"Mikeala, I need to ask you something, but you don't have to answer. I may not have to use what you say, but..."

"What is it, Sela?"

"I need to know if Natasha ever mentioned how William felt about end-of-life issues," I said.

"You probably hoped I couldn't answer that, but I can. Natasha and I discussed what we'd do for each other. As I recall, we didn't ever agree, but Natasha said, 'William always says if he can't be awakened after an accident and his organs are in good shape, he'd want them to save as many people as possible.' That I remember as clear as day because it gave me such a different view of Natasha's husband. He was always just *the professor* or *a guy who liked riding better than playing tennis* or *a poet always entangled in pretty words*. This statement about donating his organs always showed such dimension to the man. Natasha always laughed it off. 'That'll never happen,' she'd say."

"It sounds like William to me, and now the burden is mine."

"He might not make it?" she asked.

"He's had surgery for a brain tumor. He's on powerful drugs, has a feeding tube, and is still in a coma. It hardly seems survivable to me, but he is breathing on his own. I don't know what I'd want, but I had to know what he might want. Thank you for coming," I answered.

"Sela, I want to tell you why I reacted like I did when you called awhile back. I did still partly blame William for Natasha's death. Why didn't he get her into treatment? Why did he allow alcohol in their home?"

"I don't know, Mikeala. I do know some things about William that would really surprise you. Maybe someday, he can tell you himself."

"God willing," she said, and we parted on friendlier terms.

I waved to her and hurried back to the hospital. There was a note for me from Dr. Hastings. She had worked a double shift, mostly for William, and would be gone a couple of days. It read: "Dear Sela, I can come back very quickly if needed. I think Bill is holding his own. In case you were wondering, I believe it's too early to discuss end-of-life decisions. You may stay with your husband for longer periods of time now. He's been moved to a semiprivate room with another coma patient who rarely has visitors, so two of Bill's friends may be there with you now. Dr. Rhys Taylor is the neurosurgeon on call. I have seen Bill move his hand a couple of times. He seems to be searching for a connection to something, be it life or heaven. Yours, Sonya Hastings."

Before I went in to see William, I called my grandmother. "Hi, Grandma, just checking in."

"How's our boy today?"

"About the same. He can have more visitors now. Do you want me to come get you?"

"No, darling. I have a neighbor who'll bring me. I'm waiting for Applause to bloom," she said.

"Oh, Grandma, that would be just perfect."

"I think in a few days if this sun hangs on."

"Okay. Let me know, and I'll meet you at the main entrance."

We said good-bye, and I looked for Dr. Taylor, who took me to my husband's room. He told me the lab results showed William's tumor to be benign but that it was of a kind that ultimately would have damaged his brain function and threatened his life. He squeezed my shoulder and told me I had done the right thing, allowing Dr. Hastings to operate. I thanked God silently. I was afraid to be too open about the divine moments. I said hello to the woman in the other bed. She was probably not much older than I was, in need herself of a divine moment. Then I kissed William's cheek. Did it feel warmer today? Did he move slightly when I leaned over him?

I pulled a chair close to the bed. You can't imagine how difficult it is to talk to someone who cannot respond. I told him about Grandma watching the blue rose beginning to flower. I described how Lee and Melissa were riding Chisholm and Malibu now. I described the outfits Marjorie Skinner was finding for me and how Lois La Monde had told her classes she loved us both, about his father and Daudi speaking in Swahili. Then I stopped suddenly. William had opened his hand. I put one of mine in it, and he closed his down, weakly, on mine, but it filled me with such hope.

What does he want to hear? What words make him long for more? I opened my phone with my free hand and called Lee. He answered right away. "Sela, everything okay?"

"Yes, but Lee, I need some of those letters kids have been writing to William."

"I think Miss La Monde has them all, but I'm still on campus. I'll see if I can find her."

"Great."

When Lois walked through the door about forty minutes later, I hardly knew what to say. She took a step back and said, "I had no idea. Oh, Lord, he's so still, so… not real."

"Miss La Monde, he just closed his hand on mine. I think he's waking up."

"What about the tumor?"

"The tumor was benign," I told her. "There are some things the doctors don't know yet, but we know how strong this man is, don't we?"

"Yes, Sela. You have made him strong. You did something no one was able to do after Natasha died. You put a light back in his eyes. I thought it was me, but I was wrong. It was you! Now, here are those writings from his students. There's one from me in there too. Do you think you can read that one?"

"Miss La Monde, I'll read that one first," I said.

When she left, I looked at William again. The tubes and wires and cast and head bandage and IV drip overshadowed the man that was my husband, my teacher, my friend. He would not want to live like this. He had great things left to do, to write, to say to me, to his friends. I had to make him understand that he had to wake up.

I began reading the letters, still holding his hand that was cupped tentatively around mine. I read slowly; I read as if he could hear every beautiful word, poems about transcendence, short stories about revival, notes about strength and grace under fire, metaphors from the sea. I read to William the words he had taught them to use, the language of surprises and revelations, clear points of view and imagery that sang, his own unique lessons coming home.

He opened his eyes and said, "See..." And then he went back into the River.

I punched the call button. Dr. Taylor came in with a nurse.

"He opened his eyes," I said. "He spoke to me."

"Good. Good," the doctor said.

I could see on the monitor that his pulse and blood pressure had gone up. The doctor shined a small beam of light in William's eyes and said, "Mr. Langley, you can wake up now. You're okay. It's safe to wake up. We're taking care of you."

But my husband drifted in another dimension. *Oh God, my story, the eleventh story, the one he hasn't heard. I have to read that one,* I thought as Dr. Taylor continued to check all the equipment that was keeping William alive. The story was on my computer. I hadn't printed it yet. How could I leave just now and drive to Malibu? Lee had brought the truck back to the hospital lot, but I couldn't bear to leave my husband. He had opened his eyes. He had opened his battered body to the inevitability of pain and confusion. I couldn't leave now.

They made me go to my room after a while but said I could come back at midnight. But at midnight, I was in the dream of the blue car vaulting over the bridge on the Chalice River.

I woke with a start. I had fallen asleep with my clothes on. It was light. The clock on the wall by the door said seven thirty. I jammed my feet in my shoes and ran down the hall. A nurse was changing William's IV bag, but all was quiet.

"I think he has a little more color today, Mrs. Langley," she said.

"You do? Really?"

"I do." She patted my arm. "Can I bring you some breakfast?"

"Some cereal and fruit, if it's not too much trouble."

"Mrs. Langley, everyone wants to make this as easy as possible for you. Just let us."

"I will. *Asante...*"

"What's that?"

"I was going to say 'thank you very much' in Swahili," I told her.

"Swahili? Like that African who comes here sometimes?"

"Yes. He's a dear friend," I said.

"He brings things to Mr. Langley's room, but we're told to remove them. I've saved everything in case they are important to you or your husband."

"Oh thank you, Miss..." I looked at her name tag. "Jenko."

"Say it again, in Swahili," she said.

"*Asante sana.*"

"That is so lovely. How do you say, 'How are you'?"

"Hujambo."

"When that black gentleman comes again, I'll surprise him," she said. "Now I'll get that breakfast for you... and do call me Sharla."

I swear, when I looked back at William, he was smiling.

Daudi didn't come that day, but Grandma did. She filled William's small closet with peach jam and books, but the staff said no to her perfect blue rose in a crystal vase. "No flowers allowed in intensive care units," they said, seemingly not certain William could stay in his room, that he might go back to the ICU for some reason. Someone kept it watered at the nurses' station and promised to bring it to William when they could.

Sharla asked its name.

"Applause," I said.

"Oh, a worthy name, and you know, it's kind of the color of your eyes."

"My husband bought that plant for my grandmother for that very reason," I told her.

"This guy's a keeper," she said.

"Don't I know it," I said.

When Grandma and I were talking quietly around noon, William began to moan and make circling motions with his hands. Dr. Taylor came in and said sometimes those motions were involuntary, but he was keeping track of everything William did for Dr. Hastings's assessment.

But I knew what was happening. William had hit a rough patch of water in the River.

Grandma agreed to stay with William so I could go to the canyon. I picked up some clothes that William would recognize, my laptop with the poem for Mae and Dorothy, and the eleventh Quantum Crossing story. I drove back to the medical center as fast as I dared, but there had been no change. Grandma's friend needed to get home, so she said a tearful good-bye, resting her hand on William's heart.

I felt very alone after that. I rubbed William's forehead, practically the only part of his body that didn't have tubes or bandages. He seemed to breathe a little more rapidly under my hand, searching for reassurance.

"I'm here, William. I'll always be here."

I opened my computer and brought up the poem I had printed and mailed to Dorothy and Mae on the way back from Malibu. I thought hearing the words might bring that image to his mind, that day on the beach seeing Mae and Dorothy embracing, so I read.

Out and Back

It is time to go.
Pools of sea green gather.
Horse stamps
edging homeward.
I rein through the last breakers
safer than he knows.

I've seen two women
walking on the fringe,
feet in damp sand,
heads bent whispering
arms around each other
as if there were no land.

Tide is strong.
I let it whip me
long after they are gone.
I swallow waves,
my clear self
curling earthward
unchecked.

I go
where I'm expected,
keep my promises
in the dark,
dry-mouthed.
While they.
in some wet cove,
some sea-escape,
stay wrapped in sunlight
and truth.

William got very still but not in a deep coma way—in a way of listening, seeing that scene played out behind his closed lids.

Sonya Hastings returned the next day. She was interested in William's "progress," as she called it, saying I should keep doing what I was doing.

"I'm just reading to him. Talking is just too… futile. I know he'll hear the disappointment in my voice. Reading to him seems normal. It gives him permission to be quiet, not to struggle to respond when he's not ready."

"You are a very wise young woman," she said.

"*Asante sana.*"

"Yes, what is this? All the nurses are greeting each other and *patients* with *hujambo!*"

"Oh, gosh. Sharla Jenko asked me a few words, and the whole thing got out of control."

"Well, the patients love it. Mr. Pearson had his wife bring him a Rosetta Stone. He came out of his coma yesterday and asked for the course. Sharla said she'd asked him a few times that morning, 'How are you doing?' in Swahili, and he woke up saying 'I want those Swahili tapes.' For heaven's sake! How is *that* possible?" Dr. Hastings mused.

"The brain in a coma may understand more than it does awake," I said.

"Well, it was a first for me," she said.

Two more days passed. Sonya began to look worried. The Wards and the Hilliards sat with William for a while each day, and I was able to get some fresh air, albeit in pressed white cotton slacks and a navy-and-white-striped tank top with spaghetti straps.

"You are much too pale," Marjorie had said and told me I should get about twenty minutes of sun every day. "At least for your vitamin D, dear."

I sat on the bench on the quad where William and I had read "A Story in Two Hearts" to each other and he'd given me his leather jacket to wear.

I called Daudi. "*Habari, baba?*"

"Oh, mama, must come see baby rhino. William too."

"He's not awake yet, Daudi."

"Magic work soon, you see."

He wanted me to come to the zoo so badly, but I couldn't make myself drive down the Conejo Grade. I could go along Highway 1 following the ocean, but what if William woke up or died and I wasn't there? I thought of the years I had waited in line to get into one of his classes. I was waiting in line again, just to see his eyes.

When I went back into the hospital that day, Dorothy and Mae were in William's room. They threw their arms around me. Dorothy said, "You really get it, don't you?" She clutched my poem in one hand and Mae's arm in the other.

"I hope I do. There can never be too much love in the world. I had that vision and wrote those words many years ago. My poetry teacher, who was gay, loved one line so much she gave me an A for the whole poem."

"Oh, which line?" Dorothy asked. I could tell that they both wanted to know.

"I'm keeping that to myself in her memory," I said.

"She died?" Dorothy asked.

"Yes."

"Did you love her?" Mae asked.

"Very much," I answered.

"You have had a life, girl," Dorothy said.

"But without William... I close myself down a little more each day that he doesn't know me."

"One day you'll say the words he needs to hear," Mae said.

"But it could be too late. Even 'I love you' may be too late."

"What do the doctors say, Sela?" Dorothy asked.

"They say the longer he's in the coma, the harder his recovery will be, that he may not be the same person or remember any of his life," I said.

"I don't believe anything will change Mr. Langley. He has the heart of a saint," Mae said.

"And you, my dear, the pen of an angel," Dorothy added.

"Oh, I wouldn't go that far," I said. "I'm just trying to be the writer William expects me to be and live up to the standards of my dear mentor of the past."

"Sela, may we share this poem with our friends?"

"Of course. May I meet some of your friends?"

"Definitely," Mae said.

William shifted a bit in the bed.

"We should go," Dorothy said. "We'll come again."

"Chin up, girl," Mae said.

Then I was alone with William again. I put my mouth on his, something I hadn't done often because his lips were cold and it scared me. Today they were warm. I kissed him again. Nothing.

"William?"

"See," he said.

"See what, my love? Can you see me?"

"See..." He struggled to say more but couldn't.

"Now you listen, William. I'm going to read you 'The Ending,' the last story of *William and Angela: A Quantum Crossing*. You wanted to hear this, and I need to know what you think, Professor. I need you to wake up. No one has heard it, and if you don't wake up, no one ever will. If you are down there in the Chalice River, you listen as if your life depends on it."

The story has an ending, and you know the ending before you start, he always said. So on that day in April, I picked up the copy I had made when I copied "Out and Back" for Mae and Dorothy, and I read as if my life depended on it too.

When William Hathaway was seventy-five, he was diagnosed with liver cancer. He was still quite handsome but thin and pale from fighting the disease, which had gone on too long before he sought a medical opinion. He sat in the oncologist's office gripping the sides of the chair while the doctor went on about how it was too late for treatment and that he should get his affairs in order.

William did not tell this doctor about the only thing that mattered to him, the love of his life, a woman who had been with him in his darkest moments. He thought of the day she had slipped in beside him and taken his hand at the graveside of his oldest daughter. He was the only one who saw her, but it eased the grief of losing Sela to have her there. She lived to comfort him, lived to love him, lived because he lived.

In the times when he was alone or working (he had been a well-known and admired actor since his twenties), he called out her name, so desperate was he for her presence. Years could go by. Then, when he was ill or exhausted, she whispered his name and flew into his arms. Her touch drove away all the demons of his complicated life. Her voice soothed his fears, his discomfort, his disappointments. She said she would never leave him. Surely she would come now, he thought, and smiled.

The doctor looked over at him and said, "I'm glad you're taking it so well."

"Oh, I'm not taking it well. The one I love most in the world is not with me."

"Can I call her for you?" he asked.

"I don't think so," William said.

He drove home slowly, shaking badly.

"Angela…," he whispered in a broken voice.

He sat in the car a long time trying to decide what to do. It seemed there was only one thing, finally, that made sense.

He went to the Chalice River.

There was no one there. He set out a few things on the bank by the bridge—a camp chair, blankets, water, the few things he could eat. He had shaved and put on the shirt that Angela had touched the night of his premiere of *Chosen One*. He had been surprised to find it neatly washed and ironed in one of his wife's closets after she moved out. But he had saved it all these years.

He called his youngest daughter and tried to stay calm.

"Denise? This is your old man… No, I'm not okay. Listen, don't worry. I'm going to say good-bye… No, don't try to find me… I *do* love you…"

His throat closed up, and he could say no more. He had been obsessed with Angela and barely knew his daughters, but without Angela, he would have been nothing to them. At least he cared, and he had tried to make amends over the years.

The first day on the river was cold. He climbed into his sleeping bag and stared at the river and the place on the bridge where Angela's car had gone over. At dusk, rain threatened, so he crawled into the car and closed his eyes. Memories and pain kept him awake. He had ridden his horse for the last time a few months ago. Angela had galloped beside him, her long, dark hair unfurling in the rush of air. He hadn't told her how bad he felt. He let her go… again.

The second day he sat closer to the river, needing some drugs even more than the day before but didn't want to dull his senses. He would be alive for death or for Angela. That's when she touched him, the moment he accepted the death that coursed like the river to its end.

She came up behind him and encircled him with her arms, leaned over, and put her cheek against his.

"William, what is happening? Why are you here?" she cried.

He grabbed her hands and brought them to his lips before saying, "I'm dying, Angela."

"Oh, God, William," she said in a hoarse whisper, "but why are you here? Why aren't you home? I'll stay with you… you know I will."

She came around and knelt on the ground and laid her head in his lap. He stroked her still-wet hair and told her how her love had saved him so many times but that his path seemed so clear now. He would go into the river.

"William!"

"You know it's the only thing I can do, my love," he said, lifting her face up and kissing her.

She hugged him to her then and sobbed into his chest.

"You are all I have," she said.

"You are all I have," he responded, reeling from a pain that was like no other.

"I can heal you," she said.

"No, Angela." He could barely speak. "This is too much for you. I've thought about this for a while. I welcome it. But I'm grateful you came before I went into the Chalice River."

"I won't let you do it alone," she said. "I will go with you."

"Yes, stay with me. It's the only choice left to us."

He struggled up from the chair and let her support him in the climb down the rocky bank. The river was high and turbulent, like the night years ago when Angela was swept away and never found. They stepped in, embracing at the edge of death, and when the sky was black as the river, they moved deeper into the water. William's pain receded as the water deepened until all that remained was Angela's face pressed against his and the final wave of the Chalice carrying them to its killing depths, holding them with its terrible power, as they were holding each other. Soon they were under the bridge and gone...

They woke up in a spacious hotel room clinging to each other in a white outfitted bed, still wet and shivering. William pulled a thick down blanket over them, and they didn't speak for a long time, hungry for warmth and kisses and gazing into each other's eyes.

She was twenty, he twenty-nine. Built into one wall of the room was the latest 3-D, gold-ray television, and on the screen an old movie was beginning. The credits were rolling: *The Range* starring William Hathaway. They didn't watch at first, but then they heard William ask in his movie voice, "Are you real?" and a girl who looked just like the girl in the bed say, "Some people think that I am."

William sat up suddenly.

"They caught you on film! Angela, look, it's you!"

She stirred from the comfort of his arms and the soft white covers.

"I see Katie Turin," she said.

"I see *you*!"

"You always see me, my love," she said and hugged him again.

Later they dressed and ventured out into the brilliant day. Low-flying commuter planes sped on their accustomed routes. Buildings were unimaginably tall, and there were many decorated walkways between them. Some had rows of flowers and vines that hung down over the streets like banners, streets that were coated with a kind of red plastic. There were few cars, no curbs, and no traffic lights.

William and Angela didn't seem to notice these things. They wandered into a café. All of the patrons had gorgeous bronze skin. Their own whiteness stood out.

"Where are you from, friends?" a waiter asked.

"The Chalice River," they answered together.

"I don't know that place," he said, still interested.

"It's very far from here," William continued, "and we need to eat."

"Of course. Our special today is eland steak on a cotton seed roll with wilted cannabis lily pad salad and nematode soup."

"We'll just have the sandwich," William said, and then he turned to Angela. "What is possible now, my girl?"

"Everything," she said. "Everything I ever believed."

When they left the restaurant, a man in a silver suit flew by trailing a sign that read,

"Welcome to the New Year, 2063"

When I finished the last line, I looked at my husband's face. He smiled. So I read the last few lines again: "William said to Angela, 'What is possible now, my girl?' 'Everything,' she said. 'Everything I ever believed.' When they left the restaurant, a man in a silver suit flew by trailing a sign that read, 'Welcome to the New Year, 2063.'"

William Langley opened his eyes and looked at me. "See... la," he said.

Dr. Hastings had just come into the room. She turned and went back out into the hallway. Nurses and attendings and families of patients not awake yet began clapping softly, then people in the waiting room who heard the news, none of them William's visitors. I was the only one there. Then Sonya returned quickly and began ministering to my husband as he searched for full consciousness.

Sharla thought to bring the rose Applause from the nurses' station and place it on a tray at the end of William's bed. It stood in its crystal vase, seeming as if its recently misted blue petals had risen from a dark river into the open air.

from the river

you pull me from the river
with the promise of a blue rose
and a hand on my heart
where you know I love it to be.

you kiss me trusting I am there.
the scent of you stays in the room
the lines you read as fresh as air
lines as far back as "released in dew
like shattered glass."

you said I dared you to touch that poem
when you were sixteen.
I have remembered that again
deep in the Chalice River.

I am caught in the rolling dark
like an anchor
with a blue car farther down
and someone with silver hair.

I ache for you in the river
but all my cries are washed away
and those of friends along the shore
and though they shake me with their grief
and pray to a lonely god

it is for you that I will wake.

William Langley, 2013

Appendix

spring storm
(the complete poem by William Langley, the last two stanzas of which got Sela into his Writing the Short Story class)

listen
reach for the flashlight
4 a.m. darkness like an animal crouched
that sound
my fear spills out the front door
with the pale beam
it's snowing
wind from the death-season stirred up

listen
is the lion down on the path
where I saw him last week
waiting in April for the red colt
who sleeps in the grass at noon?
the sound has a hunger
what is it?
the licking of a gaskin sheathed in ice?
a chestnut throat strangling?

listen
the horses are circling circling
hooves thrum on the blossoms
the white blooms from the night sky

listen
grey geese cry overhead going home
the cougar pads his soft retreat
snow whispers to the blind ground

Serengeti
(Sela's poem that Daudi read to Langley's fifth-period class in Swahili)

Tulisafiri katitka bahari ya nyasi fupi,
kwenye vilima vilivyoumbika
kama mashua chini ya anga,
swala wanatupungia mbele ya mashua yetu,
wakiwa na mavumbi.
Duma wanasubiri visiwani,
wanatoa milio kuwaashiria wanawe wajifiche.
Tai kahawia wanatua kwakasi kama abatrosi
juu yakiumbe mdogo mbele yetu.
Pundamilia wanaogelea,
kujiokoa na kinywa cha simba,
fisi wanaogelea majini mizoga.
Nyuma ya mashua yetu kuna chole,
mana taji na mbuni.
nyasi ndefu zinatuyumbisha yumbisha,
tukiwa na mbweha na tembo,
nyumbu wanaendelea kupiga makasia,
kipondya afrika wanaelea angani,
digididigi wanaibuka hapa na pale,
namiguu yao ya rangikahawia.
Nguruwe pori wanafukua fukua vidibwi
haraka haraka.
Twiga wamekuwa sunami
kwenye migunga,
huku wakipepesa macho yao kututazama,
nakutazama pembeni huku wakishika makasia,
kurudi kwenye asili ya uumbaji
mahala ambapo waliotajwa
na wasiotajwa
wanakusanyika ndani ya safina
katika mawazo yetu.

For Joan / Three poems
(my ever-remembered and loved poetry teacher)

how can I write a poem
she will never see?
or edit with red pen
or read aloud with secret smile?

I could name a darkness
or a prayer
put hazy metaphors upon the page.
she knew exactly what I meant.

now I cross out more than I leave.
words fail
like storms that never reach the ground.
who would they nourish anyway?
I am empty of secrets that matter.
I am washed clean
of remarkable words.

but I will always hear her voice
speaking the lines,
finding the ones that are true.

she was my connection
to everything,
everything I could feel,
everything I could say.

am I cut loose from her?
am I silenced?

or will that heart of hearts
beat on in me?
that poetry still sing
when I, too, am gone?

I cannot speak
with her voice.
I cannot write
the turn of phrase
that clutched the heart
when she revealed
those risky pieces
of her life.
I cannot see
with her pure vision
the perfect line.
But I can tell you
how I felt when she said, "Bravo,"
to my words,
when she allowed my wandering
among her words
to find my voice.
I can tell you
that I became a poet,
discovered language
again and again
when she would smile
or touch my hand.
I put my darkest self
to paper.
I learned to pare
complexities of mind,
to peel back layers of pain
and desire
with a word.

Oh, that was true joy,
her eyes upon my soul,
her "yes" upon the scattered shards
of all my dreams
that she made whole.

I can see her
with her little horses
among the roses.
They dance and she laughs
as if there is enough air for forever.
She writes a poem that day
about Georgie
and everyone cries at the tale.
We all long to touch people like that,
to make our own verses
wrench the heart.
She takes us through the steps,
syntax and rhythm
and metaphor.
Dance! dance! she says,
but we are winded by the climb.
Some fall by the wayside.
I stay.
She leads me among the blossoms,
shows me the magic words,
the high and shining ground of my own poems
where I can unfold,
where I can breathe.

To Lee 11/11/91

(my friend who died on November 11 at 11 a.m., 1991)

into the light
of beginnings and endings
he's still with me
in everyday romps through the gold fields
and swinging from trees
his face
his eyes
his arms reaching for branches
follow me follow me he would cry
then his legs hugging the bay mare
where we raced through the sun-dappled oaks
and leaped little brooks on the Sespe

sometimes I think I can go there
it's just a moment away
that joy
that connection
those crazy sweet games
that we played

I remember the light
of beginnings and endings
the time he stood up for me
hushing the classroom
taking the blame for the wild kids
trust me trust me he would say
whispering the truth
on the way out the door

I remember the backcountry days
on the Hondas

telling stories and dreams
riding high in the hills
of our own separate landscapes
crossing one bridge
to be friends

in the heart's light
of beginnings and endings
are memories and letters
and photos
all piled into corners
of who I am
with him
without him
our secrets
lost in the ghost soul
bound in the living ones

and love
forever bright
forever real

Literary Works within the Novel

The *William and Angela: A Quantum Crossing* short story collection is dedicated to William Shatner, the only actor I can imagine with the exquisite equestrian skills and the dramatic grace to portray William Hathaway and love the ghost of Angela Star.

SUGGESTED READING

The Faith of a Writer.......... Joyce Carol Oates
Just Six Numbers .... Sir Martin Rees
By Cold Water .... Chris Dombrowski
Breathing In .... Joan Raymond